A STIFF

Kiss

AVERY OLIVE

www.crescentmoonpress.com

A Stiff Kiss
Avery Olive

ISBN: 978-1-937254-33-9
E-ISBN: 978-1-937254-34-6

Crescent Moon Press
1385 Highway 35
Box 269
Middletown, NJ 07748

Crescent Moon Press electronic publication/print publication: February 2012 www.crescentmoonpress.com

"There is no love without forgiveness, and there is no forgiveness without love."
Bryant H. McGill

Chapter One

Xylia

When I was twelve, I found my mother dead on Christmas Day. Since then, I've always found death fascinating. My father thinks I'm still coping, still trying to understand why my mom left. He hopes my interest is a stage I'll grow out of. But I'm not so sure it is.

* * * *

As I push through the door to my house, I'm happy. I can't help but throw down my messenger bag and yell, "I'm free." At least, until Monday morning. But winter break is only a week away. I've been waiting for what feels like my whole life for this moment.

"Free from what?" Dad emerges from the kitchen. His gray hair is slicked back with gel, exposing a large forehead and a severe widow's peak, signs of both his intelligence and his pain. He wears brown cords, a plaid button-down shirt, and a tie—one that goes with neither the shirt nor the pants. It's thrown together as though he has nothing clean to wear and nothing that matches. His outfit makes me a little sad. Since losing Mom, he's let himself go.

"Uh, duh, it's the weekend of course. And the countdown is on."

"I swear, just yesterday I was walking you to

~ ☾ ~

kindergarten," he says, smiling.

"Dad…" I whine. "Don't say that. It's embarrassing."

He looks over his shoulder, eyeing the area in the foyer. "'Cause all these people are going to hear." He indicates the empty space with his hands.

"Just don't, okay?"

"But honey, it's a father's right. I'm allowed to create embarrassing memories."

And he does, all the time. Personally, I think it's his way of dealing with my mom being gone. His way of reminding me that since she isn't around, he's stepped up and taken her place.

"Are you ready for tonight's game?" His voice takes on a serious tone.

Tonight's game. I hold in the groan that begs to be released. For as long as I can remember, going to soccer games has been our thing. And I hate soccer. But I love my dad.

Silversprings, Oregon, has nothing going for it except its high school soccer team. Soccer here is more important than church. The town closes down early on game days and everyone proudly wears blue and yellow to support the Rams. And if you're not sitting in the bleachers you had better be dying, in the hospital, or have some sort of contagious disease to stay away.

This is the championship game, the last I'll attend. Next year I'll be in college. "Of course, Daddy." I lay on the charm and smile wide. "Wouldn't miss it for the world."

Dad reaches out and ruffles my hair. "Great. I want to get there early. We need to snag the best seats."

I have to laugh, because although the bleachers aren't assigned, no matter how late or early we arrive, we always sit in the same spot. It's a town thing—you just know where and where not to sit. Everyone has their place.

~ ☾ ~

"Sure thing, Dad. I'm just going to freshen up. What's for supper?"

He rolls his eyes and laughs. "Honey, it's game day. You know exactly what's for supper."

It's a good thing I don't have ulcers or high cholesterol, because the food they serve at the soccer field is fried in lard, bathed in cheese, and showered with salt. They don't have anything to eat that requires a fork or a table. But like the games, the food is also a tradition. Corn dogs, chilli fries, and orange soda await me. Better take a swig of Pepto before we leave.

"Come on, go get ready. I don't want to miss the warm ups. And please, at least for tonight, wear something with a little color. Blue and yellow perhaps," Dad says, hope filling his tone that this is the one day I won't wear black.

"Alright, alright. I'll see what I can do." I stalk up the stairs, the hard soles of my knee-high Doc Martins thudding against the wood. I'm only a few steps from the top when the shrill sound of the phone reverberates through the house. I instinctively clutch the rail for support. *Shit*. I don't need to look at the caller ID to let me know who's going to be on the other end of the phone line.

Dad disappears into the kitchen and I hear him answer the phone. Following me up the stairs is his voice, a lot of *I sees*, *uh huh's* and then a final, *yes of course*. Dad slams the phone against the countertop, and it's clear from the loud bang that I'm in trouble. I probably should have scurried to my room instead of planting my feet on the staircase, waiting for what I knew would surely come. *Three, two, one...*

"Xylia!" Dad yells, the pounding of his shoes on the floor telling me he's fast approaching. "Xylia Morana, come here this inst—" He sees me standing on the stairs and stops in his tracks, then slams his jaw shut.

~ ☾ ~

I had assumed I might very well find myself in this situation when I'd decided to ditch school this afternoon. So it comes as no surprise when Dad folds his arms across his chest, points his chin up, and narrows his eyes at me.

"Something you want to tell me?"

Playing it off as no big deal seems best, so I shrug. "Um...I may have missed a few classes today. But in my defence, who doesn't skip the occasional class?"

"Apparently two hundred other students. Where were you?"

Shopping. Movies. Library. Any response would be better than the truth. "Vinyl's?" I offer.

He stares me down. "Right. You want me to believe you skipped school to go to a record store?"

"Hey, they got in some new stuff. If I didn't get there first, someone else would have," I reply.

"You're grounded. That means no trip."

He says it, and it stings, though I know the punishment will never stick. But that doesn't stop my chest from growing tight and my throat from constricting. I say, "But Dad..." This trip means everything to me. He knows it and I know it.

"Don't *but Dad* me. I know you weren't at Vinyl's. Dammit, Xylia, I better not find out you were traipsing around some cemetery—or worse, at someone's funeral—so help me!"

"I haven't done anything wrong. Don't—don't say I can't go, please." It's going to be a blast, a trip with just myself and a list of cemeteries, churches, and spooky houses, all waiting for me to discover them. I'd have to stay at hotels my dad okayed and would pay for, and I'd have to check in with him like, ten times a day, but I've wanted to do this forever. It had taken me ages to convince him I'd be safe traveling alone.

And all I'd needed to do was to stay out of trouble for

~ ☾ ~

one semester and the trip was mine. Maybe I should have thought about that before I'd decided to ditch. My stomach twists a little with guilt. I know punishing me isn't easy on Dad, but that doesn't stop me from pushing out my lip and frowning.

Dad clutches the back of his neck and lets out an exasperated sigh. "Stay out of trouble until break and maybe you can still go."

And with that I know the conversation is over, because if someone saw me earlier today, holed up in a church three towns over watching strangers say farewell to Joshua Adams—I'll find myself in a shit storm, up shit creek without a paddle, eating a shit sandwich, or worse. It will be a grounding that will stick, one that will have me locked in my room, and no amount of sweet charm would ease him up.

Because I've promised. I've promised countless times that such occurrences would never happen again. And I'm pretty sure I've used up my last lifeline.

Dad storms out of the foyer, but not before adding in a slightly lighter tone, "Hurry up, get changed."

I let out a sigh and trudge up the last three stairs, head down the hallway, and go into my room. I yank open the doors to my closet. They squeal in protest, jerking along the tracks. When open, they expose my wardrobe—or lack thereof. Really, it's a funeral procession's dream: black, black, and more black. Tired and worn cargo pants, flowing floor-length skirts, and shirts of all shapes and sizes. However, if I push everything to the left, there are a few items I'm almost ashamed to admit I own.

I shove, and a small pop of color emerges. One very clean and crisp Rams jersey, a pair of torn yellow fishnets, and a blue tutu. Everything needed for a game day outfit. In my small-town world, game day is like Halloween. It's the one day you dress up in a ridiculous

~ ☾ ~

costume and no one can say or do anything about it. I'm pleasing Dad by wearing the Ram colors, but with my own style.

I toss the game day outfit onto my bed and head for the shower where I stand for ten minutes in steamy bliss. Once clean, and wearing a towel wrapped around my head, I toss on a pair of sweat pants and a worn Rams T-shirt. Normally I'd waste time downstairs in front of the TV until it's time to leave, but with Dad upset with me, I'd rather stay holed up in my room.

Since I have nothing better to do, I work on my homework, then flip through a gossip magazine, and finally, when I'm really bored, I just stare up at the ceiling until it's time to get ready.

After slipping on my get-up, I pull a brush through my hair until it's smoothed down. Sometimes I hate that I inherited my mom's hair: raven black, thick, and majorly unruly. Then I part my hair, make quick work of the length, and suddenly my hair is separated into two French braided pigtails with yellow and blue ribbons wrapped around the elastic bands. In my opinion, if you're going to do something, no point in doing it halfway. This is Rams fandom to the extreme. Although I draw the line at painting my face. Unlike my dad.

"Okay, honey, you've primped long enough. It's time to go!" My dad's even voice carries up the stairs and into my room. I'm thankful his tone is back to normal. There is no hostility in it, no leftover semblance of our earlier altercation.

I grab a book for halftime, since reading is way more exciting than looking at cheerleaders, and head downstairs.

In the foyer, Dad taps his foot against the hardwood and tosses his keys from one hand to the other. He's got so much paint caked on his skin I can barely recognize him. He's wearing his jersey and *the* signature pants.

~ ☽ ~

These pants are as old as I am, I'm sure. He forced my mom to fashion them just to wear to soccer games. Blue and yellow plaid MC Hammer parachute pants. Gag. But my mom had made them.

"I'm happy to know that this might be the last time I see you in those pants," I joke. Even through all the hard times we've had, taking me to the games is the one thing my dad's been able to keep constant.

Outside, the sky is blanketed with an overcast of gray clouds. There's a nip in the air and signs of the impending rainy season are everywhere. The trees have become skeletons, having lost their leaves, and the once green grass is now brown, giving our yard and Silversprings a dreary facade.

I squeeze into Dad's tiny smart car. Good thing we're a family of two and never go on trips, because this car holds nothing besides the minimum amount of oxygen for two passengers. We sit in silence, as if speaking would use up the allotted oxygen, all the way to the field.

~ ☾ ~

Chapter Two

Landon

In the locker room the guys wander about, towels around their waists, leaching the stench of sweat off their bodies and into the air and engaging in more conversations about girls than sports.

As I put my stuff in my locker and change into my uniform, I try to tune everything out. Usually I'm with the team, talking about their latest conquests, but tonight I'm trying to get into the zone. There's a lot riding on this game. My entire future, actually. My parents have made it quite clear that they don't have enough money to send me to college. Without a scholarship, I'll be lucky to be able to afford community college. I desperately need to impress the scouts in the stands. I need a full ride to school, and a ticket out of this town. But when a certain name comes up, I can't help but lose focus on my pre-game strategy and listen.

"I heard Charity kicked him to the curb, *again*," the guy on my left says.

Another adds, "So she's available? 'Cause man, what I wouldn't give for a piece of that."

I lean in. "Change the subject," I say, shutting down the conversation.

"So it's true? She dumped you after you did it in the janitor's closet?" Daniel, my wingman and my cousin, jumps into the conversation.

~ ☾ ~

My jaw snaps shut. "That's not what happened." I'm pissed but can't say I'm all that surprised. Charity's known for her exaggeration.

"And what, you're saying you were the one to call it quits? Why would you throw her away before a game? That's bad luck," Daniel says as he juggles a few rolled up balls of socks.

Besides soccer, Daniel's the only good thing about Silversprings. There are pictures of us as babies, wearing Ram colors and holding soccer balls. As captain, I'm close to all my teammates, but Daniel is like a brother. I look out for him. But sometimes he can act like a pain in the neck.

"Yeah, I broke up with her."

"Who are you kidding? You guys always end up back together," Daniel says.

I raise my chin. "We. Are. Done." But Daniel's right. Charity and I have been on and off since I moved to Silversprings freshman year. Sure, there were the odd flings in between, but nothing substantial. We always did end up right back in each other's arms. But not this time. We'd grown too far apart. My heart and hormones just weren't into her anymore.

"If you're serious, you mind if I ask her out?"

Daniel would be just about the last person she'd end up with, and his request defies the bro code, but I'd been honest when I'd said we were done. But that still doesn't stop me from saying with some sarcasm, "Sure. You guys would be great together. My best friend and my ex."

"Really? Sweet!" Daniel pumps his fist in the air, completely missing my meaning.

I put the last of my stuff into my locker and shut it.

Daniel turns away from me, our conversation apparently forgotten, and hops up onto a bench, boxers hanging dangerously low on his hips. I wonder if he's

~ ☾ ~

thought of becoming a plumber. If he doesn't make it as a pro soccer player, that is.

That's what we both want.

"Who's gonna win tonight?" he hollers.

The rest of the team stops what they are doing, then yell in unison, "We are!"

I get a little pissed. It's about time the guys quit with the yapping and take the game seriously again. They might not have scouts and scholarships on their brains, but I do.

A wide grin on his face, Daniel cups his hand around his ear and shouts again, "I can't hear you!" then bellows, "Who's gonna win tonight?"

Aw, heck. I take a moment and yell with the team, "We are!" Our voices echo off the lockers, filling the air.

Daniel says, "Damn right we are. Boo-yeah!" Then adds, "Rams on three."

We huddle together like we do on the field. "One, two, three—go Rams," we cheer.

The excitement that's filled the room seeps in through my pores. If our team is on point, we can win. If we win, no more Silversprings. I'll be able to ditch this town, concentrate on getting an education, and on going pro. That's what matters.

Second to having fun and beating down The Eagles, of course.

~ ☾ ~

Chapter Three

Xylia

At halftime, when the team runs off the field, I'm ready to dig my nose into my book. Dad's finally forgotten that he's mad at me for skipping school, and I'm able to relax and enjoy our time together. The team's ahead and the crowd's crazy happy. Nothing like a championship game to get our small town all revved up. I'm even a little excited, but mostly because I've been able to check out number 17's butt. I might hate watching a bunch of guys kick a ball around, but I will fully admit to checking out Landon Phoenix's rear. But in truth, I like looking at Landon's face more than his butt. He's gorgeous.

I may not like hanging out at soccer games, but for me, not only is this the time when I can bond with my dad, but it's also the time when I can freely and openly check out Landon. At school I tend to keep my head down and eyes averted when Landon's around, not wanting to call attention to myself or tick off Landon's girlfriend Charity. But at the games, I secretly swoon when his body's covered in sweat, when his shirt clings to his muscled abs, and when he flashes that winning grin at the stadium. Neither he nor anyone else has any idea I gawk at him.

I can secretly pine for him and hope one day he might look at me as intently as he looks at the soccer ball.

~ ☾ ~

The players are back in the locker room, having their half-time pow-wow. I scan the crowd for Dad, who decided to make a pit stop. Off in the distance I can see him juggling enough food to feed a starving country for at least a week. But that's tradition. Gorge yourself on food that will make you break out in zits, add at least ten pounds to the thighs, and end up with the worst indigestion ever.

Had I known Dad would buy out the concession I would have stuck around to help carry the load, but at least he's leaving a trail of popcorn, French fries, and nachos in case he needs to find his way back to buy cotton candy and a foam finger.

"Think you got enough?" I ask as Dad takes a seat. I start relieving him of food, setting it on the small space between us.

"I figured if this was our last game, we should go out in style, so I bought most everything they were selling." He looks at me, then with raised eyebrows he gives me a shrug and adds, "Too much?"

I let out a small laugh. "Yeah, Dad, you went a little overboard."

"Huh...and here I was prepared to make a second trip."

"I think you got it covered," I say, tossing a chilli-covered fry into my mouth. Looking at my sauce-covered fingers, I ask, "Did you grab any napkins?"

Dad snaps his fingers. "Ah, crap. I knew I forgot something," he says.

I lick my fingers then reply, "I could go get some."

"No, that's okay. I think I can make it there and back before the game starts back up. Besides, I'm sure you have some reading to do." He gets up and starts to wade through the line of knees in front of him.

"Daddy?" I call out.

"Yeah, honey?"

~ ☽ ~

"Could you bring back some cotton candy?" I toss another fry into my mouth and lick my fingers clean.

He grins and nods, and I dig into my bag to find my book, then settle in to wait for my treats: cotton candy and Landon Phoenix.

~ ☾ ~

Chapter Four

Landon

There's two minutes left in the game. The crowd's been cheering wildly since the second half, but now complete and utter silence has fallen over the field. All eyes are on me. The score is tied, 4-4.

Up until now I've put on a stellar show for the scouts, scoring two goals and assisting with others. Daniel's done a great job of protecting our net. But now, it's up to me. I've got the ball on the sidelines. This might be the last chance we have to score the winning goal, my last chance to win a scholarship.

The most important moment in my life.

But for the first time tonight, I hesitate. I have that feeling people get when something is off and everything feels wrong. I'm standing just out of bounds, ready to throw the ball I'm holding back onto the grass, toward my teammates, but the world is getting fuzzy. I juggle the ball in my hands, buying a few extra seconds. The ref eyes me, waiting for another round of play to begin. I throw the ball with all my strength toward Steven, the only player who's open and closest to the other team's net.

The ball, however, doesn't make it. It flies through the air and lands clean in dead space. Nowhere near any of my teammates. Every player on the field rushes to the ball.

~ ☾ ~

I'm shocked. It was like there had been no power behind my throw. Shaking my head, I jog toward the ball, though I'm winded. I never get winded. Ever. My heart pounds fiercely in my chest and thumps loud in my ears. Sweat soaks through my jersey. It's blurring my eyesight. Now the tiny black and white ball seems miles away. I'm stumbling forward. The ground beneath my feet swirls, making me dizzy.

I look to Daniel. He's not watching the action. His eyes are trained on me as he raises one eyebrow. He mouths something. I can't make it out. Instead, I force myself to shake my head. Then his arms raise in the air. It looks as though he's calling for a time out, but no one's listening to him. I can hear the loud voices of my teammates echoing in my ears, though the sound is muffled. But I know the ball is still in play.

I can't move. Everyone's running around me but I'm frozen in place. The entire stadium gasps loudly. Peripherally, I see the fans rise to their feet. They point with worry and confusion. Daniel runs full bore toward me, but it's too late. My lids droop over my eyes and suddenly I'm falling, in slow motion, until the turf slaps me hard.

"Coach! Coach!" Daniel yells frantically, his voice like a loud siren in my ear, but I can't see him. My eyes won't open.

"Landon, wake up Landon," he yells.

My body jostles back and forth, likely from him shaking me. I can feel my stomach doing flips. I don't want to barf.

"Open your eyes, son!" Coach yells sternly.

But I can't. I try to force my eyes open, to see the light. I just want to shake off the feeling that everything is terribly wrong. I just want to stand up and finish the game.

Then I hear other voices, anxious voices, calling, "Dr.

~ ☾ ~

Morana! Is Dr. Morana here?"

   Like slipping into a deep sleep, everything goes silent. I lose all feeling in my body. And then...

~ ☾ ~

Chapter Five

Xylia

I'd been looking back at the crowd, enjoying their enthusiasm at the tie in the game, but then I notice a man is yelling my dad's name. I flip my gaze to my dad and see his eyes are wide, his body tense. I turn to quickly scan the field until I understand. Landon, my gorgeous Number 17, is on the ground. The goalie, Daniel, stands over him, frantically flailing his arms.

Landon doesn't move.

My stomach twists in knots and my chest constricts with worry. Get up. Get up, I scream inside, but with each passing second, his still body doesn't move.

Swarms of people start to crowd around Landon, including coaches, referees, and players. Dad is already on his feet. I stand too, trying to get a better look, as does the rest of the crowd. My view is now blocked and I can't tell if Landon's okay, if he's moving. The entire stadium is silent as they wait for the star player to rise to his feet and finish the game.

But when I hear someone else scream out, "Dr. Morana," I know something is horribly wrong.

Like a fireman hearing a fire station's bell, Dad leaps to his feet. He flies down the bleachers, taking them two at a time, pushing and shoving worried fans aside. No way am I staying behind. Not when Landon's hurt. I knock over my soda and shove my way down the aisle. I

~ ☾ ~

try to keep up, following the brightly colored parachute pants, pushing through the wall of fans and onto the field. Dad doesn't ease up on his speed until he skids onto his knees beside Landon.

Dad is like a well oiled casket hinge, not making a sound as he assesses the situation. He tilts Landon's head back to open his airway, then presses his fingers to Landon's neck, searching for a pulse. "Call an ambulance," he snaps out. "Now."

Everyone within a ten foot radius pulls out their cell phones and dials 911.

"Step back. We need some room," Dad says, his gaze never leaving Landon. Hands cover mouths, eyes fill with fear, but the group of worried fans staggers back. Dad places his mouth over Landon's, covers his nose, and blows a breath of air into his lungs. He raises back up, then says, "Xylia, I need you."

I fall to my knees beside him. "What can I do?" My hands shake. My heart pounds loud in my ears. This is bad. Really bad. But Dad can save Landon. Dad's a great doctor, one of the best.

"I need you to begin chest compressions."

My eyes grow wide. "But Dad..."

He looks away from Landon and glares at me. "Just do it!" He takes another deep breath, then tries to fill Landon's lungs with air.

My mind races as I try to recount what my father had drilled into me from the time I was able to perform CPR on my dolls. As the steps come flooding back, I assume the position. I place the heel of my hand in the middle of Landon's chest, then gasp as a surge of death sparks my skin.

I focus and interlace my fingers, then compress his chest down. I wait for it to completely recoil before doing the next compression.

"That's right honey, now twenty-eight more," Dad

~ ☾ ~

says as he checks for a pulse again.

From somewhere among the sea of distraught onlookers I hear, "He just—just fell. I don't understand."

There's an eerie silence then as I press my hands down on Landon's chest and pump again. "One-one thousand, two-one thousand, three-one thousand…" I mutter.

A few seconds later my father says, "Okay, last one, Xylia." He does the head-tilt, chin-lift thing again, opening the airway. Then he blows more air into Landon's lungs, twice. "Okay, go!" he says.

I resume compressions. My arms begin to ache but I don't let fatigue stop me.

"Where's my ambulance?" Dad demands.

"There," someone says. My gaze stays trained on Landon. Bright red and white flashes light up his blue and yellow jersey but cast an ugly glow around us.

A fierce wind blows up, whipping my pigtails against my neck, rustling the starched crinoline of my tutu. It causes my concentration to falter. I look away from Landon's chest, only no one else is bothered by the ferocious force of air or the loud howl it causes. They stand still, wide-eyed and shocked, staring at me as I stare at them. Everything starts to whirl around in front of me and I go dizzy, like when I used to twirl on the swing set in my backyard.

That's when I see him. The man is out of place at a soccer game. He's wearing a charcoal gray suit, has a toothpick dangling from his firm, set mouth, and has striking eyes, like a movie star. He's moving through the horde of people. His posture is bone straight, his strides so calculated it's as though he's floating and a current of air is what propels him forward. And he's staring right at Landon. Another doctor?

A wave of nausea sweeps over me. I swallow, forcing the bile back that rises in my throat. However, the

~ ☾ ~

feeling is only heightened. My stomach lurches with unease. Even my head begins to spin as an unsettling amount of wooziness is added. Bright lights flash, coming in and out of focus. The blinding whiteness scorches my eyes. I'm forced to blink rapidly, to shield them from the hurt. Then, suddenly, whispers fill my ears. Murmured words come at me from every direction. Voices. But they're too hushed. I can't make out what they are saying. What they could be trying to tell me.

"What's happening here? What's the situation?"

The paramedic's question snaps my focus back to Landon. I shake off the dizziness. Stress must be getting to me. The lights are playing tricks on my eyes, because people don't float. And there's about a million fans and players around us, all muttering about Landon—those have to be the whispers I heard. I just lost my focus for a second. But I can't lose my focus. Not when Landon's heart depends on my timed compressions.

My dad doesn't answer, just barks out, "Get me a vent bag!"

"But sir..." The paramedic sounds young, confused.

"I'm a goddamn doctor, do what I say. Bag, now! We need to get this kid to an ER."

This is the closest to the process of death I've ever been. I go dizzy again. I swear I can feel the life force being sucked right out of Landon. His soul is clawing its way out, trying to move on. But we won't let it. Dad is still forcing air into Landon's lungs and I'm pumping his chest, keeping his blood circulating.

To me, this moment is amazing. Freaky, frightening, but amazing. A life is in my hands. This is even more frightening than finding my mom dead, even more freaky than sneaking into the morgue of the hospital, and even more sad than finding out the old people I visit at the hospital have died. I see now why my dad wanted to be a doctor.

~ ☾ ~

The paramedics roll a gurney alongside us. The bed lowers with a loud screech until it's only a few short inches away from the ground. Once in position, they ready Landon to be moved.

"Don't stop. Listen to my voice, and whatever you do, don't stop compressions." My father's voice pulls me back to reality, yet again. "Okay, on the count of three we are going to lift. Just move with us, Xylia, but don't stop."

Dad and the paramedics lift Landon up and onto the gurney.

Dad looks at me and to the gurney. "Now, climb on."

I raise my eyebrows. "What? Why?"

"Please, Xylia. Just do it," Dad says. His forehead creases as he brings his hand up and wipes off beads of sweat that have formed. He looks tired. Frustrated.

I do as Dad says. I climb onto the bed, my knees on either side of Landon's still body as I continue compressions. I don't stop. Not for anything. Dad gives me a nod, and together he and the two paramedics lift the bed up and begin rolling it across the field.

"Oh god, Landon! Is he going to be okay? What's happening?"

The familiar voice of Landon's mother touches my ears. I look up from her son's chest and see her and Landon's dad come to a stop just before us. Landon's mom is frantic. His dad supports her as her son is rolled away. We pass his girlfriend, Charity, who stands with her hands covering her mouth, silently sobbing. Tears stream down her face.

"We're doing everything we can," Dad says. We leave the crowd behind. Somehow we manage to get the gurney into the ambulance, never having missed a beat or breath. The small quarters force me to stay where I am instead of getting off of Landon and sitting on the bench.

~ ☾ ~

"I can take over from here." A paramedic, different from the young one, says to me.

I look to Dad for an answer, but he just shrugs, then presses the bulb on the ventilation mask, forcing it to breathe for Landon.

"I want to stay, I want to keep going." My voice comes out stern.

"Okay, honey, keep going. Let's move out."

"But doctor..." The paramedic scowls.

"Just let her continue." Dad orders. The paramedic shakes his head but complies. My knees are killing me and my arms feel like I've been weightlifting for ages, but there's no way I'm stopping now. I won't let Landon die.

As the ambulance doors swing closed, I notice the man.

The perfectly pressed suit he wears and his heavenly blue eyes are a direct contrast to his penetrating stare. The blood in my veins turns ice cold. The hairs on my arms rise as a chill courses up my back. I'm not hallucinating. This guy is here for a reason. And I'm scared the reason is Landon.

* * * *

The hospital is a ten minute drive away. Dad and the paramedics hook up monitors and an IV, then inject things into Landon's arm as I keep pumping his heart.

"How long has he been down?" the young paramedic with sandy blond hair asks. He looks no older than me.

I see Dad look at his watch, then frown. "Too long," he mutters.

"Eight minutes out," the driver calls over his shoulder.

But not too long, I think. Landon could still come back. After all these years, I'd never worked up the

~ ☾ ~

courage to talk to him. What's the worst that could have happened? He could have laughed in my face. But as I look down at him, at his long eyelashes, slender jaw, the things that make up his kind face, I'm almost sure he wouldn't have. Not Landon. He isn't like all the other jocks. He doesn't think he's better than everyone else.

The ambulance slows to a stop. The driver lays on his horn and curses loudly.

Dad looks up from Landon. "What's the problem? Why aren't we moving?"

The driver pounds on the horn. We lurch forward only to come to another abrupt stop. I tighten my legs, squeezing them against Landon to hold myself as steady as possible.

"There's traffic, doctor, I'm—"

The sound of the horn squeals again.

"Get us out of here. Find another route."

Precious time passes as the ambulance forces its way through the traffic. The driver continues to honk the horn and swear at the other cars each time he's forced to brake and bring us to a stop.

The hospital is so close. If Landon can just hold on a few more minutes, we'll be there. Hold on Landon, my mind screams. But time keeps crawling by. Too much time.

"Maybe you should call it, doctor."

Ice fills my veins and I freeze for a second. "Dad, don't call it. He could still come back, right?"

But Dad doesn't give me the answer I'm looking for. Instead, he looks away from me as he says, "They're right. He's been down far too long. Even if he came back, there would be extensive damage to his brain."

"But Dad—" I protest, and for the first time, I miss a compression. I go to restart, but Dad stills my hands. Looking into my eyes, he solemnly shakes his head.

"No...no..." I whisper as I stare at Landon's body. No

~ ☾ ~

one will get to see him kick another goal, see the slight hint of dimples on his cheeks when he smiles. And no one will see how when the sun shines atop his head, his hair almost looks like strands of glittering gold. But most importantly, he'll never know how I felt about him.

It's the water that fills my eyes that catches me off guard. A single, stray tear rolls down my cheek, then another and another. Quickly, I wipe them away and force myself not to let another slip out. I'm surprised by my reaction.

Dad glances down at his watch, "Time of death...nineteen thirty-two."

Stiffly, I climb off Landon and squeeze onto the bench next to Dad. My stomach twists with grief and regret. I'm reminded of all the things I never got to say to Landon, and now never will.

"You did everything you could," Dad says. He presses his lips against my head, as if it would be enough. As if that wipes away everything that's happened. He doesn't know, though. He doesn't know how my heart aches right now for Landon.

As I rest against my dad, feeling the comforting touch of his hand against my head, realization begins to set in. It's so fierce I think I'll barf. I've seen more than a dozen dead bodies, but this, *this* doesn't even compare. I want to pound Landon's chest more, force his lungs to breathe, do anything to bring him back. This is the one death I wish I wasn't a part of. And yet I can't pull my gaze away from him, can't control the emotions swirling around my head.

Landon's dead.

~ ☾ ~

Chapter Six

Landon

Finally, I hear something. I have no idea how much time has passed, but a small sense of relief blankets my body. It warms me through to the bone. I strain to hear the faint music playing in the background and try to open my eyes, but I can't. Then bickering voices override the music.

"This one's so young."

"So? What does that matter? They come in all shapes and sizes, young and old."

"But I hate doing this to the young ones. I wish we could send him back and take some old, withering person."

"We can't. That's not the way this stupid process works."

"Fine. Let's get this over with already."

"Or maybe..." the first voice pauses. "Maybe we *could* have some fun."

"No. Oh, no. This isn't supposed to be fun for us. Our job is to maintain the balance and take him. Don't make this personal because you're unhappy."

I open my eyes. A searing white light floods my vision and a splash of fireworks explode in front of my eyes. I blink rapidly, my eyes burning, and try to focus them, to adjust to the brightness, though all I see is white. I'm alone. There are no bodies to the voices I swear I'd

~ ☾ ~

heard.

I stand up on shaky legs. The white is everywhere. I rub my eyes with my fingers, hoping they just haven't had time to adjust to this new surrounding, that the bright lights from before have me unfocused. I take a step forward. My body doesn't hurt. I flex muscles, and my brain tells every part of my body to acknowledge that it's in working order. Then I notice something is off as I look down the length of my body. I'm not in my uniform as I'd expected. A crisp white suit covers me, and shiny white shoes are on my feet. Touching the fabric, I feel it's soft against my fingertips, but more importantly, it's real. This isn't some weird dream.

After the surprise of my outfit wears off, I survey the room. But it's not a room. There are no walls. There isn't a roof above my head. I'm standing in a white globe, where there's no beginning and no end. I'm still encased in pure white. What the heck?

"Hello?" I call out. My voice carries forever, nothing for it to echo off. Beyond strange.

"Am I dead?" I ask into the vacant space.

No one answers me. This feels familiar. I have to rack my brain, curious if all my memories are still filed away somewhere. I know my name—Landon Phoenix—my age—eighteen—my parents' names...it's all there. And then I remember why this feels familiar. This scene is playing out like a movie I once saw.

I look around as I say, "God? Are you here?" I almost expect Morgan Freeman to appear out of thin air. But nothing happens.

"I want to go home now." My voice comes out shaky as the last word resonates against imaginary walls.

I'm not confused anymore. I'm freakin' scared.

~ ☾ ~

Chapter Seven

Xylia

I stand in the corner of the waiting room we've all been ushered into. Tears and tissues surround me. Paisley patterned chairs line the walls and are scattered across the grey and white speckled floor. Lame stock photos with words like *courage* and *strength* are pictured in big block letters. But they don't give me courage or strength. They don't cull my fears and worries.

There's a flurry of activity. Students, teachers, friends, and Landon's parents fill the space. Nurses scurry by, going about their business, clueless someone's just died. But everyone here, huddled together, want the same thing. They're waiting for my dad to come out and tell them what went wrong.

We're forced to wait. Things like this take time. I figure Dad will be doing whatever is necessary to declare someone dead, like running tests. That's not where my mind is at, though. I picture Landon, lying on a cold metal table. Or maybe they've zipped him up in one of those black bags. Slowly, the situation eats away at the little strength I have left.

I could grab a cab, or even ask one of the men in uniform for a ride home, but instead I head for the elevator. Dad had said he'd be at least an hour, and I can't take the sobs and sniffles that fill the waiting room

~ ☾ ~

anymore. I head to the floor where I work, figuring I could put in some time on my job.

I work at the hospital. I got the position based on my dad's recommendation and on the pull he has. I don't care—money is money. In a way, I get to experience death of all kinds. It pours from the walls of this place, filling up the halls with its stench and emotion.

The elevator doors open to the third floor, the Geriatrics ward. Nurse Joyce stands up from her stool behind the nurse's station and smiles. "What are you doing here so late?" she asks as she wipes her hands on her scrubs. She's been here forever, an institution on this ward. Her light brown hair is cut into a short bob with a severe straight line of thick bangs. It slims down her slightly pudgy round face, but the fact that her cartoon-covered scrubs are pulled taut against her bulging belly doesn't hide her weight issues. Or the cookies she always seems to have on shift, shoved in her pockets or shared with the patients. I like her. She's warm and cuddly and makes me smile. But not tonight.

"My father's working. I came with him. Thought I might check on some of my patients," I say, avoiding the truth.

"Okay. But I'm not sure how many are still awake."

"Doesn't matter. Do you have any spare scrubs behind the counter? I think this outfit might scare them," I say, motioning to my unusual clothes.

Joyce laughs. "I think it's cute. And a heck of a lot more cheerful than what you usually wear." She walks over to a stack of shelves just off to the left, then pulls out a pair of pants and a shirt. "Here, this should fit," she says, walking back toward me.

I take the blue scrubs with Silversprings Hospital stamped on the breast pocket. "Thanks."

"Let me know if you need anything."

I flash her a smile and take the long hallway in giant

~ ☾ ~

strides, heading to the changing room. Quickly I replace
my Rams blue and yellow with the powder blue scrubs
Joyce gave me. The pants are a little too big. I have to
cinch the drawstring. They still hang down, reminiscent
of Dad's parachute pants. The shirt, on the other hand,
is a little tighter then I'd like it to be, but it will do. I
stuff everything in my locker, grab my kit—full of books,
cards and gossip magazines—and head to my first
patient.

The first room I pass is dark. Loud snores echo off the
walls of the tiny space. I keep moving, and after three
failed attempts, I finally find someone awake. I knock
lightly on the open door to announce my presence
before I say, "Mr. Cambel, are you awake?" I take a few
steps inside the room.

The scratchy blankets and sheets rustle and a throat
clears. "Xylia? Is that you, dear?"

I walk the rest of the way into the room, then pull
back the curtain to expose a heavyset man lying in bed.
Mr. Cambel's fairly new. He's only been here a few
months, but has quickly risen through the ranks to
become one of my favorites. Well into his seventies, Mr.
Cambel is dying of liver failure—too many years of
scotch and brandy. And by the time he realized he was
doing damage to his body, it was too late. He lectures
me on steering clear of alcohol, like he's taking on the
role of my grandfather or something. Old age has
treated him well, though. Besides a few wrinkles, he still
has a full head of silver hair, a personality that can keep
you on your toes, and chocolate brown eyes that gleam
with the little life he has left.

Though I call him and the rest of the elderly in the
ward my *patients*, they aren't. I don't check their vitals
or serve them medicine, and thankfully I don't have to
clean up after them. Instead, I mostly just keep them
company, try to lift their spirits, and no matter what,

~ ☾ ~

show that people still care about them.

It's easier to form bonds with people you know aren't going to be around too long. They have few expectations. And most of all, they don't judge. They want a friend just as much as I do. Death is our common denominator. They know they are going to die and I know they are going to die. No expectations of life here. Besides, I know that I've left an impression on them, and most of all I don't have to try too hard to please them. They take whatever I'm willing to give.

"Well, quit standing around and get on over here," Mr. Cambel says, tapping the edge of his bed. I take two steps, then sit on the small amount of free space he's offered. Reaching into my kit, I pull out a book.

"What'll it be?" I say as I flip the pages.

"Anything you want."

I scan the pages of the book and search for something to read. This is what Mr. Cambel prefers; along with simple conversation, he likes me to read him poems. Some people like playing cards or watching TV, or even Scrabble, but Mr. Cambel likes poetry. I do, too.

When I find the page I'm looking for, I clear my throat and begin to speak. "I was angry with my friend; I told my wrath, my wrath did end. I was angry with my foe; I told it not, my wrath did grow," I pause for a moment, and Mr. Cambel smiles eagerly. I swallow, take a breath, then finish the poem, letting the words from "A Poison Tree" wash over me.

When I finish, Mr. Cambel sits for a while in silence before finally speaking. "Ah, interesting choice. I do love William Blake." He pauses again, maybe taking in the whole of the words I'd spoken, or maybe just organizing them in his head.

"Another?" I ask.

"Sure, why not? I've got no place to be." He chuckles.

So that's what I do. I find another poem, then

~ ☾ ~

continue. He stays silent most of the time, but
sometimes gives me a small taste of what he likes about
my choice. But he never frowns on what I've selected.
Never tells me he doesn't like it, or that I chose
something too sad. I push through another poem until I
realize that my eyes are watering, that the sadness in the
words pulls at my own heartache. I still can't believe
Landon's really gone. That on Monday at school, he
won't light up the halls with his infectious smile. But Mr.
Cambel doesn't know my misery, so I flip the pages, find
another poem, and begin to read, taking only a brief
moment to clear my eyes of the wetness that's
accumulated.

"Wasn't lights out over an hour ago, you two?" My
father's voice startles us.

I set the book down and turn slightly to see him. "It
was, but Mr. Cambel doesn't mind," I say. "Did you find
anything out about why Landon died?" I ask.

"Nothing. So far his death is completely unexplained.
We finally got the family to agree to an autopsy," Dad
says. "They'll start tomorrow. I hope they find an
answer."

"Strange," is all I can come up with to say.

"You about done here, honey?"

"Can I finish the poem?" I look back to Mr. Cambel,
who smiles.

"Sure," my dad says. "I'll be in my office. I have to
finish up some paperwork anyway." He pauses, then his
body stiffens. "I just want to say...I'm very proud of you.
I mean, proud of what you did today. I know it was
tough, but you did great, kid."

Hearing Dad say that makes me a little gooey inside.

"Alright. Come find me when you're ready," he says,
then turns from the doorway. I listen until the sound of
his feet hitting the linoleum floor can't be heard
anymore.

~ ☾ ~

But as I pick up the book and start to find where I left off, the full brunt of the emotions I've been trying to push aside come at me all at once. The poems in this book may be helping Mr. Cambel, but they aren't helping me. Instead, the despair that's written on every page has me thinking more and more about Landon, and death. "I've got something I have to take care of. Can we finish tomorrow?" I ask.

"Sure, no problem. Though I hope I'm still around." Mr. Cambel winks.

"Thanks," I say as I hop down from my perch. "Tomorrow," I add, then head out the doorway and into the hall.

At the elevator, I press the button to the basement. More importantly, I'm pushing the button to the morgue. I've never seen anyone die before. I want to know what happens when someone dies. That man in the suit, the one who seemed like he'd glided across the grass—was he really part of my imagination? Had I really hallucinated him? Or was this some sort of cosmic joke—guys in suits escorting dead people. I need to know if that's how my mother left. If that's what's on the other side.

~ ☾ ~

Chapter Eight

Landon

In the White Room as I've come to call it, time is at a standstill. I have no idea if seconds are passing, or minutes, or hours, or even years. Sure, I could count in my head forever, judge time that way, but as for what's happening outside the room, I'm at a loss. How do I know the seconds I count here are the same seconds that are passing back home? Instead, I choose not to dwell on the passage of time and decide to move my feet and head in one direction. I'm hoping to find something or someone, or at the very least, fall off the edge and return home.

Unless this is home. Maybe I'm drugged up and in surgery. And this is just all one big hallucination. If that's the case, I never want to do drugs, ever again. Highs like this aren't worth it. This is just plain freaky. I'd rather settle for a dream.

One, two, three...wake up. Putting one foot in front of the other, I try to walk in a straight line. The whiteness never falters. The more steps I take, the more things look exactly the same. It's as though I am on a never-ending treadmill, heading nowhere fast. For all I know I could be walking in circles. The idea that I am getting nowhere makes me uneasy. Add that to the confusion over what the heck is going on and this might just be the worst kind of purgatory. In my eyes, this is neither

~ ☾ ~

heaven nor hell; this is some waiting room in between. Either way, I want to go home, now. This never-ending whiteness and silence is enough to drive anyone insane.

Ahead, appearing almost out of thin air, gray fog swarms toward me. It's moving fast, creating a scene of menacing shadows, taking on a strange form as it flies through the air, coming closer. I turn and run. After believing nothing exists in the White Room, this fog has me terrified. My heart pounds and I hear the thuds.

An deep laugh echoes off nothing, and suddenly it's not just the charcoal fog that has me terrified. And then, through the fog that is now encasing me in a ghostly mist, the nothingness speaks to me.

"Time to go."

I'm dead. I have to be. Or at least, soon I will be dead.

~ ☾ ~

Chapter Nine

Xylia

As I step off the elevator, the cool air sends chills up my spine, raising the tiny hairs that cover my skin. I cross my arms over my chest and rub my bare arms, hoping the friction will warm me.

The lights overhead buzz and flicker, creating an eerie atmosphere. I don't think twice about how spooky the basement seems. What I think about is what I'm about to do. I find my legs are propelling me forward. I want to see Landon's dead body. These circumstances are different from any other time I've seen a dead body. Some of the other corpses I hadn't known when they were alive. But I'd felt Landon's life slip away beneath my fingers. I just *have* to see him one last time.

I don't know how many times I'd tried to sit as close as I could to him in the library just to hear his voice. Run behind him in gym class so I could stare at his lean, athlete's body. Even the smell of his deodorant and the sweat that wafted off his body was like an instant aphrodisiac that would send me into a fit of daydreams.

The hallway is long, with brick and mortar on either side of me and cement beneath my feet. I pass the occasional door. There's a lot more down here than just the morgue. Records, storage, offices, the incinerator and laundry are all housed in rooms somewhere in this expansive dungeon. But I know where I'm headed.

~ ☾ ~

I keep my nose to the ground and push forward, but am startled when I hear footsteps closing in. A security guard walks briskly toward me. Fear that I might be busted speeds up my heart rate. After hours, the basement is restricted. I drop my arms to my side, raise my chin, and push my shoulders back, trying to give the fast approaching security guard the impression that I have every right to be here. As we cross paths, I notice his eyes fall on my chest. I assume he's noticing the employee badge I have pinned to my pocket and not my breast size. He gives me a flick of his chin and continues to stomp down the hallway. I keep facing forward and hear the sound of his footfalls dissipate. I let out a sigh of relief and feel my muscles relax as I near the end of the hallway.

As I push through the thick metal doors, the morbid truth of my name resonates within me. Dad does all he can to save lives. However, I do whatever I can to immerse myself in death. My last name, Morana, means just that, death. Whether a coincidence or fluke, it seems I was born to have some sort of affiliation with *The End.*

I slip inside the morgue. Goosebumps prickle my arms at the change in temperature. The metal doors of the morgue close with a loud click. I look back, hoping this isn't one of those moments where the door is locked from the outside and a knife-toting killer is waiting for me on the inside. I shake the image out of my head and turn back toward the room. Nothing living is down here. Just me.

Long metal tables fill the center, and trolleys lined with silver tools glisten in the light. The space is cramped. I work my way toward a desk at the back of the room. On the wood surface is a thick black binder. It's in plain sight, so I'm not really snooping, I think, as I flip open the cover. My eyes scan the page until I find what I want—a name associated with a number. Quickly,

~ ☾ ~

I close the binder.

The walls are lined with thick, square doors, clearly marked with numbers. I stop in front of the one I want. In the middle of that wall, at waist height, is number twelve. Beyond the door, lying on a sliding metal table, is the body of Landon Phoenix.

I've always had a crush on Landon, ever since freshman year when his family moved to Silversprings. I've watched him grow into his looks, no longer a gangly boy with braces. I've always wondered what it would be like to share the same air as him. To hear my name roll off his tongue in that deep voice I've come to long for. To press my lips against his as he holds me in a tight embrace. Though, now those things are impossible, except one. I can pull open the door, slide the table out, and at least for a moment, share the same air as him, whether his lungs are breathing it in or not.

I hesitate, my hand on the handle. Besides my mother's frozen stiff body, this will be the only other dead person I *really* knew and can see up close. The others have just been people, random ones at that. The guy from the grocery store who jumped off Whibley Bridge into the icy waters below, the occasional patient of mine who succumbed to old age, and many, many others. But this is personal. This is someone I'd known, or at least had held secretly in my heart.

I suck in a deep breath of air and pull on the latch that separates me from Landon. It opens with a sticky suction releasing sound. A haze of foggy, frigid air surrounds me. When it clears, the sandy blond hairs of Landon's head come into focus. I yank on the table handle and slide his stiff body out of its cold crypt.

I take everything in. I try to commit to memory everything about him, from the exact color of his hair to the tiny freckles that cover his bare arms. The perfect shaped eyebrows to the unique lines of his once rosy

~ ☾ ~

lips.

I touch him; my body chills with death's influence. I breath deep, drinking it all in.

Then the startlingly loud sound of my ringing cell phone pierces the air and makes me jump. The moment absorbing Landon's features wasn't long enough. Quickly, I dig my hand into my pocket and pull out my cell. It's Dad, probably wondering where I am. I press the ignore button on the screen, amazed I even have reception in this metal encased tomb.

I take one last look at Landon, release a sigh full of sadness, and realize I need to put him back in the compartment. But this is the last moment I'll ever have with him. Forever. I can't help but lean over him for one last look, one last time. From this angle, his skin looks severely pale. Tiny blue veins crisscross over his face, and I can even see the thin hairline cracks in his lips. I reach out and smooth down his unruly hair, tucking a few strands behind his ear. I pull my hand back slightly, but then I place my fingertips gently against the cool of his cheek. My heart tugs in my chest, my eyes well with tears. Another rush of regret envelopes me. If only I'd been stronger, I could have saved him. Or worked up the courage to talk to him...

If only.

This is it. This is the last time I'll ever get to see him. I want to say goodbye. All I want is to be close to him one more time. My heart speeds up, my palms grow clammy, but I inch closer and closer until the cool soft skin of Landon's lips are touching mine. I hold still for a second and feel that odd buzzing of death I always feel when I'm close to someone dead. It grows, deepening, until it's almost too much.

I force my lips away from his. I'd wanted one last look, one last touch of his skin, but how did that turn into a kiss with a stiff? I shake off the moment, and

~ ☽ ~

when my eyes open, a small amount of relief washes over me

But that relief is quickly rinsed away when Landon's body shifts.

And then the impossible happens.

Landon sits up.

~ ☾ ~

Chapter Ten

Xylia

The phone that's still in my hand falls and shatters against the hard cement floor. I blink, hoping it's just my wild imagination working overtime. But Landon's eyes fly open. I jump back a step as he gasps for air. I can't believe what's happening. Leaning in close, I come within inches of his face. His chest rises and falls. A strangled cry pushes through his mouth as he falls back against the metal table. His eyes close.

My heart drops. I clap a hand over my mouth to hold in a scream. I stumble back and crash into a gurney. I rush to the door, slamming against it with my hands when I reach it, pushing it open. My feet don't seem to be moving fast enough as I run down the hallway to the elevator. When I get there, I push the button repeatedly, trying to force the elevator to hurry up. My breath is coming fast, and my hands are trembling when the door finally slides open.

When the elevator reaches the first floor, I slip through the opening, not wasting any time. The nurse's station is straight ahead. I race to the desk.

"You need to get someone to the morgue now—he's still alive!" My voice comes out strangled, rushed. The nurse just eyeballs me, confused.

This time I try and slow everything down as I repeat, "The morgue. He's still alive!" It still comes out frantic.

~ ☾ ~

The nurse's features shift, suspicion taking over confusion. "Who's still alive?"

"L-Landon Phoenix. I saw him...*move*. He's still alive. Just get someone down there, please!"

"Okay, miss, you need to calm down," she says, clearly not believing me.

"Please, just call my dad, Dr. Morana. Tell my dad to get to the morgue."

The nurse rolls her eyes at me. When it becomes apparent I'm wasting my time, I turn my back on her and start running. I head down the hall looking for a different nurse, a doctor, anyone that might listen to me. At the end of the corridor I see a security guard.

"Excuse me! Please stop," I call out. I sprint forward, pushing myself harder.

The security guard turns around and I grab his shoulders, saying, "There's a kid in the morgue. He's still alive. Please, you have to help him."

"Whoa, slow down, Miss. What's going on?" the security guard asks as he pries my hands off him.

"God dammit, doesn't anyone in this place know how to listen?" I yell, angry. "Please, just get a doctor to the morgue. You're wasting time!"

The guy reaches for his radio, pulling it from his shoulder to his lips. "I have a situation in the north wing. I'm going to need—"

But I don't stick around to listen. I know how his message will finish—something like, "there's a crazy orderly running around." I have no idea what kind of condition Landon is in, nor do I really know if he's still alive, but this time I'm going straight to a doctor.

I push the door open that leads to the stairwell. I pound up the stairs, two at a time, my hand gliding along the railing. I barely slow my pace when I reach the door. I shove it and it swings open with a loud bang. My father's office is to the left and down the hall a little

~ ☾ ~

ways. Just as I round the corner, I see another security guard is fast approaching. "Shit," I mutter.

"Dad. Daddy!" I start yelling a few feet from his door.

Just as I reach Dad's office, the guard wraps his arms around me from behind, squeezing me.

I gasp as his strength crushes me. "Get off me."

"Calm down, stop struggling."

The door to Dad's office finally opens and he emerges, groggy-eyed. "What's going on? Xylia?"

I still fight against the guard's clutches as I say, "Daddy, I—I was in the morgue. Landon Phoenix is—he's alive."

"That's impossible," Dad mumbles as he pushes his glasses up the bridge of his nose.

"Dad, I'm not lying, I swear. Just believe me, please," I beg as my body, my mind slowly stop fighting.

"Is this really your daughter?" The security guard still holds me tight.

Suddenly Dad seems to see the guard, whose arms are wrapped around my chest. Dad's eyes grow wide. "Yes, she is my daughter. Let her go," he says, his tone full of authority.

Reluctantly, the guard loosens his grip, then, when he gets a glare from Dad, he lets me go completely.

I push myself away from him and scramble to Dad. I grab his hand and tug him to me. "C'mon, Dad."

Dad says to the guard, "Call Dr. Chase. Get him to meet us in the morgue."

The guard pauses. "You don't actually believe—"

"Of course I believe my daughter, now go! Get Dr. Chase."

When the guard is out of earshot, Dad looks at me. "What the heck were you doing down there? We've had this discussion."

When I'd first started this job, I'd been caught in the morgue a time or two. To the hospital and to my dad, it

~ ☾ ~

was a big deal to have someone snooping around. Not to mention the fact that the hospital Board found my actions just odd. It makes people squirm, having someone so comfortable yet intrigued with death. After the third time I'd been caught, I'd promised to never go to the morgue again.

"I know, Dad, I'm sorry, but—" I don't really have an explanation. At least, not one that would satisfy him.

Dad lets out an annoyed sigh. His eyebrows are knitted together, like he's thinking of ways to punish me, but he knows now is not the time.

We ride the elevator in silence. When we get to the morgue, I almost expect the table I left out to be empty, that I had imagined the whole thing, but Landon's still there. He's lying with his eyes closed. His chest moves rhythmically.

"Stand back," Dad says, looking first to me and then to Landon. Unwrapping the stethoscope from his neck, he puts the buds in his ears. Dr. Chase bursts through the door. Ignoring the commotion, Dad takes another step toward Landon. "My god, he's breathing—he's alive!" he says.

Dr. Chase pushes past me to stand by Dad, who's pressing the metal of the scope to Landon's chest. "I can hear his heart," Dad says. "Gary, get an IV and a gurney. We need to get this boy upstairs stat."

I clear my throat. "I-I told you, Dad. I wasn't lying." But how? How is this even possible?

The doors to the morgue open again, letting in a puff of warm air; it's the guard from upstairs.

"Xylia, outside. You there," Dad points his finger to the guard, who I can't help but scowl at. "We need help. This boy is alive!"

"But Dad..." I don't want to leave.

"Outside, now!"

The guard gets on his radio and barks orders to

~ ☾ ~

someone as my father and Dr. Chase start searching the drawers of the morgue for medical supplies. Not having anything else to do, I march out the doors. My mind, however, is running a mile a minute. How the hell could someone die...but not be dead?

Briefly, my mind replays the moment where my lips pressed against Landon's. I shake the memory away, trying to shatter the image as I swear to myself never to think about it again. A kiss could never bring someone back to life. That's impossible.

Only a few minutes pass, then the hallway is filled with echoing footsteps and voices. A flurry of doctors and nurses round the corner and rush toward me. Some carry medical supplies, some carry blankets, and some are empty handed. I press my back against the cool brick, allowing them room to pass. Wheels of a gurney squeal loudly as the people push open the doors and hustle inside. The door clicks shut and the commotion that filled the hall is gone. Now the only sound is the buzzing of the fluorescent lights overhead.

I push myself off the wall, go to the door, and press my forehead against the glass window. On the other side, the morgue is filled with doctors and nurses moving about. I can't see a thing, can't tell what they're doing to Landon. However, I know enough about Dad's role as a doctor to guess. They'd be starting an IV, pumping Landon full of saline, probably giving him oxygen, and transferring him to the gurney. I can't help but feel as though I should be in there doing something.

I stand, face still plastered against the window in the door, hoping to see something, anything that will tell me Landon's okay. Instead, I get shot with a cool breath of air. It chills me to the bone, just like when I touched Landon. I shiver and bring my hands up to rub the bare skin of my arms. Then a low whisper reaches my ears.

I whirl around, but there's no one in the hallway.

~ ☾ ~

Maybe it was Dad or a nurse, I think as I turn back toward the door. But the people inside are going about their work, oblivious to me and the voice. I let out a sigh. Exhaustion must be taking over.

The minutes tick by slowly as I wait. What's taking them so long? Just then there's a rush of action. I step back from the door, which swings open, almost hitting me. Several people push the gurney past me. I manage to find Landon's face. His eyes are still closed. But I can see the rise and fall of his chest as he's rolled down the hall. Dr. Chase follows closely behind. Finally, Dad exits the room, along with the guard.

"Is—is he okay?" I ask when Dad stops in front of me. But I can't look him in the eyes.

"We need to run some tests. But you saved his life. Had you not been there, he would have suffocated when he came to."

I put my hand over my mouth. I had never thought about that. Never having believed in miracles before, this is an excellent time to start. Had I not been there, Landon would have died. *Again*. But that's not it—that's only half the truth. That kiss, that moment of connection, just can't go unnoticed.

The guard coughs, reminding me of his presence. "I'm going to need to ask you a few questions, Miss Morana."

"Yes, of course," I say, really having nothing to hide. Just as my father said, I had just saved a life. No one could give me flack now about being in the morgue.

"Let's get out of this cold basement. I need to notify the family," says Dad.

In the elevator, the guard wastes no time pulling out a pen and small pad of paper. "Now exactly what were you doing in the morgue at this late hour?"

Looking to my dad, whose eyebrows are raised, I realize he too is waiting for the answer. I swallow. "I

~ ☾ ~

have a nasty habit of exploring where I don't belong," I say.

"And you chose the morgue?"

"I-I knew him. I just...wanted a last goodbye?"

The guard scribbles on his pad. "So what was it? Exploring or saying goodbye?"

"Both." I gulp.

"You know you're not supposed to be down here, especially since you are of no relation to the victim."

"I'm sorry. I won't do it again, but he's only alive because I was there."

"Which seems odd, doesn't it?"

Now my eyebrows are the ones that are knitted, "I don't understand. How is that *odd*?"

"Was this some kind of prank? A high school joke, perhaps?"

My face falls flat. I'm appalled at what this man is suggesting. I'm thankful when Dad chimes in.

"I was the one to call time of death. I examined the body myself. I assure you, this has been no joke."

Shaking his head, the guard writes more down on his pad. The doors open and we're at the main floor. The guard stalks off, apparently done with his interrogation.

"I want you to go home. I'm going to be here late. There are a lot of things that need to be done, sorted out," Dad says. When he sees the corner of my lips turn down, he says, "Please, no arguing, just go." Then he reaches into his pants and pulls out his wallet. He produces a twenty-dollar bill and holds it out. "Call a cab."

Grabbing the twenty, I plunge my hand into my pocket, going for my phone—

Uh oh. "Uh, Dad...there's something else."

He makes a grumbling sound, low in his throat. "Oh, Xylia. What is it?" He's expecting the worst, I'm sure.

"I uh, dropped my phone. It broke," I say, turning my

~ ☾ ~

face away from him.

He sighs. "We'll deal with that tomorrow. Just go home and get a good night's rest. A lot's happened today."

I pull Dad in for a hug. "Love you," I whisper.

"I love you too, honey." His lips press against my forehead. Mom will never be able to kiss me goodnight again, but at least my dad still can.

~ ☾ ~

Chapter Eleven

Landon

I'm tired of not knowing. Not knowing how much time has passed, not knowing what's happening, but most of all, I'm tired of not knowing if I'm dead or alive.

"Can you hear me? Can you open your eyes, Landon?"

My eyelids flutter, brightness fills them as my eyes adjust. This time everything is clear. I can make out a ceiling, lemony colored walls, and the weight of blankets that cover my body. I can hear something, too. There are faint beeping sounds of machines, the tick of a clock somewhere in the room, and hushed voices. I'm in a hospital. I guess that answers some of my questions.

"Welcome back, Landon. We thought we had lost you."

I try to open my mouth to speak, but my throat is scratchy and instead of words, a groan comes out. My hand rises to my throat. Have I lost the ability to speak?

"Your throat's probably dry. Here, have some water."

A man steps close. He has graying hair and glasses and he's holding out a cup and straw. The weight of the water-filled cup is heavy in my hand, which shakes as I try to grasp it.

"Take it easy. Let me help you with that."

Taking the cup out of my hand, the man then holds it in front of my mouth. Leaning forward, I wrap my lips around the straw and suck up the liquid. It cools my

~ ☾ ~

throat, relieving the scratchy soreness. A few more gulps and the doctor takes the cup away.

"Do you know where you are?"

I nod, clear my throat, and try again to form words. "A hospital?"

"Exactly. I'm Dr. Morana."

The name sounds familiar, though I don't think I've met this man before.

"Can you tell me your name?"

I chuckle, but it comes out as a cough. The doctor had already told me my name. "Landon. Landon Phoenix."

"That's good. That's very good."

"What happened?"

"You collapsed on the soccer field and were, uh, brought here." He glances over his shoulder. "You need to get your rest, but first, your parents would like a word."

He's not telling me everything and it's making me uneasy, but I want to see my parents. "Okay."

"I'll let you three have a few moments, but then I really need you to get some rest." Again, he looks over his shoulder, then motions with his hand.

I see my parents approach from the corner of the room, then their faces come into view. Mom has puffy cheeks and streaks of mascara down her face. She's been crying. Even her voice sounds shaky as she says, "Thank you, Dr. Morana." My father looks only slightly better. His lips are in a frown, his face, sullen.

"Mom? Dad?"

"Oh honey, you gave us quite a scare," Mom says.

"Why am I here?"

She looks to Dad then back to me. "The doctor already explained that, dear. You collapsed on the field and were rushed here by ambulance."

My mother's never been a very good liar, this time being no exception. But the White Room, the never-

~ ☾ ~

ending cascade of whiteness and bright light, had to be something, had to be real. "I know that, but *what* happened?"

"Why don't you get some rest, son? We'll talk more in the morning. Right now, you just need to concentrate on getting well."

I look to Dad. "Did we win?"

"Yeah, son, we won." He sighs.

As though my body understands the word "rest," I'm suddenly exhausted. My eyelids even begin to grow heavy. They droop, clouding my sight. "Okay," I say. The need for sleep becomes more persistent.

Mom leans in and kisses me on the cheek. "We'll be close by, if you need anything. Okay?"

"Just get some sleep. We'll be back," Dad says, giving me a nod, then turning to the door. He puts a comforting hand on Mom's shoulder as he leads her away. Mom clicks off the overhead light as she walks out the door.

Now only the LED lights on the various machines I'm hooked up to flicker in the darkness. I'm afraid to close my eyes. Afraid that this might all have been a dream, that when I close my eyes I'll return to the White Room, or worse—return to the blackness. But I can't fight off the fatigue. My eyelids fall, sleep consumes me.

Flashes of the gray, dark shadows cloud my dreams, then a blurry figure with green eyes and black hair appears. A girl. The image flickers like an old movie. But something's not right. Something's—

~ ☾ ~

Chapter Twelve

Xylia

I've never had a nightmare, or at least, not one that I can remember. Even after that Christmas morning, the one when I'd awaken hoping to find presents from my parents and Santa—whom I knew no longer existed yet welcomed brown paper wrapped parcels from him nonetheless—but had instead found a nearly bare tree and no signs of Christmas joy. Even after all that, I still never had a nightmare.

However, this morning, I wake with a sweat-drenched body. Pyjamas wet, sticking to my skin, hair plastered damp against my head. My mind works overtime as it tries to process the dream and the whispers that pulled me out and woke me up. The murmurs I heard coupled with the image of Landon Phoenix's body rising from the metal slab still resonates in my mind and has me more than a little confused

After a soothing shower, fresh clothes, and locking up all images of Landon away tight, I stroll into the kitchen. A sugary breakfast is the only way to start the day. Brown sugar-frosted cereal is a staple in my house. I pour two bowls, adding the milk.

"Dad, I made breakfast!" I call out. Usually he's the first one awake, the one pouring the bowls. I don't think much of his lacking presence, chalking it up a very late night.

~ ☾ ~

I'm startled when the phone rings. I stand up and walk over, then pick it up and say, "Hello?"

"Hello. Is Dr. Morana available to give a statement?" The male voice on the other end of the line brims with confidence.

I'm confused. "Statement?"

"Yes. Is he available?"

Covering the receiver with my hand I yell, "Dad? The phone's for you." I'm met with no response. I figure he'd gone to work and ask the caller if I can take a message.

There's a long pause, then the man replies. "Yes, please tell Dr. Morana to give Michael Blake at the Gazette a call when he has a moment—"

"The newspaper?"

"Yes, that's right."

"Ooookay." I know there's uncertainty in my tone, but I don't want to dig into this. I take the man's number and promise to have my dad call back. I look down at the scribbled note, perplexed.

I finish my bowl of now soggy cereal, then turn on the TV for Saturday morning cartoons. Only they aren't on. I nearly choke at the sight on the screen. Hordes of people are in front of the Silversprings Hospital—news crews with their satellite radio-topped vans, reporters with microphones, people waving banners, and more.

Turning up the volume, I plop down onto the sofa and listen. The picture switches to a news studio. A thin, blond woman appears behind a news desk, wearing a red blazer and white blouse, and smiles at the camera. "Good morning, I'm Sylvia Duran. We're interrupting local programming to bring you an extraordinary story. Late last night a local Silversprings resident, pronounced dead by hospital doctors, has miraculously recovered. As you can see"—the news reporter disappears, the scene changing back to the hospital— "Silversprings Hospital has been flooded with people,

~ ☾ ~

some hoping to get a statement, some hoping to confirm their faith that this is truly an act of God, and some just rallying behind the unnamed patient. Though full details have not yet been released, this truly is an unbelievable moment for Silversprings."

The remote falls from my hand as my heart revs up and pumps overtime. I'd kissed Landon. And now he's alive. It's impossible and yet, it's happening. I want to see Landon again but I'm not so sure it's the best idea. Suddenly I don't know what I want. I don't want to get in trouble, I don't want to admit I kissed him, but I'm not sure I want to let another day go by where I'm not honest with him and myself. Not wasting any time, I change into my work clothes—black scrubs—and grab my employee badge. Time I faced the impossible.

At the hospital, the parking lot is full as I drive by on my way to employee parking, which thankfully has been left alone by the mass of people crowding the entrance. A line of security guards protect the doors. I choose to take the maintenance entrance to save myself the bother of pushing my way to the front.

Instead of going to Landon's room, I chicken out and head to Dad's office. Not feeling it important to knock, I push open the door. My father, exhausted, his eyes glazed over and his clothes wrinkled, is riffling through papers on his desk.

"Daddy?" I say with concern. He looks as though he's been up all night. He must not have come home at all.

"Xylia? What are you doing here?" he asks, going right back to the strewn-about papers.

"I was worried about you. I've seen the news, and someone from the Gazette called the house. What's going on?"

"They want answers but I don't know what to tell them. I can't make sense of what happened, honey. I didn't think things would get so out of hand."

~ ☾ ~

I nod. Neither did I. "It's okay Daddy, really. Is there anything I can do?"

"You don't have to help me. Besides, don't you think you've done enough?"

I'm taken back, like I've been slapped in the face. "Done enough? That boy's alive because of me," I say.

"Yes he is, but you shouldn't have been down there. The Board is on my case about why you were. They're talking about suspending your job. Hell, they might suspend my job," he mutters.

I feel my eyes grow wide. "What?" I say. I can hear my voice raising several octaves.

"You can't just go down there Xylia, it's restricted. *You* know that. We've gone through this before. But the Board agrees with me in thinking that letting the whole truth out would be damaging to the hospital. We're— we're going to omit the morgue fact. That's to stay between you, me, and the hospital. No one is to know. You got it?"

"Yes," I croak. I suppose it's in the interest of the hospital not only to keep me out of the story, but out of the morgue, too. How would that look? Trust in the medical system would falter if people knew that a person had woken up, in the morgue. And had a person not been there to rescue them...

Yes. A cover up makes sense.

That doesn't stop Dad from bowing his head in anguish. "One more week, that was the deal. You had to stay out of trouble for one more week."

"Daddy, I'm sorry, I am, but can we just look at the good in this? He's alive...*I* helped save a life."

"But the Board still doesn't see it that way. What they see is a troubled girl who likes to break the rules and hang out in the morgue. This has to stop, Xylia. I thought you'd grow out of it, but maybe...maybe it's time you talk to someone. Maybe you need more help then I

~ ☾ ~

can give."

"But Daddy—"

"Enough. I'm serious. Besides, it's not just the morgue. People talk, Xylia. You spend too much time in the cemetery. You attend funerals for entertainment. You hang out with dying people. It's not healthy. You need to talk to someone. I know I'd said I would let you sort this out on your own, and I know I'd promised you could go away next week during winter break, but I just think"—he scratches the scruff on his cheek—"I think you need therapy. Until you do, consider the trip off."

Anger boils in the pit of my stomach. I've been looking forward to the trip he'd promised me I could take when I stayed out of trouble a whole semester. And up until yesterday I had been doing a good job, had a clean record. I had even saved up money so I could explore a little, spread my wings and try and sort out my life. I've been planning for months, marking down famous cemeteries to visit, monuments, spooky houses, and churches. This was supposed to be like my last hoorah before growing up.

"I don't need to talk to anyone. I'm fine, I swear. I don't need a shrink."

"Xylia, it's not an option. You'll see someone and talk to them about whatever it is going on inside that head of yours, or no trip at all."

I want desperately to get out of this town, go on my trip, so I acquiesce unwillingly and say, "Fine...if that's what you want."

But I know there's nothing wrong with me, and definitely nothing a shrink could help me with. Some people collect stamps, baseball cards, go to war monuments. I like to visit cemeteries, go to funerals, and see the occasional dead body in the morgue. I don't really see what's wrong with that.

~ ☾ ~

Chapter Thirteen

Landon

From the moment the light poured into my hospital room through the window, causing shadows to stretch across one end to the other, I'd been poked and prodded. A flood of activity has gone on around me and yet I've been given no answers. Nurses have been monitoring my every move, every blip on the machines, but no one will talk to me, no one will explain what is going on.

Finally, when my parents arrive, I'm relieved. Their faces even show a different story from last night. Mom's fixed her blond hair and make-up, and her jeans and blue blouse are neatly pressed and clean. She doesn't look near as upset as she had. Instead, only the faint red around her eyes shows any sign of distress. Even Dad appears calm and cleaned up after a good night's sleep.

"Mom?" I ask. "When can I leave? I feel okay, but they keep running tests."

"They just want to make sure everything is fine before they release you."

"But why won't anyone tell me what's going on? I mean, if I just collapsed on the field, why are they doing so many tests?"

"Just precautions, there's nothing to worry about. How did you sleep?"

"Fine...but I still don't understand," I say.

~ ☾ ~

"Don't worry about it. Just relax and get some rest."

This angers me, because all I've done is relax and sleep. I've slept enough for a lifetime. "I want to go home."

A nurse's aide interrupts us, bustling in with a tray of something that slightly resembles food. Her hospital attire is bright and covered in colorful flowers. It's a change from the boring blue most of the nurses and aides wear. She seems young but is obviously experienced in how she juggles the tray in one hand as she pulls a rolling table up to the bed. She positions the tray in front of me and places the hospital sludge down.

"You two are going to have to give him some space, let him eat. You can come back in a little while. I'm sure by then the doctor will be ready to see you," she says, standing at my side.

"Alright, we'll be back. You eat all that breakfast—it will keep you healthy," Mom says. She kisses my cheek.

"See you in a bit, son," Dad adds, following Mom out of the room.

"Do I really have to eat this?" I ask the nurse, who is still standing near me. "It looks like dog food."

This makes her smile. She has crooked teeth just like Charity's, and in a weird way, the reminder is almost calming. "I bet it tastes like dog food too," she says, then laughs.

"Thanks. I really didn't want to hear that."

"Plug your nose. You probably won't be able to taste it then."

This nurse is different. She's relaxed and easy to talk to, unlike the other stuffy nurses who have been in here. She might give me some answers. "So, what's wrong with me?" I ask.

The smile falls from her face. "Uh...I think you should wait to talk to Dr. Morana. I'm really not at liberty to discuss anything with you."

~ ☾ ~

"Oh," I reply.

She takes a step away, but I reach out and grab her wrist. My reflexes surprise me. There's quite a difference from last night. "No one is telling me anything," I say. The nurse looks down at my hand. I let go, giving her a look that I hope comes across as apologetic. "Sorry."

"It's okay." She takes another step away from me.

"Please."

She stops, her back turned away from me, possibly pondering how best to proceed. She takes half a step, then walks to a small table in the corner. It's covered in magazines and a TV remote. She picks up the remote and brings it over to me. "Here. You're all over the news."

I raise an eyebrow at her. "Huh?"

"Just turn the TV on"—she flicks her chin at the dark screen—"and see for yourself. But if anyone asks, I didn't tell you anything, okay?"

"Um, yeah. Sure, okay."

She leaves, and I turn on the TV.

What flashes across the screen, across every channel I flip through, are headlines. I can only presume they are about me, judging by what the nurse said. I turn up the volume as a reporter "on location" talks about a Silversprings resident who suddenly came back to life after being pronounced dead. A kid who collapsed on the soccer field. I rise up in my bed, taking it all in. I can't believe the words I'm hearing, what I'm seeing. They don't say my name, but I know—that kid who'd died was me.

So I had been dead. The White Room, that annoying, never-ending depth, makes sense now. I *was* waiting around for someone to either pull the plug completely or to bring me back to life. I compose myself, control my features, just as Dr. Morana comes through the door.

"Oh. Um, you shouldn't be watching that," he says,

~ ☾ ~

then takes the remote from my hand. He turns the TV off.

"I was dead?"

Dr. Morana takes the stethoscope from around his neck. He places it in his ears and then on my chest. "How are you feeling? Any shortness of breath? Aches or pains?" he asks, completely ignoring my question.

"How long was I dead for? What happened?"

"Please, just answer the questions." He moves the scope to another part of my chest.

"How about I answer yours if you answer mine."

He takes a step back and sighs. "Yes, you were pronounced dead."

"For how long? Is there anything wrong with me?" I'm ticked off when Dr. Morana tilts his head to the side but doesn't answer my question. I roll my eyes. "Fine, I feel fine. No shortness of breath, no pains, no aches. Now please, tell me what happened."

He scratches his head. "You were dead for two hours and thirty-two minutes. And as far as I can tell, this is a true medical miracle. I have no idea what happened. All the tests we preformed came up inconclusive," he rambles on, fast, as though he's extremely nervous.

"Okay...so...I died. Like, really died? But I'm fine now? How is that even possible? And why is it all over the news?"

The doctor shifts his weight. "As far as I can tell, your heart stopped then restarted all on its own. The tests we ran are inconclusive. You are in excellent health, and though I'd like to keep you a little longer for observations, I think you'll be just fine. As for the news...I have no idea how *that* happened, nor am I particularly pleased about it."

"But I just...died?" I'm still having a hard time to wrapping my head around everything.

"You didn't die, honey," my mom says, eyeballing the

~ ☾ ~

doctor as she comes back into the room. "He didn't die," she repeats.

"Now, dear, don't get all worked up," Dad says, right behind her.

"What? He didn't, he just...was sleeping. That's all, sleeping."

"Mrs. Phoenix," Dr. Morana said, "that's not what we discussed, but however you want to look at it—"

"He didn't. If he'd died, he wouldn't be here, so he was just sleeping."

"Mom, it's okay, I can handle the truth, really. I'm a big boy," I say.

A stray tear rolls down her cheek. "He didn't die," she whispers.

Dr. Morana clears his throat. "With the recent involvement of the press, I feel obligated to make a statement. But I need your consent. I am looking into all possibilities to best describe the situation. And I can assure you, the press will want a family statement as well, so prepare yourselves," he says, then adds, "Now if Landon continues on the way he has, I don't see anything wrong with releasing him tomorrow." He turns to me. "As long as you promise to take it easy."

"I promise," I say. "I just want to get out of here."

"Then just hang out, son. We'll let you get some rest," he says. I cringe at the mention of *rest* but ignore the word.

Just as Dr. Morana turns to leave I speak up. "Doctor? Were you the one to...uh...I mean, were you there when I woke up?"

His eyes jerk to the left and he pauses, just a little longer than necessary, "Um, yes, why?"

He's lying, I know he is. There's something off with him. He's even more stiff and awkward than when he was telling me I had died. I should call him on the lie but somehow I know he still won't tell me the truth. "Oh, no

~ ☾ ~

reason."

"Right." He swallows. "Well, I'll be back."

What is he hiding, and why? For some reason I wonder if it has something to do with the image, the face that keeps flickering behind my closed eyes. The girl I'm sure I saw just before the White Room disappeared.

~ ☾ ~

Chapter Fourteen

Xylia

Seeing my father upset with me is hard. I know I haven't been easy to deal with since my mother's death, but I don't see why he thinks a shrink will change all that. As I walk through the halls of the hospital, I decide to help him as best as I can.

There's nothing wrong with me, but if I can find out information about Landon's abrupt recovery, maybe I can sway Dad into letting the shrink idea go back into the casket where it belongs. Not to mention, if I can redeem myself, prove to him that I'm responsible, then maybe he won't take my trip away from me either.

So even though I know this could get me in trouble again, I risk slipping into the first open office I see. I hope my good intentions and research will be enough to get me out of trouble if I get caught yet again. I eye the computer that idles on the desk and flop down into the chair. I move the mouse about the screen. The screensaver flicks off. I'm thankful, letting out a sigh of relief when the desktop appears instead of a password protected start menu.

I click on the internet browser and the window to *Google* opens up. I type in *Patients who awaken after being pronounced dead* and click enter.

The screen flickers and produces a list of sites. I know Dad's busy sifting through Landon's medical records

~ ☾ ~

and test results. This might just be my ticket to helping him.

The first page comes up with nothing of use. The second one too. It's not until the fifth site that I start getting somewhere. There's an article about a twenty-three-year-old man, who after being pronounced dead, came back to life seven minutes later. Though he had severe brain damage and died a few short days later, at least it's a case that shows it's possible.

Continuing on, I find even more information. I write down the details, satisfied with myself. I have enough to help Dad out. Sometimes you can't rely on only what you've learned. But this is a real phenomena, although extremely rare. Thanks to *Google*, I've got the medical answer Dad needs.

I close the browser and make sure I've left everything exactly how I found it, then exit the office to find Dad.

* * * *

"Hey, how's the research been going?" I sit down at the cafeteria table where Dad's sitting. I hope the research I've found is enough to get me out of talking to a shrink. I don't want some shrink messing with my head. There's nothing wrong with me.

He shrugs. "Between regular patients and the fact I haven't slept since the night before last...not so good."

I can't help my smile, even have to control myself from bouncing in my seat. "Then I have something for you. I think it will help, a lot." I pull out the paper from my pants pocket and slide it across the table.

Dad picks it up and scans the page. A small grin plays on his lips. "Wow, Xylia, this is excellent. Where did you find this?"

"The internet Dad. It's more than just Facebook and MSN," I chuckle.

~ ☾ ~

"The internet?" He scratches his head. "But are you sure it's real? I mean, did this information come from a viable source?"

"Yes Dad, it did. This condition has even been mentioned in medical journals. It's the real thing. Though every case is different, with different initial symptoms and time frames, these patients all came back to life, so to speak."

He nods with approval. "This is great, really. Though this won't get you out of talking to someone." He pulls out a card from his breast pocket. "I've made an appointment for you on Monday with Dr. Evans. She's easy to talk to."

My heart plummets. It had been a long shot, and maybe I'd been silly to think that one right move in a long string of wrongs would really redeem myself in Dad's eyes. I was hoping this would be enough, but I guess I'll just have to try harder. I take the card then slip it into my pocket, knowing I'll be anywhere but here Monday at one o'clock.

Dad slides his chair back and stands up. "Guess I have a statement to give."

"I'm coming to watch." I smile, but I wonder if he notices the disappointment it tries to veil.

* * * *

Watching my father standing at the front of hundreds of people is quite amazing. The crisp air of the winter afternoon touches everyone. The hordes of people stand, huddled together for warmth outside the main entrance to the hospital as Dad stands behind a makeshift podium. I look up to the sky and see thick gray clouds, wishing I'd grabbed a jacket. It could rain at any moment, dropping the temperature down even further.

All eyes are on Dad. The crowd is silent. The only

~ ☾ ~

sounds besides Dad's voice are the camera clicks and flashes and the small buzzing sound of video cameras recording him for the six o'clock news. But he stands there—a man who is normally shy, reserved, and a little odd—with such poise and grace. His voice is full of confidence and authority. He makes me proud, even if deep down I'm disappointed about the trip and the shrink.

"Landon Phoenix collapsed yesterday evening during the Rams soccer game. After learning Mr. Phoenix did not have a heartbeat, we immediately began CPR in order to attempt to revive him. We continued life-saving techniques en route to the hospital, but everything we tried failed to bring back a heartbeat. Prior to arrival at the hospital, Mr. Phoenix was pronounced dead."

As he continues, I'm mildly let down by the fact that I'm not mentioned. I mean, I understand about not being named as the one who found him in the morgue, but I was the one who pumped his heart, pressing up and down continuously for those nineteen minutes.

"There have been thirty-eight cases of Lazarus Syndrome on record, possibly even more around the world. Though each case differs slightly, and the exact cause that restarts the patient's heart is still unknown, what we can take from this is both a medical miracle and a chance for this teen to have another chance at life. All of us here at Silversprings Hospital are always pleased when someone gets a happy ending. Thank you for your time."

"Have you considered a misdiagnosis, perhaps prematurely calling his death?" a reporter holding a microphone speaks up.

Another one asks, "Why take so long giving a statement? Did anything else go wrong that you are worried about getting out?"

"What's the hospital's opinions about miracles from

~ ☾ ~

God? Do you believe in God?" a short bald man asks, pen and paper in hand.

My dad steps away from the microphones and heads toward the main doors of the hospital.

Many reporters shout out questions, one right on top of another, two or three people speaking at once. I don't fault my dad for not wanting to answer them. I've seen the media take things out of context and twist words to make just about anyone look bad, so it's no wonder my dad turns and waves one last time to the cameras before walking through the doors of the hospital.

Following his lead, I too walk through the doors. "Dad," I call out. He turns and smiles. I run to him and fling my arms around his neck. "You did great. I'm so proud," I say.

"Thanks, honey, but you did all the work."

"Yeah, I did. So does that mean I can get a new phone?" I wink.

My dad tells me to get to work. Apparently I haven't been fired. Yet.

* * * *

"Good afternoon, Evelyn," I say, walking into one of my favorite patient's rooms.

"Ah, Xylia, I was wondering when I would see you." Evelyn smiles. She looks small, wrapped in blankets up to her neck and propped up against the hospital bed. Her hair is coiffed into a perfect curling iron set of silvery waves. She's been here for a few months, waiting for a permanent bed at another care facility since falling in her shower and breaking her hip. I like her because she has such an optimistic personality. Also, despite being laid up in a bed, she hasn't let her looks go. Every few days a hairstylist from the salon comes in and washes and sets her hair. Her daughter even brought in

~ ☾ ~

her night creams—those ones that fight against wrinkles, though I don't have the heart to tell her they aren't working.

"We going to play some Scrabble today?"

Evelyn scoots up to a sitting position, pressing her finger on the button that slides the bed higher. "Or we could talk about all the commotion that's going on around here."

I raise my eyebrows in surprise. "Oh, commotion? Whatever do you mean?" I say.

"Nothing gets past these ears." She winks. Evelyn is the ward's gossip hound. She knows everything that goes on in the hospital, and not just what goes on in the geriatric ward.

"Um...I don't know what to tell you."

"Uh huh, I bet you don't," she says and rolls her eyes. "I hear you had a great deal to do with it, so c'mon, fess up and tell me all about it."

I walk over to the bed, take a seat next to her, and scoot the chair closer. "I'm not sure you can keep a secret."

Her eyes grow wide and she brings her hand to her chest. "Of course I can," she says, sounding hurt. But I know it's just a ruse to get the information.

Truth is, since Evelyn came onto the ward, she has been like a second mother to me. She's easy to talk to, and not only does she have a knack for hearing the latest news, but she's also a good listener.

"Alright, I was there," I say.

"And..." she prods, adding, "so was that handsome doctor dad of yours too?"

"You know I don't like you talking about my dad like that." I wrinkle my nose.

"What? He *is* handsome. I'm not the only one who thinks so, either."

"Ew! That's too much, Evelyn, really."

~ ☽ ~

"Oh, grow up," she says and laughs. "Now hurry up with the gossip. I don't have all day."

"Why don't you just turn on the TV? It's all over the news."

"Because the best gossip comes from the horse's mouth, Xylia, and don't you forget that." She eyes me and then winks.

I look at Evelyn. She's so eager to hear something. She leans her small body slightly forward and raises her eyebrows. Her long, hot pink fingernails drum against her blanket covered thigh as she waits. But I'm not supposed to say anything. What happened in the morgue is supposed to be kept secret.

I sigh. If I don't tell Evelyn, then I'll have to carry this weight around with me forever, and I'm not sure I can do that. I'd kissed Landon. I'd *wanted* to kiss him, and now he's alive. If I had a mother, I know I'd talk to her about this, I'm sure of it. Maybe I can at least get Evelyn to keep her mouth shut. Your pseudo mother isn't supposed to tell your secrets is she?

"Alright, alright, just twist my arm why don't you," I say. "I might have been down in the morgue when he woke up."

"He? Oh, I didn't know this was about a *he*..." She grins, twisting her fingers together. "Do you know him? What's he look like? Handsome, perhaps?"

"Yeah, he is a *he*, alright, and of course he's hot. We go to the same school," I say, thinking Evelyn is always focused on looks. I bet she has all the guys around here wrapped around her finger.

"So, what were you doing in the morgue? I thought you'd learned your lesson the last time."

The last time was really *one* of many adventures in the morgue; however, that time I'd been caught. I was taking a look at Mr. Whittaker, one of my former patients, when his body fell from the table. The

~ ☾ ~

commotion alerted the guard. I was caught and poor Mr. Whittaker's body suffered some damage. Facial bruising, broken nose and a dislocated arm had his family thinking it best to have a closed casket

"Well…this was different. I mean, I was there when he died. I swear I felt the life being sucked right out of him as I tried to revive him with chest compressions. I just wanted a last look. Then he just decided to wake up."

"You know, people don't just wake up after being dead. Something must have happened. Did you do anything while you were there?"

Yes! My mind screams, as my stomach twists with guilt. I kissed him! "People do just wake up," I argue. "It's called Lazarus Syndrome—"

"No, they don't. There's a reason. God doesn't just bring people back to life for the fun of it. He doesn't work that way."

Of course it doesn't work that way. If it did, my mother would still be here.

"Xylia," she prods. "What did you *really* do?"

"I don't know…I touched him?"

I let out a breath of air, turning slightly in my chair to look out the window. The rain has finally decided to fall, and it splatters against the glass. I lose focus for a moment, the hypnotic sound of the rain pattering against the hospital and the drops landing on the window have me mesmerized. A chill suddenly zips up my spine, catching me off guard, and with it comes a husky whisper. Indecipherable words.

I whip my head around toward Evelyn. "Huh? What did you say?"

I must have been daydreaming, because Evelyn glances down at her pink nails, unfazed, and lets out a "humph," then adds, "I said, that's it? You just touched

~ ☾ ~

him?" She's jabbing me in the ribs, like she knows I did something more.

"I don't know why I did it, but..." When I hesitate, Evelyn gives me a gentle smile and motions with her hand for me to continue, like nothing I say is going to make her think any less of me. I plunge on. "I kissed him, okay? That's what I did. I kissed him goodbye, then he started breathing."

Evelyn snaps her fingers, a smile stretching wide across her face. "That's it! He's meant to be yours."

"What?" I say. No way can she be right.

"It's a modern day fairytale, a reverse Sleeping Beauty scenario. You just became his knightess in shining armour." She claps her hands. "Believe, Xylia. This is meant to be."

* * * *

After leaving Evelyn, I'm still not sure I believe her and her silly fairytale thing. But her words do compel me to take the long way to my car. I take a path down a corridor completely out of my way so I have time to think. Or so I tell myself.

I stop short of Landon's door and press my body tight against the wall. I peer in. He's asleep, looking so peaceful. I lean a little farther, trying to get a better look. Life has certainly changed him since the last time I saw him, in the morgue on a metal gurney. His face and arms are no longer pale and road mapped with blue veins. His lips are rosy and plump.

As though he senses someone's presence, his blue eyes open. He lifts his head up and looks deep into my eyes. I swallow. My feet are planted in the ground. I can't seem to move. His head tilts to the right a little, like he's trying to remember something. His eyes

~ ☾ ~

continue to bore into me. I have to force my feet back and away from the door. As I rush down the hall, my heart races along with my footsteps.

~ ☾ ~

Chapter Fifteen

Landon

I'm staring. I can't tear my eyes away from the doorway where the girl stood a second ago. She looked familiar, but I couldn't place her. Now she's gone.

The cheery nurse from earlier strolls in, pulling me out of my daze. "Do you know who that was?" I ask.

"Know who *who* was?"

"Didn't you see her? A minute ago, in the doorway," I say.

She lifts an eyebrow, walking over to the end of my bed to retrieve a clipboard. She flips through the papers. "Says here we don't have you on any morphine or sedatives." She smiles.

"Very funny. I know what I saw."

"Right, well, I was just in the hall, at the nurse's station. I didn't see anyone around. Don't worry though, sometimes after someone experiences something traumatic they *see things*," she shrugs, "and maybe *hear things*?" Her voice taking on a questioning tone.

"I'm not crazy! I know what I saw. There was someone there."

"Okay, let me give you a piece of advice. If you're not crazy, then don't tell anyone else you saw something like that, or they *will* think you're crazy."

I grumble. "Yeah, whatever," Then mutter under my breath something about wanting to go home. Maybe this

~ ☾ ~

place *is* making me crazy, but no, I know what I saw.

"And"—the nurse waves her pointer finger at me— "that talking to yourself business, shaking your head as though you and *you* are having an argument is not good kid, not good at all."

Annoyed, I reply, "Don't you have some place else to be?"

"Yeah, yeah, I'm going. Just came in to check your IV. But remember what I said. You're in a hospital; it takes no time at all to move someone to the psych ward instead of pushing them out the door."

"Fine. I didn't *see* anything and I don't *hear* anything. Got it."

"See ya later, kid." She waves as she walks through the door.

* * * *

When Mom comes in the room I ask, "Where's Daniel? He's probably worried sick and going crazy." I'm a little mad at myself for not asking about him earlier. He's my best friend and I'd kind of forgotten all about him.

"He was here all night. I sent him home this morning and told him I'd call when we had some answers," she says, then adds, "Charity was here, too. I had to practically push her out the door."

It's sweet Charity cares, but I feel sorry that she can't seem to let go this time.

"Can you call him? I mean, I'm fine now, so I'd really like to let him know I'm okay. Maybe tell him to come by for a visit?"

"Sure, but first, some reporters want to ask you a few questions. The doctor made his statement a little while ago, but they want to see and hear from you. Can you do that for me?"

~ ☾ ~

"I'd really rather not. I just want to see my friends," I say.

Her eyes become more pleading. "This would really help." She bites her lip, then says, "They offered us some money to come and interview you. We could use it, so please put on a smile and answer their questions. For me?"

It's not so much that she said "please," it's the tone her voice has taken on. It worries me a little. "Mom?" I ask.

"Yes?"

"Is there anything wrong? I mean, like, financially? Are things okay?"

"Of course they are. Don't worry about the money. The medical bills are just a little more than we had originally expected, that's all."

I know there's no money for college, but to see the worry on her face, to hear it in her tone, I'm concerned. Medical bills aren't cheap. Sure, I'd assumed we had coverage for disasters like this, but I can't shake the feeling that something else isn't quite right.

"Okay, then. I'm ready whenever the reporters are," I say. When my mom's eyes light up, I know I'm doing the right thing.

* * * *

When the camera crews are all set up, it's like I'm back in the White Room, but I'm not. Lights are strewn about, all pointing at me, bright and blinding. There are a dozen people crowded around the small space, taking up every inch. Someone from somewhere in the room says, "Alright, you ready?" The voice is male, very deep and gruff.

I nod.

"Now just stay relaxed, answer the questions, and

~ ☾ ~

then you'll be done, okay?"

"Okay." My throat's dry. The lights beaming down are hot. Beads of sweat form on my forehead.

"Alright, we're going live in five, four, three..." The male voice trails off.

A female voice takes over, and I try to locate the speaker through the blinding beams of light. "Hello, I'm Sylvia Duran, and we're here today with Landon Phoenix, the Silversprings teenager who miraculously came back to life after being pronounced dead by doctors. Landon, first off, how do you feel?" The reporter is straight and to the point.

I shrug. "Fine."

"Does anything feel different? I mean, since the incident?"

"Not really."

"So what you are saying is, you don't feel any different, that the episode hasn't changed you in anyway?"

Did we not just clarify that? "No, I don't feel any different, really. I feel just the same as I did before."

"Do you believe in God, Landon?"

I don't understand what believing in God has to do with anything. "Well...I...uh, I'm not too sure."

"Some are saying that this maybe was an act of some sort of higher power? Do you agree?"

Religion was never a huge thing in my house. We never went to church, never said grace at the table, never recited prayers before bed. When it came to God, I'd never put much thought into it. "I'm really not sure. Maybe?"

"So how does it feel to be a medical phenomenon? That besides yours, there have only been thirty-eight cases of the Lazarus syndrome recorded, *ever*."

"Well, to be honest, I never really thought about it."

"You're being released tomorrow, I hear, so what are

~ ☾ ~

you going to do now?"

"Um, finish out the semester?" I chuckle nervously.

"I hear you play for the Rams. How did you feel when you heard they won the championship based on the fact that the other team forfeited after you were rushed from the field?"

I look over to the right, toward my parents, whose silhouettes I can just make out. I narrow my eyes. They'd lied to me. "I'm disappointed. I really think we could have beaten them fair and square," I reply.

"Are you worried that your 'accident' might tarnish your chances of being picked by any scouts that might have been at the game?"

I take time to think about this question because it never really entered my mind. I knew scouts had been at the game and that this had been my last chance to show everyone out there what I had to offer. I never thought that my being carried off the field on a gurney would look bad to those scouts.

"No," I say finally, adding, "I'm not worried because those scouts are the same ones that have been watching me all season. They know I can perform, and with the clean bill of health I've been given, they should know I *can* win and *will* win for any team I play for in the future." I nod, knowing that it was a damn good answer. I know I can win."One last question for our viewers, if you don't mind?"

"Sure."

"Can you describe to our viewers what it was like, what happened to you during those two hours and thirty-four minutes you were supposedly dead?"

I'm taken back by the question. I have no idea how to respond. My mouth opens and closes a few times but nothing comes out. I shouldn't have to tell anyone what it was like, what I'd experienced when I was dead. I believe that should be for me, and me alone. So I'm

~ ☾ ~

thankful when I hear a throat clear from somewhere in the room.

"Mr. Phoenix has been through a lot. I think it best we give him some space, let him rest. You all can come back later." It's the cheery nurse who thinks I'm crazy.

I hear the reporter signing off, more murmuring in the background, and then the bright lights dim. A cameraman and some fancy looking woman with a microphone—probably Sylvia Duran—as well as hospital staff head out of the room, leaving it empty except for me and my parents.

I say, "No more interviews," to my mom and dad.

"But—"

I shake my head. "C'mon Mom, this isn't right. I shouldn't be put out on display like some kind of freak, answering their lame questions." My hands tighten into fists. "And hell, maybe if you had been honest with me about the game, I wouldn't have looked like a fool when they brought that up."

Mom opens her mouth to say something but I quickly hold up one of my hands, forcing her to stop. "I just don't want to do it again. What happened when...how I feel...it's my business, okay?"

Mom wrings her hands together, a *caught with her hand in the cookie jar* look about her face. "You're right. We shouldn't have pushed it on you. It seemed like a good idea."

"Well, it wasn't, so no more, I just want to see Daniel, do whatever I can to make the day go by faster so I can go home, then pretend like this never happened."

"Sure thing son," Dad says from behind Mom.

I'm not sure if I can ever really pretend like I hadn't died, like it never happened. It's here with me, the memories I have of the White Room, the pain, and agony of the burning sensation and the calming, soothing feeling I'd felt on my lips before I came back.

~ ☾ ~

How does someone forget that? How do they put dying behind them?

And that face, the one I see every time I close my eyes, somehow, I'm sure it has something to do with why I was brought back. Maybe there is a reason for the way things happened, or why. And that girl I keep seeing in my mind just might have the answer. I just need to find her.

* * * *

"You sure you want to go to school today?" Mom asks as she places a plate of toast in front of me. "The school said you could write your exams after winter break if you need more time to recover."

Mom always made sure that for all the hours I put into sports, I put as many or more into actual schoolwork. She wanted to make certain if I didn't make it as an athlete I'd have good grades to fall back on. So the English test I have to take this morning should be a breeze. I'd looked over my notes last night, hoping to clear the webs in my brain that might have been spun by spiders while I was "out." I figured I was ready.

"I'm fine. I feel great. I can handle it. Besides I'm sick of lying around. I just want to get them over with," I say, picking up a piece of toast and tearing off a bite. I'm not really hungry, but with Mom hovering over my every move, I can't help but eat to please her.

"Do you need a ride? I know the doctor told you to take it easy, not to drive for a few more days, just in case."

"Daniel should be here any minute, but thanks," I say between mouthfuls. I'm tired of being coddled.

"Hey, Mrs. Phoenix," Daniel's voice booms. "The door was open. Hope you don't mind that I came in. Hey man," he says to me, "we need to get going."

~ ☾ ~

I stand and push the plate of food away, but then quickly pull it back when I see Daniel eyeing the buttered and jammed toast like a puppy dog. "Daniel, you hungry?"

"If you're not going to eat," he says, snatching up the halves, then shoving one into his mouth. "Thanks."

"Alright, let's go," I say, ignoring the crumbs on his chin and the jam stuck to the corners of his mouth. At least Mom's efforts at breakfast aren't going to waste.

In the car, Daniel says, "Boy, what I wouldn't give to have extra time to study," not wasting any time expressing his disbelieve in how eager I am to take my exams. "Maybe they'd even forget about exams and grades and just hand over my diploma." He cranks the wheel hard to the left.

I instinctively grab the handle on the door, like I do every time Daniel drives. "I feel fine. I'd rather just get it over with."

"Yeah, well, we aren't all as smart as you. Hey, do you think being dead and brought back to life gave you any super powers? 'Cause dude, that would be so cool."

I sigh and shake my head. Is he serious?

"Dude, it happens in the movies all the time."

"You know those are fake. As in not *real*."

"I'm not an idiot, but it still would be cool."

Clutching the handle a little tighter as Daniel makes a sharp right turn, I say, "you're right, it would be."

"So...are you ever going to tell me what it was like?"

I don't have to get him to elaborate. I know what he's talking about. It's what everyone keeps asking. They all want to know what it's like to die; if I saw God and the pearly gates, or if I was sucked into a black hole and shot out into the universe.

My forehead is pressed against the window. I let the coolness calm down my revved up energy and say,

~ ☾ ~

"Nope," popping the 'P' for a little more emphasis. It's enough for Daniel and he lets it go. I just wish everybody else would too.

~ ☾ ~

Chapter Sixteen

Xylia

"The balance between this world and the next—between life and death—has been completely thrown off."

A man's voice. Distant. Young.

"Blast that kid. We need to find him, bring him back. It's the only way to right what has been wronged."

Another man's voice. Cranky this time.

"It's never that simple. *You* never make it that simple."

"Of course not! We've been made a fool, but mark my words, I will get the body."

"It's always about you and your ulterior motives. Have you ever paused to think that if you do your job *and* be nice, you'll get what you want? Move forward?"

I wake, gasping for breath. My heart races at max speed, thumping hard against my rib cage. It hurts, coupled with the nausea, the feeling of being on a roller coaster that just won't stop makes me want to die. I force myself upright, pushing against the plush of my mattress.

I search my room for the source of the voices. There were voices, men in my room. I'd heard them. But when I find myself alone, I untangle myself from the black sheets and flop back down onto my pillows.

It was just a dream. It had to have been. Yet it was so

~ ☾ ~

real. This time I swear I could make out what they we saying.

I shake my head and look over at the clock. Green numbers illuminated against the dimly lit surrounding of my room show me it's early. Too early. I stifle a yawn with my hand and rake fingers through my tangled mess of hair. What wrong needs to be righted? I ask myself as exhaustion begins to cloud my mind, my memories. It must be something important. I try to hold on to the thought, but quickly my eyelids fall over my eyes. They spring open, only to flicker closed, again. I can't seem to hold on, I can't seem to focus on anything except the need for sleep. Another yawn escapes through my lips, and this time, when my eyes close, they do not reopen.

When my alarm rings, I roll out of bed with just enough time to throw on a black floor-length tattered skirt, a long-sleeved shirt and my boots. I don't bother messing with my hair or makeup. The tangled mess and yesterday's leftover makeup kind of adds to the look. I head downstairs and out the door for my exam, even though there's a distinct feeling of something nagging at me and yet, I just can't seem to remember what it was

With winter break just days away, the only thing left at school begging for attention are end of this semester's exams. It's the last thing I need to really focus on before I run away on my own adventure. Exam week is simple. Since there's a whole lot of students and a whole lot of exams, basically you just have to show up, take your test, and then leave. It's a perk of being a senior.

This morning I'm writing my English final. I'm not too worried. If there's anything my dad really passed on to me through the magic of genes, it's being smart. I've always earned good grades and have never really had to work hard, either. So when I file into the gymnasium with the herd of other students, I know in less than two hours I'll be back home, lounging on the couch with the

~ ☾ ~

satisfaction of having at the very least earned a B on the test.

What has me worried, though, is Landon. I doubt he's going to be here, having died and all. But how can I ignore what happened? How can I pretend as though I had nothing to do with Landon coming back to life? Was I supposed to force myself to believe I hadn't been there, hadn't seen his dead body, and hadn't watched that body come back to life after I'd kissed him?

I heard he'd given an interview after my dad gave his. I had to force myself not to watch. It was too much knowing that even though Landon will get a second chance at life, I'll never be able to tell him the truth. I should, but I know I won't. I'll never have a chance with him.

I sit in a seat and wait for the test to be passed out. My number two pencil sits idle, waiting for the chance to color in the tiny multiple choice bubbles. Taking a moment, I glance around. Others aren't nearly as relaxed as I am. From where I'm sitting there are pencil chewers, foot tappers, and people who are green faced with sweat covered foreheads. And there, two rows over from me, is Landon Phoenix.

To say I'm surprised is an understatement. I'd assumed that being dead for a couple of hours might have earned him a free pass. However, I wouldn't want that on my conscience. I mean, it would bug me for the rest of my life, knowing that I got handed my grades because I spent a little time in the county morgue. Maybe Landon is more than a pretty face and a star soccer player. Maybe he actually wants to earn his grades. Or maybe now he just wants to bask in all the attention. People keep staring at him like he's a freak. Or a god.

"You have two hours to complete your test," the principal says. She's short, plump, and hard to hear.

~ ☾ ~

"Make sure you have your name and student ID on the top of the answer sheet before you start. When you are finished, you may stand up and hand your test in to one of the waiting faculty members, then you are free to go unless you have other exams to complete today. Good luck. You may start."

Hundreds of test packets tear open as students pull the enclosed question booklet from the envelope. Pages flip, pencils tap, even desks creak as students hunker down and pray for a passing mark.

Midway through the allotted time I hit a snag, having worked through all the questions I can confidently answer without thinking twice. Now, however, I am working my way backward, trying to answer the ones I've skipped. It's taking longer than I expected and some are harder than I thought; a few I'm plain at a loss as to how to answer. And I'll be dammed if I can't ignore the fact that the living dead is sitting so close, taking the very same test.

Setting down my pencil, I fill my lungs with a few deep breaths of air, then stretch my arms over my head and extend my legs. I survey the room and see to my left that all eyes are trained on tests. I look over to my right and see the same thing. Except for one pair of blue eyes that are looking right at me.

Landon.

He's appraising me, looking me up and down. It's startling. I drop my gaze and lower my head, then force myself to concentrate on my test. But I have that feeling, the one that tingles your skin and raises the hairs on the back of your neck because you know someone is looking at you. That someone is *still* looking at you.

A few minutes pass but I can't shake the feeling I'm being stared at. I let my hair fall forward, draping the side of my face so I can peek without having to look at him head on. His eyes are still focused in my direction.

~ ☾ ~

Had he even moved? Even marked down a single answer in the past few minutes?

Not liking the idea that someone is watching me, that Landon's eyes are paying more attention to me than his exam, I start speed reading the questions, marking down answers. What if he remembers me, and...the kiss?

If I do the math, I should at least still get a passing grade, even with the carelessness of marking down random answers just to say I'm done. It'll do. I stand, and a few heads pop up at the sound of my shuffling feet against the hardwood floor. I ignore the prying eyes. I don't even chance a look over my shoulder at Landon. Instead, I walk to the back of the room and present my exam.

"Are you sure you are ready to hand this in? You still have a little less than an hour to complete it," the school secretary says, hesitating at the idea of taking the paper out of my hand.

"I'm sure," I reply and smile, though it's forced.

"Okay." She takes the paper and puts it into a box. "You are free to go. Sign out here," she says, sliding a clipboard across the desk.

I flip through the paper until I find my name, scrawl on the line, and pass the papers back. The secretary gives me a slight shrug. I ignore her and head out the doors.

Outside, fresh air fills my lungs. The sun beats down, instantly warming my bare arms. It's quite a change for the usual Oregon drizzly weather this time of year. It's nice—comforting, like my childhood stuffed animal.

"I know you, don't I?"

My body freezes, like the warm sun has been replaced with rain so cold it's turned to ice. Slowly, I turn around. Landon's standing in my personal space, only inches away.

~ ☾ ~

"Uh, yeah, you do. We've only been going to school together since freshman year." I've never noticed how blue his eyes really are, how good they look this close. Now why couldn't he have come up to me *before*, when I didn't have to ignore him?

He rolls his eyes. "Yeah, that's not what I meant. I've seen you somewhere else."

"Um...how about every class since freshman year...soccer games, class field trips..." I'm being hostile because I don't like where this conversation is going, not at all. It's making me uncomfortable. I know I can't tell him where he really knows me from, because it could risk my job, my dad's job.

And there is no good way to say, "hey, I kissed your dead body."

What's also making me uncomfortable—besides his proximity—is the buzz of death that is wafting off him in dull, lapping waves. It's something I've noticed around the dead, and maybe others feel it too. Like the energy that makes up the living hasn't quite dissipated yet. But he's alive. He's healthy. That weird death feeling shouldn't be there. It's strange, weird, even troublesome. I pinch my eyes shut, open them, focus on the tiny mole on his neck.

He shakes his head and says, "Yeah...maybe."

He leaves, stalking off until Charity meets him halfway across the lot. She looks at me, her nose wrinkling as she says something. Her hand brushes through Landon's sandy hair, caresses his cheek, but he shakes her off and walks back into the school, Charity tight on his heels.

The sigh of relief that escapes my lips loosens my body, relaxing me. It was nice to hear his voice and have him say something to me. If I think back, I'm sure it's been years since he's said a single word to me, if ever.

~ ☾ ~

* * * *

At home I count down the minutes to one o'clock. I should be at the hospital for my meeting Dad arranged with the shrink, but I'd already made up my mind not to go. Dad will be upset, maybe even a little mad. But I know he'll forgive me, eventually.

However, I'm pulled out of my afternoon cartoon marathon by the loud and persistent chime of the doorbell. I take the bag of chips from my lap and set them on the table, then brush stray crumbs from my shirt. I drag my boots as I walk to the door.

The first thing that comes to mind when I pull open the door, is *whoa*, my dad's good. Maybe knows me a little too well. The second thought is *shit*. Standing on my steps is a woman in her late thirties, with blond hair pulled into a taut bun, wearing a neatly pressed blue blazer, a matching skirt and a very nice looking pair of pumps. What completes the look? She's holding a binder and has a smug look written all over her face.

I know who this is. Dr. Evans, I can only presume. She's standing on my porch and not at the hospital where she's supposed to be. Where I'm supposed to be.

"You must be Xylia. May I come in?" the shrink lady asks politely.

"Um, no." I'm ready to push the door closed in her face, but she's fast. She puts out her hand, even wedges her leather pump in the doorjamb, keeping me from closing her out.

"Your father said you would be difficult, but I'm not giving up so quickly. Just let me in, we'll talk—heck, I'll talk, all you have to do is listen. If that's what you would prefer."

"I really don't need a shrink, despite what my *father* has told you."

"Well now, that seems to be up for debate. Why don't

you let me be the judge?"

"Uh...because I don't know you, nor do I feel like talking to someone who's going to twist my words until *I* start to believe *I'm* crazy," I say.

Her face shifts, the smug smile gone. "Okay, let's get one thing straight....Your father is paying me a lot of money to talk to you, so either you talk to me and put his good money to use or"—she shrugs—"I'll tell him we're talking and take his money." She folds her arms and tilts her chin upward.

My jaw falls to the floor. "What? You can't do that. That's stealing," I snap out.

The smug grin is back as she says, "Well, yeah, maybe. But who's gonna know?"

"I am! I'll tell him what you're up to. That you're lying and taking his money."

"Uh huh, right. And who do you think he's going to believe? Me, the PhD, or you the troubled teenager with a track record of lying as long as I am tall?"

Truth be told she isn't that tall, five foot three at the most. Short, really. But sadly, she has a point, and like the shrink I know them all to be, she has twisted things in such a way I have no choice.

"Fine."

"Great! Let's get started. *Now* may I come in?"

"Uh, no."

Her eyebrows dip down. "I thought we had a deal."

"We do. I'm just not about to let a crazy shrink into my house," I respond, pushing the door open far enough for me to slip out.

My mom loved the wrap-around deck, even though our deck doesn't wrap all the way around. Its length only extends across three sides of the house. In the front, Mom had asked my father to put in a wooden swing. She'd sewed fluffy pillows for the swing and would sit out here for hours watching the cars drive by.

~ ☾ ~

I kick my feet up and drape them over one of the pillows. I motion to a rickety old lawn chair a few feet away. "Have a seat," I say, smiling arrogantly.

Shrink lady sits down on the edge of the seat, her nose clearly pointed straight up to the sky. "I'm Dr. Stephanie."

"Dr. Stephanie? Your last name is Stephanie? Tough break."

"No, actually my first name is Stephanie. My last name is Evans."

"Well then...why the whole Dr. Stephanie thing? I thought people always called doctors by their last name."

"I've found that my patients prefer being able to use my first name. It's friendlier and makes them comfortable."

"Right."

"Let's talk a bit about why I'm here—"

"Which is? Why exactly *are you* here?"I had planned on doing the whole *Good Will Hunting* thing; sit the entire time not saying a word, but the idea of Dad wasting hundreds of dollars does seem kind of silly. I should at least say something while *Dr. Stephanie* is here.

"I'm here because your father has some concerns about you and thinks this might help."

I nod my head. "Uh huh, right. Concerns. And what might those be?"

She opens her binder. "Let's see here..." she mumbles, then flips to another page, then another. "You've been getting yourself into trouble the last few years," she says.

I counter right away by saying, "Yeah, so? Lots of kids my age get into trouble now and then—"

"Really? Do lots of kids your age sneak into the morgue? Abuse corpses?"

"That was one time and it was an accident!"

~ ☾ ~

"One time too many. It's not just that, it says here you spend hours on end in the cemetery, you insisted on burying your pet rabbit—"

"What's wrong with that? There's nothing wrong with wanting a proper burial for a beloved pet," I say.

"The problem was that you snuck into the funeral home and cremated it."

"So? You would rather be embalmed and stuck in the ground to rot? 'Cause I didn't want that for Chester." I stiffen slightly and take a deep breath.

Wow, this Doc Stephanie had done her homework. I didn't even think Dad knew about Chester's trip through the incinerator. Either way, I don't like my life being scrutinized. I don't like being shrinked, and I certainly don't like that now I'm starting to believe my problems aren't *normal* kid problems.

"You are missing the point here, Xylia. It's not necessarily what you're doing, it's how you're doing it. Normal kids don't hang out in cemeteries and morgues, sneak into funeral homes and—it says here you've played the occasional prank on your father?"

"Stop saying 'father.' It's not right. He's my dad. And a prank or two? I'm getting grilled by a shrink over a few pranks? This is ridiculous," I say, flopping my arms over my chest, almost knowing, however, what she is going to say next.

"Pranks, Xylia, are putting salt in the sugar bowl, turning the clock back a little bit. Not pretending you are dead," she says.

I press my lips into a hard line. I'm not sure why some of this is relevant. Once or twice, when I was like, twelve, I'd tried to see if I could hold my breath and regulate my breathing enough for me to seem dead. I wanted to know if there was a way to get in touch with the *other side*—if there even was an *other side*—without actually going there. Dad almost had a heart attack

~ ☾ ~

when he found me.

Afterward, I was no closer to trying to talk to my mom and Dad sure didn't think what I'd done was normal behaviour. That was the first time he thought a shrink might be in order.

But before I have a chance to defend myself, Doc Stephanie adds, "What I am trying to do here is just get to the bottom of this behaviour, learn who Xylia Morana really is, what's underneath the"—she looks me up and down—"black, frumpy exterior."

I feel my eyes grow wide. I'm not frumpy! I'm an individualist. "And if I don't want help? If I don't want to show you what's underneath all of this?" I rake my hands over my body.

"We've already discussed that. I'll just pretend I'm 'shrinking' you."

"You're kidding right? You really wouldn't do that, would you?"

She laughs. "Of course not, that's unethical. But I had you going for a bit, didn't I?"

A smile creeps across my face. "Yeah, you did." At that moment I kind of like her. But not enough to spill my guts.

"But seriously, if you don't want to talk, I can't make you. I just hope you do. Maybe not for you, but for your dad."

I consider this for a moment. I'm not doing this for me. I'm doing this for Dad I think, then say, "So are you going to shrink me now?"

"If you want to talk, then yes."

I adjust myself in the swing, getting just a little bit more comfortable as I say, "Alright, first question?"

"Have you ever tried to kill yourself?"

"Whoa. Are you allowed to just ask me that? I thought we started off slow. You know, you ask me what my favorite color is, what I like to eat, then get to the

~ ☾ ~

tougher stuff."

"This isn't a date, Xylia. I don't care what your favorite color is or what you like to eat. What I care about is what's going on inside that head of yours. Now unless you have something to hide, which you shouldn't, answer the question," she says.

"No," I say simply.

"No as in you haven't tried to kill yourself, or no as in you do feel like you have something to hide."

"Well, to put it more bluntly, *no* I have not tried to kill myself, and *no*, I don't have anything to hide." Except maybe kissing a stiff. And those weird voices I keep hearing. The ones that say things like, "we need to get it back." Is it possible I really have been hearing something from the other side? I'd figured each time I'd heard something that there was a rational reason, but maybe the rational reason isn't of this world. But if I've been hearing voices, who are they, and what do they need to get back? Do the voices mean they want Landon back? Or is my dad right and I do need a shrink because I'm going nuts?

Shaking my head clear, ignoring what I don't possibly have any control over, I listen as Doc Stephanie says, "Do you want to die?"

"What the hell? What kind of questions are these?"

"Let me repeat: *Do you* want to die?"

"Who would? I mean, there is no proof that there is anything on the 'other side,' so why risk it?" Though now, I'm not so sure. Maybe there is something on the other side. Maybe that's what has been talking to me. I notice as she takes a pen from the front of the binder and begins scribbling notes. "Wait, what are you writing? Did I say something wrong?"

She chuckles. "There are no right or wrong answers here. I'm just making notes."

I bet she's just drawing happy faces and doodling

~ ☾ ~

circles.

"So if you've never tried to harm yourself in anyway, and you don't want to die, what's with the death fascination?" she asks.

"I don't know—something to do?"

"Sleeping in open graves is something to do?"

"That was just an experiment. I wanted to—" I clamp my mouth shut.

"Wanted to what?" She scribbles more into her binder.

"Nothing. You wouldn't understand."

"It's my job to understand, so what was it you wanted to do? What was sleeping in an open grave going to accomplish?"

"How did you even hear about that? I didn't think my dad knew about that." Jeez, does my father know everything?

"You're avoiding the question. What did it accomplish?"

"Maybe I'm avoiding it because I don't want to talk about it," I say.

"Okay...what do you want to talk about?" she asks.

I shrug.

"Now we're back to square one. Can't you just give me a little something to work with here? Because right now it's not looking good."

"What do you mean *not looking good*?"

"You're not dumb, Xylia You know what I mean. But if I must spell it out, you're heading down a dangerous path. I'm worried if you don't get the help you need, you will need more than anything I can offer."

I roll my eyes. "Whatever." This is stupid. If it wasn't for my dad and his need for me to be different from what I am, I would have walked away sooner. But I just can't figure it out. I'm not seeing what really is so wrong. "So what that I've had a few mishaps? I'm not a danger

~ ☾ ~

to myself or other people."

"Yet."

The blood in my veins starts to boil. Redness flushes over my cheeks as I grit my teeth. Who does she think she is? She doesn't know me, she knows nothing. I would never hurt myself, or anyone else for that matter. Ever. "Alright, I think we're done here. Besides," I say, glancing at the hands on my watch which now reads two o'clock, "time's up."

Dr. Stephanie glances at her own watch, a surprised look crossing her face. "You're right, it is." She writes more in that dumb binder of hers.

I stand up. "Thanks for the enlightening chat. I feel totally different. You've helped me out a lot and I thank you for that," I say, extending my hand.

She grasps it, shakes my hand firmly, and looks me in the eyes. "We're far from done," she says, letting go. My hand falls to my side as Doc Stephanie walks down the steps and the pathway that leads to her silver hybrid. I stand there watching as she tosses her purse and binder in first before she takes a seat. Through the window, a shadowy silhouette waves as the car pulls away from the curb.

I'm a little annoyed at Dr. Stephanie. Thinking she shrinked me without my knowledge. Because I can't really come up with a good reason for everything. I have no real explanation for my behaviour. I can't pinpoint an exact answer that could sum up why I'd turned to dead people, cemeteries, morgues, and funeral homes when my mother died.

~ ☽ ~

Chapter Seventeen

Landon

When I get home I actually feel bad. Even though that mysterious girl was the one who'd been mean, not me. But I still have no idea who she is. She said we had classes together, that I might have seen her at games and whatnot, but I'll be damned if I can put a name to her. I thought about asking Charity, but with that nose so wrinkled and stuck up I knew all I would get is some long drawn out reason why I shouldn't care. But I do care. It's like that girl haunts me.

Daniel seemed like the next viable source; however, I really didn't want him to get the wrong impression. That I might be interested in someone else so soon after Charity. Not that there would be anything wrong if I was, but still.

So now I'm in my room, searching every inch of it for a yearbook, *any* yearbook. This is one of those times I curse the fact that I haven't been listening to my mom when she tells me to clean my room. It's dirty and disorganized. Though there aren't any dishes covered in old food and growing fury things, there is about a week's worth of laundry scattered across the floor. I swear, at one point I had a desk. Now I can't find it. There's a bookshelf on one wall but no actual books. Who knows where they are. Probably deep under the burial mound that's my laundry. And I'm actually afraid to open my

~ ☾ ~

closet. I assume that if I pull the door open, a plethora of junk will spill out and bury me alive. So the last place I decide to look is under my bed. It's the hide-all kind of place.

I get on all fours and peer underneath, where it's dark and dingy. I can't see a damn thing. I need a flashlight. I have one in the closet in case of blackouts.

I get off my knees and wade across the room to the closet. Clutching the knob I slowly turn it, bracing myself for the onslaught of crap that's going to torpedo itself at me, all desperate to escape the confines of the crypt. As the door inches open, I'm surprised. Nothing moves. There are no sounds of impending junk-slides. I flick the light switch on. There's a whole lot of stuff, piled high, but I'm drawn to the box on the top shelf labelled "books."

Funny, here I thought books would be on the *book* shelf, but apparently not. I kick a few things out of the way so I can stand inside the closet, then grab the box. It's heavy.

I place it on my bed, then flop down and open it up. I pull out the first book, an old science text. Boring. The next is an old math text. I keep pulling out books until I find a brightly colored yellow and blue glossy book with a ram in a ready-to-charge stance.

I let out a sigh but it does not relax me. Instead, I find my heart speeding up, thumping forcefully in my chest as I open the cover. In thick block letters is the year and something in Latin—the school motto that I can never remember.

I prop up pillows against the headboard of my bed then lean into them, adjusting until I'm comfortable, and begin scanning the pages. Flipping them faster and faster as the anticipation builds.

Finally all movement stops. I stare at the image of the girl I'd been searching for, who only now I realize has

~ ☾ ~

the most purest, brightest green eyes I've ever seen besides the image who haunts my dreams. My fingers trace the curves of her face as I read the name beside the girl with the fair skin, raven-black hair and emerald eyes: Xylia Morana. Had to be Dr. Morana's daughter.

In this picture she's at least two years younger, not having quite grown into her looks yet. Her hair is tied into two braided pigtails and she's wearing a black shirt slashed at the edges. Though her eyes are full of sheer beauty, they show an emptiness I can't fathom. But it's her. I know she's the one.

* * * *

Now that I know Xylia had something to do with my death—or my awakening—I'm desperate for answers. She's the girl from my vision. I want to understand what happened to me, why she was there, and why I can't get her out of my head. If I could just talk to her, maybe I can make sense of the White Room. Why I'm alive in the first place. I don't know *how* I know, but I'm sure Xylia can help me. People just don't come back. There must be a reason, and maybe Xylia is a part of a larger picture I don't yet understand. I need to talk to her.

I'd waited all last night and this morning to talk to her, and now as I rush out of our history exam, I hope to get some answers.

I see her, down the hall racing toward the main doors of the school—a flurry of black speeding down the hallway. I catch up to her when she stops at her locker and say, "Can we talk?"

Xylia's eyes scan the halls. "Um...no," she says, and before I have another chance to open my mouth, she slams her locker shut and runs down the hall.

"Hey, wait up a sec," I yell, only she quickens her pace. I run, catch up with her again, and grab her wrist.

~ ☾ ~

She gasps. When she turns around to face me, her eyes are wide. "Let go of me."

"Not until we talk. I know you were there when I died. I know it."

"I wasn't anywhere with you. You're mistaken." She shakes her wrist loose and turns on her heels.

"You still wear your hair in pigtails," I say, then wish I could take it back. Stupid. That was a stupid thing to say. But it gets her attention, sort of.

Turning back around, she says, "What did you just say?"

"In every yearbook I have, and even in the old ones in the library from grade school—and I checked this morning—your hair is in pigtails."

"So?"

"Your hair might not have changed, but you did. I looked through every picture, studied them. I know you're the one I saw when I woke up. I know it."

Her body stiffens. "You're wrong. I'm sorry, but please don't talk to me again."

"I don't believe you. Why won't you talk to me? What are you afraid of?"

Her eyes narrow. "I'm not afraid of anything. You just got the wrong girl."

I don't believe her—the way her eyes widen, then narrow into tiny slits, the fact that her body is stiff, rigid. She's hiding something. I know it.

"You don't have anything to hide," I say, reaching out to touch her arm. She recoils and lets out a yelp, maybe in surprise.

"Please, please just leave me alone."

"I won't. I won't stop."

Xylia spins her body around and races down the stretch of hallway, not slowing her pace until she's through the doors and out into the parking lot.

I have to let her go. Because by the time I push open

~ ☾ ~

the doors to the warm air outside, Xylia is peeling out of the lot in her car.

What annoys me the most is her utter lack of courtesy. Why wouldn't she just talk to me?

~ ☾ ~

Chapter Eighteen

Xylia

I never thought I'd be saying this, but I am completely avoiding Landon.

Something happened. I mean, besides the obvious, now it seems everywhere I turn he's right there, watching me—through a crowd, casually strolling up to me, or worse, trying to talk to me. It's obsessive behaviour and it's getting kinda weird.

But that's not all that's weird. No, no. I'd have been able to handle teenage obsessive tendencies, but his interest in me is so much more than that. The hunger in his eyes, the urgent tone in his voice—it's as if I'm consuming his every thought. And I felt it, that night in the morgue. My own urgency pulling me toward him. We're connected now, and I know that. The kiss we shared brought us together. The problem is that it came with something else. Something scary.

Since the morgue and—oh, I don't know, maybe even before that—voices, whispers that come at me from all directions, have been plaguing my dreams. While I'm awake I hear them too. Not as vivid, but still there nonetheless. But even now, as I think back, I'm sure it happened on the soccer field, too. Maybe. Each and every whisper wants something, and I'm sure I'm not dreaming, that it's not all just inside my head. It can't be. And that's what's really scary. That somehow maybe

~ ☽ ~

bringing Landon back has brought with him a hint of something from the other side. Something that's not happy that he's alive. Something that wants him back.

Landon is always a step ahead, like a wasp I can't shake. Today, even when I show up at the hospital for my shift, he's there. Sure, his presence could easily be a coincidence since he was released only a few days ago. However, I don't take any chances. I duck down and shuffle across the floor, hide behind the reception desk, even scuttle into the elevator, my heart pounding a mile a minute.

"So, crossword today?" I whisper, tiptoeing into a patient named Frederick's room.

His frail body is still, his eyes closed. His chest rises and falls, as gentle wheezes escape his parted lips.

"Fredrick?" I repeat, whispering louder, about to turn on my heels.

"Don't just hover over me like that," Fred says opening one eye, then the other.

"Sorry. I thought you were dead," I joke.

"Dead? I've got many more years. Don't go cursin' me like that. Damn, we should knock on wood," he rambles, reaching a shaky arm to tap lightly with a closed fist onto the nightstand. I don't have the heart to tell him it's a metal stand with a thin layer of veneer on top that only resembles wood.

"So, crosswords?" This is what Fred likes; I read out the clue and he answers it. Even insists we do it in pen. That way he's forced to be one hundred percent sure of his answer. If only life could be marked up in pen. That way no one would ever have any doubts.

"Nope, not today, I've got me a date with a hot nurse and a sponge." He winks.

"Gross." I wrinkle my nose. "That's just gross." I shake out the mental image

"Besides, I hear you have your own, shall we say,

~ ☾ ~

admirer?"

"What? Who?" Then I mutter, "Damn that Evelyn," and groan.

"She's a quick one. Has the whole ward rooting for you and that bloke who's been all over the news."

"Meh, there isn't anything going on," I say.

"Not what I heard. And you know, that Evelyn, she sure has quite a few insights. Thinks you two are soul mates or something."

My heart lurches. Soul mates. There was a time when I'd hoped, dreamed, wanted that to be true. That Landon and I could have some sort of future together. That if I only could work up the courage to talk to him, then he'd realize something profound, something that would tell him that I was his girl. But now, with everything that's happened, it can never be. Not while Dad's job is on the line, or that I'm clinging to what little of my reputation I have left. If I got fired, if the truth came out, it could jeopardize everything.

And it hurts so much, knowing that all I'll ever have of Landon are my memories. That slight graze of his hand touching my skin, buzzing it with electricity. That smell of his mountain fresh deodorant and cologne. That way he has when he smiles and little dimples appear at the corners of his lips.

Most of all, it hurts because he'll never know what I did for him, and how much I miss something I never truly had in the first place.

"I don't believe in that, so I wouldn't go holding your breath...or you really just might die." I try to force a laugh.

"Don't burn any bridges or throw something away that's good for ya. Life's too short."

"Yeah, I won't," I say, waving goodbye and leaving Fredrick to his "hot nurse and sponge" date.

~ ☾ ~

* * * *

"You're late," Doc Stephanie says, popping out of nowhere.

The hall of the hospital is empty. How did I not see her? "How the hell did you do that?" I glare at her.

She shrugs and says, "Do what?" Even her voice comes out innocent.

I let out an exasperated sigh and flail my arms about, then say, "Pop out of nowhere. It's creepy." It's like Doc Stephanie is a panther, waiting for the right moment to pounce.

"We have a session today. So here I am."

I roll my eyes. "I know we *had* a session." I glance at my watch, even holding it out for her to see. "One that started twenty-three minutes ago...at my house."

"Uh huh. Where you obviously aren't, are you?"

"Exactly. Because I didn't want to have a session today, or any day for that matter. Hence the not being where I said I'd be thing."

"Too bad for you I'd promised your dad. Cafeteria, ten minutes," she says sternly, hands even on her hips, showing authority.

I've got two options. Neither one is very good. I can do as Doc Stephanie wants and meet her in the cafeteria, or I can run. I know it's a little childish but I'm still not convinced she didn't shrink me already. I don't want or need her inside my head anymore.

So even though I say, "Fine, you win, ten minutes," to her, I'm not going to the cafeteria. I'm going to try and get as far away from her and this hospital as I can.

She nods. "Alright, see you there."

After waiting until she's in the elevator, I run down the hall to the back stairwell, knowing that if I hurry, I can be out of the hospital and in my car before she even has a chance to realize I'm not coming. I push myself

~ ☾ ~

faster and faster, down the stairs. Even with the last flight in view I don't slow, not until I push through the door outside, stopping to catch my breath.

"Going somewhere?"

I'm startled stiff, and slowly turn around to see the shrink causally leaning up against the wall of the hospital, arms folded across her chest, that annoying smug smile spread across her face.

"What the hell!"

"Seriously, you were just going to leave?"

"Maybe," I say with attitude.

"This is for your own good. I'm just trying to help." She shakes her head. "But you know what? If you're going to act like a child, then I can't be bothered to help you. You are wasting my time and your dad's hard earned money."

"Finally you are getting it. I never asked for help and I certainly don't need it from you," I say. I walk away, knowing it might not be that easy. Dad is going to have a lot to say and none of it will be good. But Dr. Stephanie doesn't try to stop me.

I turn the corner, and when I see Landon leaning against my car, I want to scream with frustration and anger. His black slacks stand out against the sleek silver of my car, his blue button-down shirt is open, the breeze flapping it about, exposing a white muscle shirt underneath. It's sexy, but not at all what I want to deal with right now.

"Can we talk?" he says, his voice smooth.

"No. We can't. I'm late for something." I reach for the door handle.

Landon slides down the length of the car, blocking me. "When are you going to stop running? You're going to have to talk to me one day," he says.

I force my lips out of the hard line they're in and say, "No, I don't. There's nothing we could possibly have to

~ ☾ ~

talk about. Now move, *please*."

He's quiet for a moment, chewing the inside of his lip but then says, "We do. Have something to talk about, that is." He notices my uncomfortable shift because he adds, "And I think you know that. It's why you've been avoiding me."

The only sound that comes out of my mouth is a "pfft." It whistles through the small gap between my two front teeth.

"See, you can't even deny it. I know you were there when I woke up. I really just want to know why."

I swallow thickly. "I wasn't. I've said this already, you must be mistaken." Mustering up a whole lot of strength, I shove him with both hands away from my car. He looks surprised, caught off guard, but by the time he decides to do something about it, it's too late. I'm in the car, bringing the engine to life. I reverse and my heart, my poor heart, is racing faster than the car. Because as much as I hate to admit it, I'm actually curious.

I'm curious why Landon doesn't seem upset knowing I was there. But most of all, I'm curious because he's been that close to the other side.

I wish I could ask him what it is like to die.

~ ☾ ~

Chapter Nineteen

Landon

I'm drawn to Xylia like a moth to a flame, although that's kind of lame because the moth ultimately dies in that scenario. But that's how I feel. When I'm sleeping, she's in every dream, with those piercing green eyes of hers staring at me, her face hovering over my still body. When I saw her in the parking lot, I knew I had to step up my game.

I need to talk to her, to understand what she was doing in the room when I woke up, and why, even now, days after the incident, she's all I can think about. I want to know why my heart tugs in her direction, why it's like a band of elastic snapping in half, and slapping me when she storms away.

She looks so mysterious, yet pained. When she pushed me away earlier, it made me realize all I wanted to do was to gather her up in my arms, tell her that no matter what, things will be okay, and that maybe, just maybe, if she lets me in, *I* could make this okay. Could make this better.

But I couldn't speak. Couldn't stop her. After that failed attempt at reaching Xylia—God, I love the way her name sounds, the way my tongue curls in my mouth as I speak it—I head home.

The front door is open, letting the cold air circulate around the house as I stomp up the porch steps.

~ ☾ ~

Inhaling a deep breath, I walk across the threshold, kick off my shoes, and head toward the sound of clanking dishes and closing cupboards.

"There you are. I was wondering when you'd be home," Mom says, taking a plate from the dishwasher and stacking it in the cupboard. Since the accident, Mom's been desperately keeping tabs on my every move—or at least attempting to.

"You got some mail," she says, smiling. "Over there, by the phone."

I head to the small jut-out of the countertop, not really an island and not really useable space. I call it the peninsula. It doesn't take me long to locate the stack of mail, my name displayed prominently in black against the various colored envelopes.

"Shouldn't they be bigger? I mean, don't you usually get a big envelope when a school accepts you?" Mom is suddenly right behind me.

"It varies," I reply as I pick up the first envelope, my thumb tracing over the school's emblem.

"Well...open it, let's see what"—she stands on her tippy toes to get a better look— "Oak U has to say. And there's one from Cedar Hill University, too." She sounds more giddy than I feel.

This is one of those moments. The rest of my future as a soccer player will be decided right here and now. I almost don't want to open any of them.

"Go on, Landon, open them. I've been waiting all morning. I almost opened up some myself, I was so excited," Mom says, her hand now resting on my shoulder.

I turn the first envelope over in my hands—yellow—I can't help but wonder if Mom is right. This packet feels small. Like there aren't any "hey, we want you to enroll now" forms in it. This might just be a single piece of paper with the words "we regret to inform you..."

~ ☾ ~

My fingers tear up one of the corners, then I stick the letter opener in and slide it, cutting the paper effortlessly. It's only one sheet, folded three times. I pluck it out. I take in a deep breath and stare almost blankly at the words that now look jumbled up.

It's my mother who pulls my attention back to the paper. "Awe, honey, just because one says no doesn't mean the others will." She gives my shoulder a tight squeeze, then runs her hand up and down my arm in a soothing manner, which really does nothing.

"Yeah, you're right, there's at least six more here. One of them has to want me, right?" My voice sounds shaky.

"Of course. You're a wonderful player. They'd be crazy not to."

I pick up another letter, repeating the opening process, slipping in the pointy dagger end in and sliding it across.

It doesn't take me more than a second to know I won't be going to Cedar Hill. I say, "This one's a no too, Mom."

"Oh, honey, I'm sorry. But it's not over yet," she says, always the optimist.

But it is, or at least it feels like that after I open two more, both no's like the first ones. "I think I'll open the last two later," I sigh, defeated, not knowing how much more rejection I can take.

"Oh, come on, you might as well bite the bullet and get it over with."

This time I don't bother using the letter opener; instead, I just tear into the envelope like a kid on Christmas morning. I unfold the paper, eyes quickly scanning the words printed on the page.

My mom breathes over my shoulder, "See...this one isn't exactly a no—"

"But it's not a full scholarship either," I say. I needed that. Without a paid ride, I don't know how my parents

~ ☾ ~

and I could possibly pay tuition.

"Hey, we can deal with that later, right now though, they want you. Maple Grove wants you to come play soccer for them." Then she motions to the other letter. "Now go ahead, honey, open the last one."

I do. It's another no. But it shouldn't be over. I'd applied to more than six schools, and there's half a year left. They still have time to come to their senses. These were, however, my tops schools and now, after all the work I'd put in, none had offered what I thought would be a done deal. A full ride.

"Mom, I know you are just trying to help but…it's not working," I say.

I know though, that between my slightly above average grades and the accident, I'm not exactly the best candidate for scholarships. Without soccer, I'm just average. Colleges don't hunt down and offer scholarships to average kids.

"But honey—"

"Just face it. I'm probably not going to college. Or at least not a good one. One with a soccer team." I'm angry as I add, "I'm going to end up being a plumber or something." I storm away with Mom yelling after me, trying to tell me it's all right.

It's always been about getting out of Silversprings. That was my goal. Go to college, play soccer, and then maybe hit the big times. In Silversprings, community college is like a prison sentence. I know if I end up there, I'll never get out. But if I don't leave, I'll end up working at the lumber mill, like Dad, or worse. I'll be trapped in a dead end job in a dead end town.

In my room, I find my fist making contact with my headboard. I hit it as tears well up in my eyes, threatening to fall over. My knuckles burn and sting but I keep punching the thick wooden board until there's no more pain anymore. My hand is splattered with blood

~ ☾ ~

streaks, freshly torn flesh hangs loose. Maybe I would have been better off dead.

"It's not over yet, son."

I'm startled by my father's gruff voice coming from the doorway. I turn to see him standing with his shoulder against the frame, ankles crossed, and arms folded over his chest.

He tosses me a towel. "Here, looks like you might need this."

"How long were you standing there?" Taking the towel, I wrap my bloody hand up, applying pressure to the knuckles.

"Long enough. And like I said, it's not over. We'll find out when tryouts start, drive across country if we have to, and dammit, we'll get you the scholarship you deserve."

"But that's just it...maybe I don't deserve it. Maybe in Silversprings I'm a great player, but not great enough," I say.

"Well, you're wrong. They're wrong. And so what if you had an accident. That doesn't mean you can't play just as good now as you did before," he says.

I make my eyebrows furrow. "What does this have to do with my *accident*? You don't think—" Then I mutter, "Of course it has something to do with it, doesn't it? They think I'm a liability, don't they?" I can almost see my career flashing before my eyes. It doesn't matter that I was given a clean bill of health. My former death can't look good. My health's a risk, and a huge one since there is no known cause for my collapse in the first place. No one would want to take on a student like me and give them a full scholarship if they couldn't play anymore, or worse—if they would have a repeat accident on the field.

"Like I said, it's not over. We'll do whatever we have to," Dad says.

I nod but know it might not ever be enough.

~ ☾ ~

Chapter Twenty

Xylia

Dad's sitting at the breakfast nook, waiting for me, when I burst through the entryway, frustrated.

He doesn't waste any time. "I got an interesting phone call today," he says.

I hold up my hands. "Let me explain?" I ask meekly.

"No. No, I don't think anything you have to say will make this better. Dr. Evans says that you need more help than she can give you, did you know that? I'm guessing she means you're unfixable."

My face falls, a tear pricks my eye. "Don't say that, Dad. She didn't say that, did she?" I whisper.

He shakes his head and his shoulders slump. "I just don't know what to do anymore. If your mother was here, she'd know what to do."

This angers me. "No she wouldn't! She left us, so how could she know how to make things better? She was the one who made things worse!" A tear spills over and rolls down my cheek. "I'm not unfixable, I just need time. I can make things better, I swear." Even though I'm not sure if I can anymore.

"It's been over five years, Xylia. If you were going to change you would have done it by now, honey."

"Please, please don't give up on me Daddy, not yet." But the look in his eyes tells me he already has. To him I'm so far gone he almost can't bear to look at me.

~ ☾ ~

"I just don't know what to do," he repeats, head now hung.

"But...but...I'm going to graduate, I got nearly straight A's, I have a job, a car, responsibilities. How can that possibly mean I'm unfixable, that there is something wrong with me? I'm just different is all. Different," I plead to him.

"Xylia, different is the way you dress, your personality. But what you do in your spare time, that's just unhealthy. I think it means you aren't well."

Another tear rolls down my face. "I am well! Maybe there's something wrong with you! You haven't let Mom go. People let people go, they don't dwell on those who chose to leave." I stomp over to the adjoining living room, to the mantle and pick up one of our family pictures. I'm five or six. We are at the Silversprings Fair. My mother's arm is wrapped tight around my shoulders, holding on to me as we ride the Ferris wheel. Dad caught the moment perfectly as the two of us plunge toward the ground. My eyes show nothing but fear, but my mom is smiling wide, looking at me with such adoring eyes. Her mouth is slightly open, and I remember that she kept whispering into my ear, telling me everything was going to be okay.

Clearly she'd been wrong. To this day I hate the Ferris wheel and nothing has been okay.

As anger flows through my veins, I throw the picture to the ground. The glass shatters into shards with razor sharp edges. "She left us, Dad, so why the hell is she still here?"

I pick up another picture of me and my mom. She's smiling, her eyes lit up with happiness as autumn leaves fall from the trees in the background. I smash it against the mantel. Splinters of glass prick my arms as the wooden frame cracks. "You should move on. These shouldn't be here, reminding us of what she didn't want

~ ☾ ~

anymore."

Tears flow freely down my face when my father's strong arms gather me in a tight embrace. "Shh, honey. It's okay," he murmurs in my ear, then kisses the top of my forehead.

"It's not okay, Daddy," I sob. "She didn't want me, and you think I'm broken."

His hand brushes the top of my head as he gently rocks us back and forth. "We'll call Dr. Evans back, or find a new doctor. Whatever it takes. Before you know it, things will be better. In time, you'll even be ready for college."

His words suddenly grab my attention. I pull away from him, swiping at my eyes with my arm. My skin is streaked with black mascara and I know my make-up is probably smeared, but I look deep into his eyes. "What do you mean *in time* I'll be ready for college? I've already been accepted. This is ridiculous," I say because I just don't understand, not fully.

"I thought I was clear: no talking to Dr. Evans, no trip. And maybe now, no college. What kind of father would I be if I sent you away when you were sick and I don't help you?"

"I don't need rescuing!" I say, taking a step back. "There's nothing wrong with me. You're just trying to find someone to save because you couldn't save *her*!" I don't even wait for a response; I just turn and leave, racing up the stairs, my father calling out after me. I ignore every word.

When I reach the door to my room, I push it open, slam it shut behind me and lock it.

The loud thumps of Dad's feet hit the stairs full force, then his fist bangs against the door. "You're grounded, Xylia."

I want to yell at him, tell him I'm almost eighteen and soon will no longer be his responsibility, but I know I'll

~ ☾ ~

just hurt him, more than I already have. Instead, I throw my body onto my bed, burying my head into pillows, hiding.

But I can't hide from my memories. As much as I have wished, prayed, demanded that the one horrible memory would go away, it won't. It haunts me, taunts me. I fight it, but the memory comes back now.

That Christmas morning the back door had been open, creaking back and forth in the crisp morning breeze. I don't remember what was going through my mind as I slipped on my boots, zipped up my winter parka over my fleece bear pyjamas, and wandered outside. Frozen grass crunched beneath my boots as I trudged across the back lawn.

It rarely snowed on Christmas. Instead, usually frozen drops of water would rain from the sky, leaving the ground glistening with diamonds that would disappear when the sun rose. But that morning it was particularly cold. My breath billowed from my mouth and nose like fog. I didn't have a destination in mind but felt a pull, a force that pushed me deeper and deeper into the woods. I wasn't supposed to be there. My parents told me never to go into the thick, dense trees without them. But for some reason I knew it was where I was supposed to be.

The deeper I trudged into the woods the more my stomach twisted with apprehension. I remember spinning around in circles, trying to remember which way went into the trees and which way was out, back to the house. I could get lost. That's why I wasn't supposed to be there. But I remember needing to know, needing to understand why I wanted so desperately to see what was out in the woods. Like I knew what I would find, but just needed confirmation.

The surroundings started to change, and the path that I had walked a million times before became a fork. I

~ ☾ ~

followed my instincts and turned the corner and pushed forward. I remember seeing the tree, the oak. A glint of pretty pink caught my eye as it swayed back and forth. Tension eased from me and I ran up to the tree, eager to see what had got caught up in its limbs, hoping it was something magical. A secret present Santa had left hidden in a place only I'd find.

But there, hanging from my favorite tree—the big white Oregon oak, the one with branches that stretched out like hundreds of arms and fingers, devoid of leaves— was my mother. She was still wearing her housecoat and her silky pink nightgown, a gift I'd helped Dad pick out two years before, and a slipper dangled precariously from one foot. The other had fallen to the forest floor. Her stiff body swayed gently back and forth. The branch bowed against her weight, and the rope that held her in place creaked and whined.

I stood still, watching her, blinking my eyes, screaming inside my head to wake up from the horrible dream I thought I was having. But I never did. And the longer I stood looking at her lifeless body, the more I believed what I was seeing. I reached out, took her hand in mine. It was icy cold. The blood-curdling scream that escaped my lips was loud, terrified. It worked its way up from the tips of my toes to the top of my head. Everything my lungs could possibly expel came out. I remained frozen in place, tears streaming down my cheeks, screaming as loud as I could until Dad came and found me, and her.

Afterward, I never once dreamed about her. Not a nightmare, not a meadow scene where she came running toward me, smiling and laughing. The other dead people, the ones I had seen in the morgue, never left my sleeping conscious scared. The countless funerals I snuck into never left a lasting mark.

I always hoped they would, that seeing the dead,

~ ☾ ~

attending the funerals, would give me some sort of closure. That maybe they'd give me some insight as to why she left. I wish I could touch the other side enough, to believe that she's watching over me. But I never feel her. There's never enough life energy left over from the dead that would allow me to talk to her in some way.

As I pick at the pills on my black duvet, thinking back to that horrible day and all the ones that followed, I realize that maybe the answer isn't that far away. Maybe now is just as good of a time as any to figure out just how to let go.

~ ☾ ~

Chapter Twenty-one

Landon

Cold water washes away the blood, swirling it around the porcelain sink. The tender flesh stings. I grit my teeth and push through. My father thought I should go to the doctor, or worse, the hospital. I assured him I was fine. When the water runs clear, I pull my hand away and dab it gently with gauze.

The medical kit I have resting on the back of the toilet is old, with parts of it missing. Good thing I don't need a finger bandage or an eye patch. Paper wrapped gauze and tape is all I need. I even take the extra effort and smear some Polysporin on the bandage before applying it to my knuckles, then hold it in place with tape. I hope it scabs over quickly; the knuckle covering is already irritating me. But not as much as the knowledge that me being brought back to life has ended the life I thought I'd have.

* * * *

There's no conversation at dinner, no one wanting to talk about my recent misfortune, no one wanting to upset me further, I guess. Its mind numbing, the way my mom has been coddling me, how my father thinks we can just drive across the country in hopes of convincing a college to accept me. I just want to be free.

~ ☾ ~

I excuse myself from the table, say I'm going out to get fresh air. I know my mom wants to tell me no, or to stay close, but for once her mouth stays shut. I'm glad. I push open the screen door and step out onto the porch, then pull on my jacket. Clouds are rolling in—fast, dark, and full of rain. The weather matches my mood, bitter and cold. I take a deep breath and wonder if things could get any worse.

I catch sight of a car driving slowly on the street. Charity's sleek black sports car comes to a halt at the end of my drive. If the atmosphere in the house wasn't as tense as it is out here, I'd have turned and left in an instant, but since Charity stands between me and what little freedom I have left, I take a step off the porch and meet her halfway.

"I must have driven by your house a dozen times," Charity says as she comes to a stop inches away from me. She notices my hand and says, "Oh, my god, Landon, what happened?"

I quickly fold my arms, covering the bandage on my knuckles. "It's nothing," I say. "So what finally made you stop?" I don't think I've ever prayed for it to rain so much before in my life. Maybe that way she'd leave. I'm just not sure I can handle her right now.

She reaches out her hand, then pulls back when I instinctively step back. "Don't be like that, Landon. I'm worried about you."

I don't want to be mean to her, it's not really in my nature, but, "Thanks for the concern," I say and step past her.

She reaches out her hand and pulls me to a stop. "Please. Please just talk to me."

I don't turn around but say through gritted teeth, "About what?"

"I said I'm worried about you."

I take a step forward, then heave a sigh. No matter

~ ☾ ~

how I feel about her right now, she's still Charity, and I loved her once. Maybe I don't owe it to her, but I might as well hear what she has to say. Slowly, I turn around. She's still gorgeous, not that her looks were ever the problem. Her blond hair is tied up in a messy ponytail, her eyes are highlighted with charcoal shadow, and her blue and yellow Rams track suit hugs all her curves. "Thanks. Now why are you here?"

"I-I thought maybe we could—"

I raise a hand to stop her. "I'm sorry, Charity, but there is no 'we' anymore"

Her eyes begin to glisten with tears. Her shoulders slump. "I know, but...I'm sorry, okay? I shouldn't have...maybe we can start over?"

I think about it, I really do. Charity is comfortable, easy, but that's what's been the problem. It's because of her that I've never really been alone. When she'd dumped me in the past, I never really had the energy or desire to try for anyone else, and well, she'd always come back. "I think it's best if we just leave things how they are. I've got a lot on my mind, and a lot I'm trying to deal with."

She takes a step forward, quickly reaching up to brush a few strands of hair off my face. Her skin is warm, inviting, but I shake my head and take another step back. The pain stricken look that crosses her face tugs at my heart.

"I just need to be alone for a while," I add.

She bobs her head up and down, sniffles, and wipes her eyes. "You're right. I'm sorry, I...just thought, I'm sorry, I shouldn't have come." She rushes past me, down the walk and toward her car.

"Charity?" I call out after her. She stops, looking up at me, mascara trails down her cheeks. "We can still be friends?"

She nods again, "Okay. I'd like that." Her voice comes

~ ☾ ~

out a little forced. But it's the best I can do. I probably wouldn't be a very good boyfriend right now anyway, and I hate to think she's shallow, but I'd always worry that she'd drop me again, especially if she found out my chances of going pro were looking pretty slim.

I watch her climb into her car. She sits at the curb, engine idling for a few moments. I can see through the spots of rain that begin to fall on the window that she's wiping away more tears. Eventually though, she puts the car in gear and drives down the street. I stand watching her go until her black car turns the corner and disappears out of sight.

As I walk the streets of Silversprings, my mind is unsettled. All my life, I'd always *assumed* I would play soccer. Assuming had obviously been the wrong thing to do. Now with that dream crushed, I'm clueless. Without soccer, I really don't know who I am. Soccer defined me.

When I turn down another street, the light rain finally easing up, I'm almost amazed at where my feet have taken me. Not really paying attention, I've stumbled to the bottom of Snob Hill and toward someone I can't stop thinking about. Even when I think I'm not thinking about her.

Snob Hill is just how it sounds. I'm sure every town or city has one. The area with the street lined with mansions, ones so big you could probably fit two of my houses into them. This is where the doctors, lawyers, business owners, and lottery winners live. It should be a gated community, with guards on hand twenty-four hours, access by invitation only and valets in front of every door because that's how every kid imagines it. To me though, it's really Everglade Road, with big houses and sad people who have money instead of happiness.

Having no idea what house is Xylia's, I walk farther up the winding road, paying close attention to the cars. Since I'm being a little presumptuous about what street

~ ☽ ~

she lives on, I'm looking for her car, which is the only thing I can really link to her.

It's not until I pass about five or six houses that I spot a silver car parked in a driveway. I debate throwing pebbles at random windows, hoping to land on the right one and not anger a parent. It's after dinner and not late, so her parents are probably still awake. I ask myself why the hell I don't walk up to the door and ring the bell, like a normal person would. I sigh, knowing that would probably only result in the door being slammed in my face.

A few seconds go by as I debate and argue with myself until a sign falls from the sky, literally. A duffle bag lands a few feet away from me. When I look up, I see someone climbing down the trellis.

It's her. Xylia's black hair flows freely as she takes the steps to the ground. I walk over to her and stand just below. She hasn't noticed me, and for fear of startling her, I stay silent. Her foot slips. The thick and clunky Doc Martens don't quite catch the wooden ledge of the trellis.

"Shit," she mutters, but it's too late. Somehow she manages to lose not only her footing but her grip. She's falling, fast.

Stepping into her path, I hold out my arms. It seems wrong to let her fall to the ground. Though I've seen this scene play out in the movies, I've never actually caught anyone before.

The weight of her falling body hits my arms. They give just a little, and I have to bend my knees to brace and support myself.

"What the hell? Put me down," Xylia says when her eyes land on mine.

Quickly I release my grip as she hops from my arms. She sniffles, wiping her nose on her sleeve.

"Sorry...I just thought—" I can easily see she's upset;

~ ☾ ~

her eyes are red and puffy, stained with wet tears. "Are you okay?"

"What are you doing here? Go away," she says. She reaches down and picks up the duffle bag, swings it over her shoulder, then walks away.

"Where are you going?" I ask, right on her heels.

She opens the trunk of her car tossing the bag in. "It's none of your business." She slams the metal trunk shut.

"I know, but I'm curious. I just want to talk," I say, though she's not giving in at all. She walks to the driver's side and opens the door.

She's going to get in and drive away. Thinking fast, or maybe not thinking at all, I scramble to the other side, open the door, and hop in.

"What the hell are you doing? Get out of my car," she says.

Folding my arms across my chest, I lift up my chin and say, "No, not until you talk to me or tell me what's wrong."

She climbs into the car, fury igniting the green in her eyes. "God! Can't you take the hint? I don't like you, I don't want to talk to you, and hell, I don't want anything to do with you, ever."

"If that were the case, then you wouldn't be the first thing I remember seeing when I woke up after I died," I say. Almost smug.

Her mouth opens but no words come out. Instead, she puts her key in the ignition, revs the engine a little, and puts the car in drive.

When we're on the road I ask, "So, where are we going?"

"*We're* not going anywhere," she says, adding, "I'm driving you home," as she rounds a corner.

"No, you're not. *We* haven't talked yet. I'm going where ever you are."

She looks at me then grins. "Fine. But you need to

~ ☾ ~

pitch in for gas."

Giving her a questioning gaze, I say, "Gas?"

"Uh, yeah. Cars need gas, and if you're coming with me, it's only fair that you chip in."

"I'm almost afraid to ask where we're going that's going to need more than a tank of gas," I say.

"Then don't." She holds out her hand. "Cash works for me."

I reach into my back pocket, then pull out my wallet. "I don't have any cash, but I do have this," I say, waving a plastic card around.

She looks at me then shakes her head. "Figures you'd have that."

I'm taken aback. If anyone was going to flash a plastic credit card I'd have thought it would have been her, yet she seems annoyed. "It's not what you think, and clearly you don't know me that well."

"Correction. I don't know you at all, but I do know what a Visa card looks like. Must be nice."

"This coming from rich doctor's daughter," I mutter. "It's one of those pay as you go kind of cards. You know, you put money on it, then use it, and when the money's gone the card won't work."

"Oh. They have those?"

"Yeah. My mom says it builds credit, but it's not actually a credit card. It only has $358.27 on it."

"Huh...I see."

Is it wrong to feel good about putting someone in their place? 'Cause I kind of feel good about it. Sure, it's something small, and I'd bet my life savings that she has a real credit card in her wallet, but at least she's realizing there's more to me.

~ ☽ ~

Chapter Twenty-two

Xylia

First impressions are always a little deceiving. With Landon sitting next to me, his body heat surrounding me like a warm blanket, his scent wafting into my nose, I realize there's more to him than I would have imagined. People tend to judge me, but I know why—it's the way I dress, the kind of car I drive, the fact that I seem to get along with the dying better than I do the living. I suppose I shouldn't judge Landon based on only what I've seen at school. Sure, he's popular and is the face of the school and the head of the soccer team and he always manages to dress snazzy. I just assumed he came from rich parents, too.

"Sorry," I almost whisper, a little embarrassed.

He turns in his seat. "What? What was that?"

I repeat a little louder, "Sorry?"

A small grin plays on his lips. "Huh? I couldn't hear you—maybe say that a little louder?"

Throwing up my hands I say, "I said I was sorry."

He laughs. "Wow, you make that look really painful, like you've never had to say that before."

"Maybe I haven't, so just drop it."

"So where are we going anyway?" he asks as I merge onto the highway. "I have a feeling I'm not going to be back by bedtime."

"No, I don't think you will. Hope that's alright," I say,

~ ☾ ~

pressing my foot down on the accelerator. I've never run away before. Well, not really. Once I stayed in the park until after dark because Dad and I had had a fight, but eventually I got cold and hungry and trudged home. This time things are different. I know Dad will get the note; at least, I hope he gets it before he has time to worry about me too much. I hate hurting him, but it was apparent that this needed to be done. He wasn't going to stop me from going on this trip, especially since he thinks I'm broken and sick. That's not the case at all. Or at least that's what I keep telling myself.

I don't notice the awkward silence that has fallen over Landon until he says something, pulling me back to reality. "Are you going to tell me what's wrong? You look...uh, really upset."

When I wipe my hand over my face, I'm surprised by the wetness that clings to my skin. I hadn't realized I'd started to shed tears. That's how upset I am, the argument with my father, letting him down...I don't know how to fix it.

"I'm fine."

"Correct me if I'm wrong, but you certainly don't look fine," Landon says, concern all over his face.

"Well, I am. Just be quiet. I have to concentrate."

"If you tell me where we're going, you probably wouldn't have to concentrate so hard."

A few seconds pass, then I let out a sigh. "Valley View."

His eyes grow wide. "What? That's like, two hours away, at least."

I shrug. "So?"

"What's in Valley View? I mean, what's so important you need to drive this late at night to get there, that you snuck out of your window for?"

"Ivy Hills," I say.

"Wait. That kind of sounds like a cemetery."

~ ☾ ~

"Maybe it is."

His eyes look like they might separate from his skull and pop out. "Whoa, hold up a sec, I didn't sign up for this—"

"I can pull over right here. I'm sure a good looking guy like you would get picked up real quick. We're not that far outside of Silversprings," I say, but somehow know I won't be doing that. His eyes are maybe calculating the odds, or how important it is for him to get these answers he thinks I have.

"Nah, I'm okay." Then he smirks. "You think I'm good looking?"

"I didn't say that. Well, not exactly. Shut up." But a small smile creeps onto my lips. The way he's looking at me, it's attention grabbing—a look that has me bound to him. And God, the smell that is pouring off him gets me, the scent of cologne so strong and earthy, like the ground just after it rains. He could say anything and I would probably do anything.

* * * *

"I have to pee," Landon says out of nowhere. We'd been driving in silence, minus the radio, for the last hour and a half. I expected him to drill me, to talk incessantly, but once he knew where we were going, he froze up.

"We're almost there," I say. The last sign we passed said we were only about twenty minutes out.

"But I have to go now." He's fidgeting in his seat.

I begin to slow the car, then pull onto the shoulder. "Fine, but you'd better make it quick." I'm barely at a complete stop when he releases his seat belt and hops out of the car.

He goes down the ditch, presumably doing his business. It's kind of surreal, how I've known Landon

~ ☾ ~

almost four years and how we've spoken more now in
the last few days than we have all those years. It's even
difficult to believe that he's standing a few feet away,
taking a leak on the side of the road, and that I'm...lucky
enough to be in his presence.

I can't help it and look over when I hear him finish,
then chuckle when I catch him doing this jiggle hop
thing. He heads back to the car and gets in. I say, "Must
be nice being a guy, having the ability to just go
whenever you need to."

Pulling the seatbelt across his chest, then clicking it
into place, he says, "Hey, girls can do it too, they mostly
just choose not to."

"It's really not that easy for us, I mean there's
planning involved, we need cover, TP, sloped ground
preferably. Hell, one wrong move and you end up with it
all over your pants, your shoes...it can become
disastrous."

When he laughs my face flushes as heat creeps up my
neck, spreading over my cheeks. "What? What are you
laughing at?" I ask.

"We're having a conversation about...pissing. It's just
funny. I mean, I hardly know you and yet you aren't
embarrassed to admit you can easily piss on your
pants...okay, maybe *now* you're embarrassed. That's a
nice shade of red you're wearing," he says and smiles.

"Whatever. Forget I said that. I've never accidentally
peed on my pants. Or my shoes, for that matter," I add
quickly.

"Uh huh."

I reach over, yank open the glove box, and pull out a
map. "Here. Make yourself useful—we need a Wal-
Mart." I thrust the crumpled paper at him.

"This isn't going to tell us where a Wal-Mart is."

"Yeah, well, whatever."

He's wearing me down. The shield I usually have in

~ ☾ ~

place is wavering. The longer I spend with him the more I almost *want* to open up.

"Does Valley View even have a Wal-Mart?" He holds the map up to his face.

"Yeah...at least, I think it does," I say with uncertainty.

"According to this map, you're going to want to take the first exit into town, then a right at the lights, a left at the four way—"

"Hey, I thought the map wouldn't tell us where a Wal-Mart was," I say, then take one hand off the wheel to tug on the map, revealing Landon cradling a phone in his hands.

"No, but my phone does." He laughs. "One should always be prepared."

"God, you think you're so smart don't you? I would have found one. Eventually."

"I never said you wouldn't have. You look like a very resourceful kind of girl."

"Yeah, one who's not ashamed to pull over and ask for directions," I toss back with a smile. When Dad and I would go on trips, he'd do whatever possible to avoid asking for directions. I never understood that about men.

"Touché." Then he adds, "I thought we were going to go to a cemetery. So why do we need a Wal-Mart?"

"Well...As you noticed, I kind of made a quick escape. I'm not fully prepared for our adventure and neither are you," I reply. I ignore it when Landon quirks his eyebrows and take the first exit into town as Landon had instructed. Valley View is dark, except for the giant lit up parking lot and building of the Wal-Mart that is now coming into view. It's like a fluorescent beacon, a lighthouse just off the highway, guiding cars to all one's twenty-four hour shopping needs. I want to smack him *and* myself—I totally could have found the Wal-mart on

~ ☽ ~

my own, without Landon's phone. Hell, anyone could when it lights up the sky like that.

I park, and once Landon and I are inside, I grab a cart. It's crazy how many people are pushing them through the aisles this late. I know why I'm here, but what is so important for these other people that they just have to go shopping at nearly ten o'clock at night? What couldn't wait until tomorrow?

"I can push that, if you want," Landon says from beside me.

"Nah, I'm okay. Besides," I point toward the men's clothing section, "you have some shopping to do."

"You know shopping for clothes is like a man's Kryptonite, right?"

"I'm sorry you're not Superman. But I'm not sure tights would benefit you much either." I chuckle, even snorting a little, having just put the image of Landon wearing red and blue tights into my head.

He rolls his eyes and shuffles toward a rack that holds various styles of blue jeans. Flipping quickly through the selection, then he pulls out two pairs, one light washed, the other dark.

"I don't even know if these will fit," he says, holding both of them up.

"Guess you'll just have to make use of the changing rooms then." I flick my head.

He turns slightly, then sighs loudly and walks over to the row of doors.

When he disappears inside, I walk up to a rack and pull a few shirts in various colors in both medium and large and walk back to the changing rooms.

"Here, you might as well try these on too," I say, pitching the shirts over the door.

"Hey, watch it," he yelps.

After a few minutes of shuffling, hangers fall to the floor and a pair of white chicken legs are visible from

~ ☾ ~

underneath the door. I ask, "Hey, wanna come out and show me?" My mom always used to make me show her things when I tried them on, making sure they fit right. When she died and my father took over shopping duties, he could have cared less. Told me it would be my own fault if I didn't have enough common sense to buy something that fit properly.

"Um, no, definitely not."

"Oh, come on," I whine.

"No, I don't think these fit right," he says.

"I can't help you if you don't show me."

"Alright, but no laughing."

The door creaks open on its hinges, and the fact that he told me not to laugh has escaped me as I cover my mouth and…laugh, hysterically. The pants are a foot too short and yet the pants are somehow too big, sagging in the waist and between his legs, and I bet if he turned around, they'd sag in the butt. The shirt is just as bad. The sleeves are skin tight, probably cutting off circulation, though they do show off his toned biceps. Two of him could fit in the chest area.

"I told you not to laugh." He frowns.

"Sorry, I can't help it, this is just too funny. Like Candid Camera kind of funny." And with that I pull out my phone, getting ready to take a picture.

Landon's quick. "Oh, no you don't." He lunges for the phone and me. I'm still laughing as he comes at me full force then wraps his hands around my wrists. "Hand that over, now," he says seriously, but the grin on his face lightens the tone. I hold in the wheeze of air that is begging to escape as his hands sear my skin with heat and electricity.

Then I notice his proximity. His warm breath on my face is minty. His eyes look at me strangely, deep pools of never ending blue. My entire body grows rigid and I stop breathing.

~ ☾ ~

Chapter Twenty-three

Landon

As I look deep into Xylia's eyes, at the smile that's on her face, a picture flashes before my eyes. The one where she looks so sad—the image of the girl I woke up seeing. Her body is tense beneath my fingertips as the phone slips out of her grasp and falls to the floor.

I don't move, not right away, and neither does she. We stand still, taking each other in. She smells like flowers, a meadow full of freshness. Skin, soft and silky. And my heart screams a tune I don't recognize. No, that's not me, it's the phone. The phone vibrates with a shrill sound on the floor. I release the hold I have on Xylia so she can bend down to pick it up. Though, instead of answering it, she pushes a button and the loudness stops.

"Aren't you going to answer that?" I ask as she shoves it back into her pocket.

"Nope," she says quickly.

I let it go; it doesn't matter to me if she chooses not to talk to whoever was on the other end. "Can we please find something that fits now?" I say, realizing I'm standing out in the open in clothes that I have no business wearing.

"Yeah, of course," she says. Her voice is distant and hollow-sounding.

After trying on about a dozen pairs of jeans and just

~ ☾ ~

as many shirts, I finally drop a few items into the cart. It's been awhile since I've had to do any real shopping, and it's a lot harder then I remember.

Pushing the cart forward, not looking anywhere but forward, Xylia says, "Do we need to make a trip down the.... uh...undergarment aisle?" She sounds super awkward. I think it's cute.

"Stay here for a sec," I say. "I'll be right back."

I run down the aisle, stopping to grab the first package of black socks I come across and boxers that I'm not all that sure will fit. When I get back, I toss the packages into the cart and use my hip to shove Xylia out of the way. "I'm driving," I say, firmly grasping the cart, pushing it forward.

"We need flashlights." She points at an aisle.

"Oh, no, not yet we don't," I say, then smirk as I point my finger at the woman's clothing section. "I think it's only fair."

"How is that fair? I brought clothes, you didn't." She shakes her head.

"Yeah, well, I just made a fool of myself, so you're taking a turn, too."

She lets out this cute groan that's more like a whimper, then says, "Fine." At a stand, she picks up a black top, then heads straight for the changing room.

Quickly, I step in her path. "Mm, nope, that just won't do." I take the shirt from her hands. "We know what you look like in black," I say, my gaze running up and down the length of her body. "Let's try something with a little *color*." I pull a purple silky blouse-type thing off the hanger. "Here, try this."

Xylia raises her eyebrows, but before she has a chance to say anything, I also grab a ruffled skirt and push her toward the changing rooms.

She doesn't fight me; instead, she stomps in and closes the door, emerging a few minutes later. My jaw

~ ☾ ~

falls to the floor. The skull knee-high socks she's
wearing are an added touch for sure, but wow.

"So? What do you think?" she asks even twirling in a
circle. The vanilla skirt flutters in the breeze created by
her movement. The purple hues of the shirt make her
eyes pop even brighter than normal, brightening up her
face.

"That bad?"

I swallow. "No. Um, you look...beautiful."

"No, I don't." She fidgets with the hem of material.

I take a step toward her, my hand reaches up to her
face. My finger caresses her cheek, then I slip a few stray
hairs behind her ear. Looking deeply into her eyes, I
whisper, "I swear, cross my heart, you look stunning,
Xylia."

This time it's she who swallows. "Landon," she
breathes.

My name coming off her lips, from her tongue, makes
my heart skip a beat.

"We should get going."

A deep breath of air is released from my mouth.
"Yeah, you're probably right," I reply. "But I'm totally
buying you that outfit."

She doesn't respond, just gives a half smile before
retreating back to the change room. When she comes
out, she's swathed in her usual black attire.

"We've got some more shopping to do, flashlights,
munchies, sleeping bag..." she says. "Care to take me for
a ride?" She hops onto the back of the cart and smiles
cheerfully.

I never thought I'd be that happy to see someone
smile. But the dimples on her cheeks that become more
noticeable, make my heart skip a beat.

"Why do we need a sleeping bag?" I ask.

"I think you might get a little cold without it," she
replies, then points to the left. "Onward, to the

~ ☾ ~

provisions aisle."

After picking up two bags of chips, a case of pop, beef jerky, a sleeping bag, flashlights, and of course the clothes, we head toward Xylia's car, bags in hand.

Setting aside the initial awkwardness of the first outfit I tried on, shopping was actually kind of fun. We fought over what kind of flashlight was best to buy, whether or not Doritos were better than Old Dutch— hence the two bags of chips—and though it sure wasn't going to get very cold in the following nights, apparently I needed a sleeping bag that keeps one warm in the fiercest of winters. Just in case, according to Xylia.

In the car, she turns up the radio and hands me the map again. "Alright, get us to the cemetery," she tells me, and I do just that. We drive down the darkened streets of Valley View. The only lights guiding our way are from the yellow lamps overhead and the beams that shoot out from the car.

"Aren't they going to have a gate? How are we going to get in?" I ask, ignoring the twisting of my stomach as we near the cemetery. I've never done anything bad. Maybe the occasional beer at after game parties, sure, but trespassing is kind of new to me.

"Haven't you ever hopped a fence before?" she asks, pulling the car to a stop. "We're here," she says, then adds, "We have to hoof it from here."

"Hoof it?" I raise an eyebrow.

"Yeah, you know, walk?"

"Right, of course," I reply as I shoulder the door, pushing it open.

Xylia heads for the trunk, then opens it. "Better grab your sleeping bag. We're going to need it."

"We're sleeping in the cemetery?"

"You scared?" she asks, reaching into the dimly lit space, then pulling out her duffle bag. It teeters on the edge of the car as she tugs out some clothes, then drops

~ ☽ ~

them back into the trunk. Then she loads the bag up with a few cans of soda and a bag of chips and zips it up. She shoves a flashlight into her pocket and one into my hands.

"Do you make a habit of this sort of thing? I still don't get why we're here."

"This cemetery is supposed to be haunted." She grins, slamming the trunk shut. "Come on, let's go."

A small chill runs down my spine. "So we're looking for ghosts?"

"I didn't say that, I just said it's supposed to be haunted." She shrugs, then slings the bag over her shoulder.

"I'm still not understanding."

"No one said you have to understand. Just follow me."

So I do. We walk down the sidewalk, the street on one side and a thick brick vine-covered wall on the other. I can't even begin to make sense of what we are doing, but her plan has me intrigued. We are apparently going to sleep in a cemetery that's haunted, but we aren't looking for ghosts. Weird.

Suddenly, she stops and I nearly ram into her. She says, "This looks like the best place to hop over."

Taking a few steps farther up the path, I turn back. "I say we just walk through the open gate. Sure, hopping the wall sounds like fun, but this way would be easier."

"Open gate?" she says with surprise, closing the distance between us.

"It's like they knew we were coming." I chuckle and lead the way.

On the other side of the wall and gate, my eyes barely make out gray colored rocks—tombstones. I turn on the flashlight, letting the light illuminate a small, gravelled path. Xylia, on the other hand, walks straight over the graves. The ones with dead bodies underneath.

~ ☾ ~

Taking a deep breath, I follow her lead, only I'm careful not to step directly on top of anyone.

"So, do you know anyone here?" I ask as we make our way deeper into the creepy, dark, expansive burial ground. Even with the dim beam sprouting from the flashlight, the area goes on for miles. Like little soldiers standing at attention, each tombstone looks the same, but on closer inspection, each epitaph is different. They commemorate the lives of the young, the old, the rich, and the poor. Weathered by time, the stone—gray and white—has taken on a tarnished, black look. And at the foot of most markers lie withered and dried flowers, a sign that someone still cares. On the top of some of the tombstones are rocks, each one a different shape, some round and smooth, others pebbles, some jagged and dirt covered. Like the flowers, the pebbles tell me these people were once loved.

The breeze is a cool embrace, reminding me the first day of winter is near.

I glance at Xylia as she pulls her jacket tighter against her neck. "No, I don't," she says.

"Alright, I've been playing this game for awhile now. Rather good, I'd thought, but I'd really like to be let in on the big secret," I say, slightly annoyed now.

Just ahead of me she stops. "Here we are."

I'm standing beside her and at what is directly below our feet. "You're kidding, right?" I look down into an open grave a few feet deep.

"Do you really think we came all this way because I'm joking?" she asks, looking at me.

"I'll do this, but man Xylia, then you need to give me something. A few answers at the very least." I leave out the part where now I suddenly think she might be messed up in the head.

"You first?" She lowers her bag into the open pit.

"Ladies first, I think," I say. "Take my hand and I'll

~ ☾ ~

help you down." I extend my arm and feel her cool fingers lace with mine. Her grip is tight as I help her hop in, then I lower myself to the ground, letting my legs fall over the edge. With a twist and some muscle, I drop in behind her. The scent of fresh earth fills my nose and I try not to think about the creepy crawlies that are probably waiting to wiggle into various orifices while I'm asleep.

As disturbing as this whole thing makes me feel, I can't deny the small amount of relief it gives me. I pray that following Xylia two hours away from home, buying ridiculous clothes, and sleeping in an open grave is going to somehow change things between us. I've never felt so complete in my life the way I do when Xylia is around. A part of me knows that I might just have the same effect on her.

I've never believed in fairytales, but I can't refute the idea that we may just need each other in some way. Like Beauty and the Beast, or Sleeping Beauty and her prince.

~ ☾ ~

Chapter Twenty-four

Xylia

"This is kind of disgusting. You know that, right?" Landon says after we pull out our sleeping bags and set out the snacks.

"There's wood on the ground, so it's not like you're sleeping in the dirt," I say. The light that shines up between us shows the expression on his face.

"What are we doing here, if not looking for ghosts?"

"I just needed to clear my head, get away from things," I say.

"And you come to cemeteries to do that?"

"Yeah, I guess I do."

"Alright, so tell me something, anything. Let me understand this," he says, gesturing to the dark pit we're in.

I'm silent for a few intakes of breath, filling my lungs and blowing out through my nose. "I'm not sure I can...make you understand, I mean." My voice comes out shaky.

Then his hand is on mine. My heart thuds loudly inside its cage. I don't pull away, and instead relish his touch. He even gives my hand a gentle squeeze, and his shadow covered eyes encourage me.

"I'm different," I say.

"We all are, Xylia, but I want to know what makes *you* different." His tone is smooth as he gives my hand

~ ☾ ~

another squeeze.

"I think that's the problem. I don't know why I'm different. I never wanted to be...I just somehow became this." I'm surprised when my eyes fill with tears. Feverishly, I blink them back.

"What happened?"

"What do you mean, what happened?"

"When I found out who you were—I mean, when I needed to learn more about you—I looked through every yearbook I had. Then I went to the library and looked at even older yearbooks. You weren't always sad, Xylia. Something changed, taking away the cute girl in pigtails and flowery dresses. Whatever it was turned her into who you are today."

My stomach flops at the idea of him spying on me, like he's reached into my personal space and tore my past out of it.

"I don't want to talk about it," I say after a few more seconds of silence goes by.

"Please?" he urges.

"This is silly, I'm silly. I shouldn't have brought you here. I don't know what I was thinking," I say, shaking my head.

"You didn't exactly bring me here. I came of my own accord. And it's not silly, not at all. Actually, the idea of sleeping in an open grave is kind of growing on me," he says.

I laugh. "No it's not."

"You're right, it's not. But I'll do it for you."

My breath hitches. I turn my head to the side, hiding my vulnerability. His hand slips from mine. I almost whimper at the loss of contact but hold it in.

Just as I'm getting used to the idea that he's no longer comforting me with his touch, his fingertips brush my cheek. They settle under my chin, pulling me back to face him. His thumb grazes my lower lip, sending

~ ☾ ~

shivers up my back. The idea of sleeping in a cemetery is nothing, no biggie, but the idea of Landon Phoenix touching my skin, gazing deeply into my eyes, now that's terrifying.

His face is inches away from mine. His chest rises and falls and a gentle wheeze whispers through his nose. His hand is still resting under my chin. I fight the urge to pull away. Hope that it's not my eyes that are imagining him inching closer and closer. Then he licks the delicate red skin of his lips in preparation to kiss me. I know any second those lips will fall upon mine. My eyes will roll slightly back, eyelids will flutter closed as I experience my first *real* kiss.

Only it never happens. Stiffly, he drops his hand from my chin, quickly placing it over his mouth as he coughs. It's one of those dry forced coughs, more of a throat clearing, but it breaks the spell I thought I was under. It reminds me that even though I took advantage of him when he was, well, *technically* dead, he probably would have never kissed me back if he'd been awake.

"If we're not going to talk about you, let's talk about me. And why it is that every time I close my eyes, all I see is you," he says, taking his outstretched legs and folding them until he's sitting cross-legged.

"I wasn't there when you woke up in your hospital room," I say, "but..."

"*But...*"

"I was there when you died. Or at least, when you kind of died," I reply.

He lets out an annoyed sounding huff. "Can you explain it to me? I mean, what *happened*?"

"You collapsed on the field. And I'm not a doctor, so I don't know what happened. I just know that my dad and I did everything we could."

"I still don't understand why you were involved. Maybe I'm a little slow, but you're going to have to spell it out for me," he says.

I replay the images in my head like a movie on fast forward, remembering ever detail. "My dad's a doctor. He's taught me CPR, and that night he needed a second pair of hands. Since he trusted that I wouldn't screw it up, even though I didn't want to, he had me perform chest compressions on you." I pause. The tears are back, filling my eyes. Even though Landon is alive and well, this seems hard. It's difficult to tell someone you swear you felt their life slip through the cracks between your fingers as you pumped their heart to save them, but failed.

"I swear I did it the way my father had taught me, finding just the right spot, applying the right amount of pressure. I pushed down and waited for the chest to retract. I did it until the ambulance came, then I was so sure I could bring you back that I kept doing it, even on the way to the hospital. I didn't want to stop, but they made me. They said you were gone. That we had lost you. You'd been down too long." Tears roll down my cheek.

"It sounds like you did everything you could."

I wipe at my eyes and sniffle back the snot that is trying to run free from my nose. "But I gave up. *I* stopped. But maybe if I'd continued, maybe your heart would have started beating again. If I hadn't been selfish, if I gave you more attention, been better at being a daugh—" I cut my words off mid-sentence because I've changed directions. I'm no longer talking about Landon.

"You could never be selfish, Xylia, it's impossible. What you did for me was amazing. You did everything you could. Besides, my heart beats now."

"But I couldn't save you. And I couldn't save her either," I cry.

"Her who?"

I sniffle again. "Never mind. I'm sorry, I didn't mean

~ ☾ ~

to—"

"Stop being sorry. You have nothing to apologize for," Landon murmurs in my ear. "Now tell me what happened. Maybe talking about it will help."

"I can't." My body shakes a little as I take in a breath through my nose. "It's too hard." Wiping my eyes again, I compose myself.

"Sometimes things in life are hard. That doesn't mean we should hide from them."

"I'm not...hiding," I say, though now it's almost clear. That's exactly what I might be doing.

He shrugs, lips tight in a line.

"I'm not," I say, a little more sternly. "Why don't we just call it a night? We have to be up and out of here early. I think we've had enough excitement for one night."

"We'll talk more tomorrow, right?"

I don't reply. Instead, I slip into my sleeping bag and lay down, using my jacket as a pillow, then shut my eyes. Landon does the same. The bag ruffles as he gets in, the zipper sounds loud as he secures it closed. He's far away, his head at the opposite end as mine, our feet meeting in the middle. Leaves and twigs scratch and rub against concrete markers. An owl hoots from his perch in the trees, lights on the street flicker and buzz, and off in the distance car engines hum. For me this is peaceful; it is nature without the worry of getting eaten by a bear. Here you just have to hope that the dirt is sturdy enough to hold, that the walls won't cave in on you and cover your body with a waterfall of soil as you struggle to claw your way out. Only the weight, the pressure on your chest, knocks the wind out of you, rendering you mute so you can't scream for help...

* * * *

~ ☾ ~

I think I'm dreaming when an immeasurable amount of coldness courses through my body. I struggle to open my eyes, praying that when I do the freezing cold will stop.

"Should we take him now?" a voice floats to my ears.

I lift my head off its makeshift pillow and look up. Standing at the edge, looking into the depths of the grave, are two men. Staring, appraising. I want to scream, but my voice is caught in my throat.

"No," the other one says.

My eyes strain to focus on the men. Then, like a crystal ball of clarity, I recognize one of the two. Same charcoal gray suit. The other one is younger, with red hair, and is not as well dressed. The moon casts an eerie glow on them, but I'd bet my life the suited guy is the same man from the soccer field. He even has a thin stick of wood hanging from his lips. He moves it back and worth, drags it between his teeth. And like before, it's as though I'm invisible.

"Why can't we just take him and be done with it? It's taken us this long to find him again, to breach the world between this one and the next. Why wait?"

I place my head back down, stiff with worry and confusion, but most of all, fear.

"Let's see how this plays out."

"*See how it plays out*? Are you kidding? We have to take him. The world needs its balance."

"And it will get its balance. But not yet."

"We don't toy with the innocents. That's not how things are done! We need to take him."

"Just give them a little more time."

A loud crack of thunder reverberates through the air, and with it comes blackness.

~ ☾ ~

Chapter Twenty-five

Landon

The cool morning air tickles my face. My eyelids flutter open, allowing copious amounts of light to blind me with brightness. I struggle to move, my body stiff and weighed down. When my vision focuses on the area surrounding me, I'm a little confused.

I've never thought myself as much of a toss and turner, but when a head that isn't mine is resting on my arm, I panic a little bit. I have no recollection of turning my entire body around and snuggling up to Xylia. Then I question myself, is it me who stayed in the same place? Had she moved? I lift my head up as far as I can without putting too much strain on my neck. With a quick survey of the dirt pit, I come to the conclusion that it was, in fact, definitely me who did the moving. Now I just need to figure out how to get out of this position without her knowing, no matter how much I want to stay plastered to the wood beneath me and just watch and hold her.

This is one of those moments where it probably would be safer to bite my own arm off to make sure I won't wake her. I'm forced to do a hug-type roll move. I'm gentle and make sure that instead of her head landing on my arm or the wood, it lands on the jacket just beside her. It's tough to do, because Xylia snorts and moans. I freeze, waiting to see if those pretty eyes of

~ ☾ ~

hers open. When they don't, I quickly wriggle out of my sleeping bag, scramble to my feet, and head back to my end of the grave.

Having no idea what time it is, I reach for my phone in my pocket. I curse when the screen is black. No matter how many times I press the On button, it never spurs to life. The battery is dead. However, I cannot bring myself to wake her. Not yet, at least.

Sitting with my back pressed against the cold soil wall, I rest my head in my hands. In my peripheral vision, Xylia's chest rises and falls as she breathes. I wonder how I managed to get myself into this precise situation. Sleeping in a cemetery, in a half dug grave, was not exactly what I had in mind when I went looking for answers.

I'd tried to kiss her. When I realized that this wasn't just about me, that she was out seeking her own answers, she'd taken me even more by surprise than usual. When tears rolled down her cheek, her vulnerability had me weak in the knees and desperate to taste those lips.

And because I'd almost kissed her, I never did get those answers. I'm in the same place as I was yesterday—only six feet deeper. Because now, I don't think I can ever leave her.

Xylia becomes restless, her movements more frequent, until she speaks up. "Landon?" Her voice is a soft whisper, barely audible, but it's there, a faint sound almost floating on the air around us.

"I'm here," I reply.

Her arms extend above her head as she stretches and yawns. "What time is it?"

"Morning," I say, adding, "my phone's dead."

"Crap. We'd better get going before someone catches us." She arches her back for one final stretch, then rises to a sitting position. "Did you sleep alright?"

~ ☾ ~

I laugh. "You know, I'm not going to lie, I've definitely had better."

"Mm, yeah, me too." She smiles, but the smile doesn't quite reach her eyes.

"Let's get out of this dirt hole and I'll buy you some breakfast." This statement seems to light up her eyes, quickly replacing the solemn features she'd awoke with.

"Really?"

I nod. "Yup. Anything you want."

"I'll have to put some thought into that. It's not very often someone says 'anything you want.'"

I smile, then side by side, we silently pack up our makeshift camp, tossing everything into the duffle bag.

"You first," I say, bending my knees and clasping my hands together so I can boost her up.

"Now why do I have to go first again?" she pouts.

"I really don't think you can give me a boost," I say with a little sarcasm.

"Yeah, but if I go first, what happens if I can't pull you up?"

She has a point. I think about it for a moment then say, "Alright, if you think you can do it, you're right. This might be the better option."

Xylia takes a step forward and assumes the same position I just had. "Oh, I can do it," she says and smirks, holding out her hands.

"Alright, you ready?" I ask as I put my foot on her palms.

She rolls her eyes. "Just go already." In one swift movement I put some pressure on my foot as her hands push me upward. She's strong, stronger than I would have thought. I grab the ground above and hoist myself over the edge of the grave.

Lying on my stomach, I reach down for her hand. Something, however, catches my eye. "C'mon, grab my hand," I say, temporarily ignoring the image in front of

~ ☾ ~

me. Xylia jumps. Her hands graze my fingertips but they don't reach high enough for me to grab on. "Try again," I say a little more urgently.

She jumps again but still her hand doesn't quite make it. "I can't reach," she says.

Leaning as far over the edge as I can, I hold my arms out again. "We need to go faster. You have to do it this time."

"Why, what's wrong?" Her tone is now worried.

"Just jump," I say, and she does. I grab her wrist but it's not a firm hold. "You're going to have to help me out a little. Use your feet."

She pushes off the wall with her feet. I grit my teeth and pull with all my strength, tugging her up. When her feet are firmly on the ground I say, "How do you feel about running? 'Cause I think we should." I'm not looking at her, but *behind* her.

Slowly, Xylia turns her head around. "Oh, shit," she says. She looks back at me. She's startled, her eyes growing wide.

"Let's get out of here, now. That guy doesn't look too pleased."

"Landon...he has a pitchfork." All the color has drained from her face.

I grab a hold of her hand and tug her forward. "Come on, babe, run," I yell.

I chance a look behind me as we run, dodging headstones. The caretaker looks pissed, and sure enough, he's still waving a pitchfork frantically about.

"I called the cops, you juvenile delinquents," the man roars, closing in on us. "You can't outrun me, you bastards!"

We keep running but my hand slips from hers as we both push faster and faster. My heart pounds in my chest as I lose sight of Xylia. I whip my head around, desperately searching for her. I see a blur of black

~ ☾ ~

hurdling tombstones like an athlete. Relief washes over me. When the thick wall of stone and ivy comes into view, I push myself faster. My legs protest and burn. I don't let anything distract me, not even the sirens off in the distance.

"Over here, Landon," Xylia calls out to me. I follow her voice to the open gate where we came in last night. I'm thankful when I see it still hangs ajar.

"Hey, stop running you little bastards!"

I don't slow down my pace as I run through the threshold of the gate, down the street, and toward Xylia's car. She's a few steps ahead of me. She's reaching into her pocket, no doubt fumbling for her keys.

I chance another look back.

"If I ever catch you bastards in here again..." The caretaker bellows as he shakes one fist in the air and the fork in the other.

"Quick, get in," Xylia says. I scramble to the passenger side, open the door, hop in, and slam it shut in record time.

"Holy shit, that was close," she says as she revs the engine and slams the car into drive. The tires peel away from the curb. "That was...kind of exhilarating." She then laughs.

"Are you kidding? Jesus, I thought we were going to get skewered," I huff.

Panting and laughing, hardly able to speak, she manages to get out, "I'm ready for that breakfast now."

I can't help but smile. That was just about the most action I've seen throughout my entire life. "You were like a track star out there, hopping those stones," I say between deep breaths.

"Oh, yeah?" She giggles.

A short drive later, Xylia pulls her car into a lot and parks. I lean forward and read the sign overhead: *Carol's Diner.* "This is where you want to eat," I say, my

~ ☾ ~

nose wrinkling a little.

"If you hadn't noticed, there doesn't seem to be a lot of options in this town. Not to mention this is a two-in-one kind of place."

I raise my eyebrows and she flicks her head to the left. I follow her movement to see another sign that reads, *Showers, Laundry, and Groceries.* "Are you implying something?"

Dramatically, she sniffs and points her nose in the air, "Landon, you stink." She laughs. "And don't knock a place like this—they usually have the best food."

"Uh huh." I'm dubious.

She ignores me. "Let's go."

Inside the diner a small sign says *Please Seat Yourself*, so Xylia walks past the counter to a row of booths. She slides in one side. I hesitate for just a second, then ultimately decide to sit across from her.

A few seconds later, a plump woman in a much too tight shirt and pants waddles up to our table. Her apron is dusted with flour, and a small pad and pen sticks out of the pocket. Her hair is pulled up into a messy bun and a pair of glasses hang around her neck. "Coffee?" she asks. I almost choke on a laugh because her voice is deep. Man deep.

"Sure," Xylia says, and I nod my agreement.

The waitress bustles off toward the kitchen, disappearing into the back. Xylia and I have barely enough time to look over the menu before the waitress comes back to our table with a steaming coffee pot

"So, what'll it be?" the waitress asks, hovering over us.

Xylia wastes no time. "I'll have the special, the one with the eggs, bacon, and ham. But I want pancakes too." She smiles.

The waitress looks to me. "And for you?"

Staring at the menu, I hem and haw over the plethora

~ ☾ ~

of choices. Then, beneath the table, I hear the tapping of a foot. The waitress, in full intimidation mode.

"Crap...sorry, I—uh...the omelette special?"

"White, whole wheat, sour, rye, or multi?" she rattles off.

"Huh?"

"Toast, Landon." Xylia giggles. "What kind of toast do you want?"

I finally decide on white and the waitress heads off to the kitchen, frowning.

"You know, you're kinda cute," Xylia says, nudging my foot with hers.

"Oh? Am I cute because I was freaked out by the waitress? Or am I cute because I can't order toast?"

"Both." She nods with a hint of finality.

A grin creeps on my face, spreading from ear to ear. Xylia thinks I'm cute.

Chapter Twenty-six

Xylia

As Landon and I eat breakfast, I can't get last night out of my head. Had I been dreaming? I've run over what I heard—or what I *thought* I heard—a dozen times, and I'm left with a sinking feeling in my stomach.

If what I'd heard was true.

And I mean, as truthful as weird, arguing guys in suits can be during a dream sequence. But if what I saw had happened, then Landon's life is still in danger. But then again, if I *was* dreaming, then I am seriously messed in the head. I'm not crazy, so instead of dwelling on what I heard or didn't hear, what I saw or what I made up, I ignore it all. Push it as far down into the depths of nothingness and pretend it never happened. I'm not crazy and Landon's not in danger.

After filling our bellies with copious amounts of food, then using the bathroom to change into clean clothes, Landon and I are back in the car.

He reaches for the map. "Where to next?" he asks, holding up the paper.

I snatch it away. "Oh, no, I'm taking you home," I say.

"What? Why?" His lower lip juts out a little, showing me just how plump it is.

"Because I'm fully prepared for the shit kicking I'm probably going to get when I get home." I hold up my phone. "I've already got about a dozen missed calls and

~ ☾ ~

a few voice mails. But you—I can't drag you down with me," I say.

"You have all these towns circled and we've already gone this far," he says, pouted lip still present.

"So? That doesn't mean you have to come with me."

"Hey, we had a deal. I'm not leaving until I get what I want."

"But I already told you everything, so your deal is null and void now."

He tilts his head to the side. "Yeah? Well, I say we aren't done yet." He grins.

"How about I just kick you out of the car?"

Landon laughs. "You wouldn't."

Narrowing my eyes, I say, "Wanna bet?"

Then Landon calls my bluff. He extends his hand for me to grasp. "Yeah, I do."

I groan loudly, expressing my annoyance. Secretly though, it's kind of nice to have company. "Alright," I say.

He beams a toothy smile. "Great. So, where to next? Though, if you don't mind...uh, no more sleeping in cemeteries?"

"I'm not making any promises," I say. "We're heading here." I point on the map. "It's about an hour away."

"And what's in"—he squints his eyes—"Morningside?"

"You'll see when we get there."

* * * *

The highway is boring. Thick stands of evergreens flicker eternally by. The road itself is mostly straight, with only a few curves here and there, which makes the drive a little on the tedious side. Landon has his head pressed against the window and is staring blankly outside. The sun slowly makes its way higher and higher in the sky as the minutes creep by.

~ ☾ ~

It feels like we've been driving forever when Landon breaks the silence. "How about a game?"

"Um, okay?" I say with uncertainty.

He straightens himself out. "Alright, I spy with my little eye...something that is black."

"You're kidding, right?"

"Not at all. You said you'd play."

"Okay, and it's inside the car?"

He nods.

"The dashboard?"

He shakes his head no.

"The steering wheel?"

"No."

"Uh...my pants? No? Okay, my shirt?" Another no. "Um, how about my hair? It has to be that?" I'm annoyed when he shakes his head again with a no. "Okay, this is stupid. I give up."

"You can't give up yet," he says.

"But there's too much black," I reply.

He smiles. "Really...too much black, you say?"

I roll my eyes. "Okay, you're an idiot. Point taken, but that wasn't very nice."

"Maybe, but you admitted to yourself that between you and the interior of the car, there's too much black."

When he puts it like that, and when I look down at myself, he's right. My body melds into the fabric of the seat, legs disappearing like a chameleon next to the carpeted floor. Suddenly it's like I'm the invisible man—only my head and hands appear against all the black that surrounds me. Even I'm a little disgusted.

"I was being serious when I said you looked beautiful in that outfit I bought you. I'm bummed you aren't wearing it."

I shift uncomfortably in my seat. I'm having a hard time accepting yet another compliment from him. And the mixed signals. The hot and cold he's tossing out has

~ ☾ ~

me confused. "That outfit isn't really for day wear, it's more..."

He raises an eyebrow. "Date attire?"

My mouth goes dry. I swallow, but my throat burns. "Uh...I suppose," is the best I can muster.

"Hmm, good to know," is all he says.

Again with the flipping rollercoaster of confused emotions. He's got me upside down. "We're almost there. Maybe we should just keep quiet until then," I sputter.

Morningside is home to one of many supposed haunted houses, which is why it's on my list. Though I can't say for sure that I do believe in haunted houses, Morningside still seemed a fitting place to visit.

Having left home in kind of a hurry, I'd never had a chance to check to see if the haunted inn still had rooms available. My dad had planned on making all my travel arrangements when he'd agreed to the trip and to put all the rooms I'd stay at on his credit card, but with me taking off without his permission, that obviously hadn't happened.

"A B&B?" Landon speaks up, then yawns.

"Hey, you said no more cemeteries."

He stretches his arms out in front of him. "But isn't it a little early to be getting a room?"

"This is Morningside, the next stop on our trip."

I park the car and hop out. Not bothering to wait for Landon, I ascend the creaky white wooden steps. They whine in protest but support my weight. Just as I'm about to reach for the door handle, Landon nudges me over with his elbow and pulls on the knob.

"You know, that whole ladies first crap is getting old."

He bows for dramatics, gesturing me inside.

"Whatever. You love it," he says, and I don't argue.

I step inside, and it's as though we've walked through a portal. The entryway is swathed in heavy drapes with

~ ☾ ~

tassels, each thick with pastel colors. The floor beneath our feet is dark wood, polished to a shine. Even the walls, with their crown moulding, whitewashed panels, and sconces remind me of another era.

We walk toward a small desk, where a thick ledger lies open. Signatures fill the lined pages. A dusty bell sits alone. I pick it up and give it a shake. Instead of hearing a few chimes, the weight in the bell thuds against the surrounding brass. I look to Landon and shrug.

"Maybe they're closed?" he says.

"We never close, not even on the birthday of our saviour, nor his resurrection," a soft voice says as someone enters the room.

I turn, and my gaze falls on an elderly lady who has silver curled hair and is wearing a knit sweater and slippers on her feet. She's short, hunched over almost awkwardly.

"Now what can I help you with?" she asks, taking a seat behind the desk and picking up a long feathered pen.

"Two rooms please," I say.

The lady clucks her tongue as her finger runs up and down the ledger. "I have one, one room only."

"Uh…" I mutter, looking again to Landon, my lips curled down in a frown. "Maybe we should—"

I'm about to say "find somewhere else," but Landon speaks up. "We'll take it," he says in a cheery tone.

Of course he says that. After all, we'd shared a grave. Why not share a room?

"May I see some ID for the room?"

Landon reaches into his wallet and produces his driver's licence, also laying down his Visa. "Here," he says.

"No, Landon, this is on me," I say.

"Shh," he says, bringing his finger to his lips. Being shushed irritates me to no end.

~ ☾ ~

At a snail's pace, the lady fills out a Visa slip, then makes Landon sign the ledger. She slides a key across the desk. "Room 2 is yours. Up the stairs on your left." Landon and I nod in unison. "Dinner's at six, whether you are here or not. Breakfast at eight, and checkout at ten."

"Thank you," I say, then turn and leave. I pull Landon toward the door so we can grab our bags.

Outside, he says to me, "That was strange. Didn't you find that lady strange?"

I frown. "Nope, not at all. This is supposed to be a historic house. The authentic ambiance is why people come here. What I find strange is that you shushed me."

"They can't legally rent rooms out to minors, Xylia. I was just doing you a favour, honest."

"Uh, but you're a 'minor' aren't you?"

Landon grins. "Nope. I turned eighteen last month."

"Oh. I never thought of that." I'm thankful, of course, that he's here and able to bypass what could have become a potential problem. But mostly I'm thankful he's here. With me.

~ ☾ ~

Chapter Twenty-seven

Landon

I pull the duffle bag out of the trunk of Xylia's car as she grabs the Wal-Mart bags. It's almost lunch time. My stomach even growls as a reminder that it's been awhile since we ate at the diner. The sun warms my back as I follow Xylia back into the B&B. We're alone on a tiny side street lined with cars and cookie-cutter houses. The inn is a stark contrast, with its old charm of faded and weathered wood next to the bright, white-sided houses next to it.

Inside, stale air escapes from the room when Xylia pushes the door open. Dust particles swirl and float in the few rays of light that shine in through the window. Yellow drapes hang loosely over the pained glass. Heavy swirls of gold filigree coat the papered walls. The bed takes up most of the space—it's a four poster, canopy style. Even the bedding matches the colonial style of the inn.

"So, I still don't get why we are here," I say, dropping the bag on the floor.

"According to local lore, this place is haunted," Xylia says. She follows my lead, and her bags hit the floor with a thud.

"Haunted?"

"That's right." She strides over to the window and pulls the drapes all the way back, letting more light pour

~ ☾ ~

into the room.

"Let me get this straight. Last night in the cemetery we weren't hunting for ghosts, but *now* we are?"

Xylia presses her head against the streaked and coated glass. "No...we aren't. This place was just on the list. It's full of history."

I shake my head but smile. "And you're full of surprises."

"Huh. We should get ready. We aren't here just to waste the day in this dingy room."

Of course. I raise my eyebrows. "Ready?"

She takes a breath of air and turns away from the window. "Yeah. We have to go to church." The groan that comes out of me has Xylia giving me the evil eye. "Okay, you can stay here or you can come with me. Your choice."

"I'm coming," I say.

"Here, you're going to want to wear this," she says, tossing me one of the shirts we bought last night. A dark blue button-down that I'd protested against buying.

"Fine. I'll put this on and go with you to church, but only because I'm still out for answers. But Xylia, this game is getting old," I say, feeling a little bad about it. I love spending time with her, getting to know her, but so far the shit storm waiting for me at home isn't worth it. Not yet.

She coughs, clears her throat, and meekly says, "Okay," as if sensing my irritation.

Xylia disappears into the adjoining bathroom, and I quickly change into the shirt she'd thrown at me. Just as I'm buttoning the last little bit, she emerges.

I think my jaw drops open and my tongue is hanging out like a dog on a hot summer's day. Somehow, in a matter of minutes, Xylia has turned herself into a gothic goddess. Even though she's still head to toe in black, the knee-length skirt and silk blouse makes her look all

~ ☾ ~

grown up. She's pulled her hair up. Little stray tendrils frame her face, which now has a touch of color. Instead of her usual pale skin, Xylia's swept some blush on her cheeks and touched her lips with red. She's stunning.

"I'm ready," she says, giving a little twirl. "How do I look?"

"A-amazing," I stutter, taking a few steps closer to her. She looks away, blushing, wringing her hands together. I slip a lock of hair behind her ear, and without thinking, I take my hand away, but wrap it around the small of her back. I pull her to me. Her face is inches away from mine and I can't hold anything in anymore.

Tilting my head to the side just a little, I then lean the rest of the way in. I place my lips on hers. They're soft and supple. She stiffens, her body tense against my chest. I don't pull away. I hold still, hoping she responds.

It feels like seconds are passing, but I hear only one tick of a clock from the nightstand, one chirp of a bird outside the inn. Just as I'm about to give up, *she* kisses me back. I'm surprised by her sudden enthusiasm as her lips urgently press against mine. Now the whole world stops spinning, every sound dissipates, and it's only the steady thump of my heartbeat I hear. This quite possibly is the best feeling in life. Xylia's hands, which hung loosely at her sides, now wrap around me, her fingers swirling the hair at the nape of my neck. Her touch sends cool shivers down my spine.

When we pull apart we're panting, struggling to fill our lungs with air. I bring my fingers to my lips. As if they are protesting the loss of her warm kiss, they grow cold, icy. It's a strange feeling that reminds me of my last moments in the White Room. It's enough to catch me off guard, and I know a perplexed expression had crossed my face.

Xylia pulls away quickly. "I'm sorry," she says, then

~ ☾ ~

turns and practically races to the door.

"No, no, it's not you," I swear. I catch up to her and grab her hand. "That just—it reminded me of something," I add, trying to diffuse the situation.

Though the disgusted look on Xylia's face makes me believe I'm not doing a very good job of it. "Charity? Did that kiss remind you of your girlfriend?"

"No, God, no. And Charity's not my girlfriend anymore."

Her tone doesn't lighten up as she says, "Then what is it? Do I suck at kissing? Did I spit in your mouth? 'Cause it sure didn't look like you enjoyed it. I'm sorry if I'm not experienced enough."

This is one of those moments that I'm really not sure if I can say the right thing, but I try. "Xylia, that was probably the best kiss I've ever had, I swear. Kissing you made time stop, literally, but it also reminded me of a feeling I had when"—I take a deep breath—"when I was supposed to be dead."

Her facial expression lightens up. "Really, it was good? I mean, that good?"

"Babe, it parted oceans, exploded fireworks, stopped the earth from moving, but most of all, it warmed my heart to the core," I say. I take her other hand in mine and look deep into her eyes.

But then she frowns. "Then how does a kiss like that remind you of being dead? I mean...I'm not sure I understand."

I'm trying get into Xylia's head, get her to open up to me, but I sigh, look away and say, "I can't really explain it right now."

She wrenches one of her hands free. "Looks like I'm not the only one with secrets."

"You're right. Maybe we could share them with each other." I hold my breath as I hold her hand, hoping that she'll open up to me. Tell me why she'd gone from that

~ ☾ ~

happy kid to being obsessed with death. Open up.

Her eyes flick to the ceiling, her teeth chew on her lip. "Maybe," she finally says, but she looks as closed off as before. "But not now. Now we're going to church."

I know the conversation is closed and don't push further. At least she doesn't let go of my hand. She holds on tight to me all the way down the stairs, through the foyer of the inn, and out the door. She even hesitates at her car before ultimately releasing her grasp and climbing in.

As I climb in I wonder if her kissing me and agreeing to open up was maybe just her appeasing me. If her feelings weren't real. I want so much to believe things are changing between us. To believe that maybe, just maybe, she's beginning to feel for me what I can't keep bottled up inside anymore.

~ ☾ ~

Chapter Twenty-eight

Xylia

We walk hand in hand up the concrete steps toward the huge wooden double doors of the church. We're late, and I'm almost glad, because the awkwardness in Landon's stride tells me he's not keen about our location. He'll probably be even more so concerned once he figures out why we're here.

One of the oversized doors is open, and as we step across the threshold, I inwardly pray he won't be mad at me.

Soft organ music fills the air; the tune is peaceful. However, that peacefulness is taken away when pews of black-clothed guests come into view. Landon halts and his hand squeezes mine, hard. I pull away.

"A funeral? You brought me to a funeral?" Then he hisses, "Do you even know these people?" I'm pretty sure he already knows the answer, but he glares at me anyway.

"No, I don't."

"Then what are we doing here?"

Before I have a chance to say something, a gruff, "Ahem," startles me and Landon. We turn around to see a gray haired, thin, black suited man who is waiting to get by, tapping his foot. Dressed in a black pantsuit, a lady waits at his side, eyeing her long red nails.

"Sorry," I say as I grab Landon's hand and pull him

~ ☾ ~

into the closest pew. The couple walks past, then takes seats near the front. I watch them and the many other people with bowed heads. Some people are sniffling. I see from their side profiles tissues being dabbed against the corners of eyes.

A silver casket with accents of polished black ebony stands center stage at the front of the church. The lid is open and I can make out the quilted white interior, the top of a curly gray head of shorn hair, even the bridge and tip of a pale nose. The closed portion of the casket is blanketed with white roses.

"When you said church I was, I dunno, expecting Mass, or heck, maybe confession, but not this," Landon says, pulling his hand from mine. Then like he has a nervous twitch, he rubs his hands up and down his thighs.

He's uncomfortable. It's obvious. "Have you ever been to a funeral?" I've been to twenty-seven, each one very different. Some don't have flowers at all, while others use arrangements filled with every plant known to man. Even the caskets are different. I think they can be a pretty good indicator of the how the person inside lived. I attended the funeral of a deceased beauty queen once; at least, that's what I told myself she'd once been. Her casket was pearly pink, iced with crystals that glinted in the sun that spilled through the windows of the church. Even her outfit was a lavish, frilly, satin pink gown. She lacked the tiara, but otherwise she was beauty-pageant ready—except for the whole being dead thing.

"No, I don't think I have," Landon finally responds.

"Saying goodbye can give a person closure," I whisper.

He raises an eyebrow. "Is that why you're here? To get closure?"

Of course I want closure.

~ ☾ ~

For me, the obituaries in the *Gazette* are the equivalent to someone else's Sunday morning engagement announcements in *The New York Times*. They bring a certain joy—not so much in the death, but in the fact that I know I can slink into the back and observe. "Closure isn't an option for me anymore," I say, because I also know I might never get it.

As Landon's eyebrows knit together, a procession of family members silently takes their place in the front. One by one they shuffle down the lacquered oak row. A small door to the side creaks open. Hushed whispers grow silent, even a few people go as far as to shush the congregation. The pastor emerges from the doorway. White robes, red scarfy thing, and a bible pressed tightly to his chest.

God's disciple takes his place behind a podium etched with a cross and taps the microphone. He clears his throat and brings his hands together as he says, "Welcome. We are here today to say farewell to our dear friend, Frank Hamilton."

"How many funerals have you been to?"

"What?" I turn to Landon.

"Funerals." Eyes narrowing. "How many?"

I shake my head. "A few, but not the one that mattered."

Landon seems to consider my response, opening his mouth then closing it. Taking in a deep breath and then whistling it out his nose.

The robed man at the front continues the service. He lights a few candles, bows his head, and says a prayer. The congregation follows suit and bow their heads, some whispering along, other staying silent, but when the prayer comes to a close they all, including me, say in unison, "Amen."

In a hushed tone, Landon says, "I still don't get why we are here. I mean, if you don't know this guy—"

~ ☾ ~

"Can we discuss this at the end?" I say, because talking at a funeral is about a million times worse than talking in a movie theatre, and I *hate* people who talk in movie theatres. Not to mention the best part is coming up. And I say that with the upmost respect for the dead.

The pastor, with a few more kind words, opens up the floor to the grieving family members, allowing them to share their thoughts and feelings about Frank Hamilton.

I like hearing what people have to say about the dead. I also wonder what people would say at my funeral. If I died tomorrow, would I have left enough of an impression on the folks of Silversprings to even warrant an eloquently spoken eulogy? I doubt it.

A few silent seconds pass, heads turn as if people are looking and waiting for someone to take the podium, to say something, *anything* about the deceased man we are here to remember and say goodbye to.

A rustle of fabric and a creak of a pew shoots all eyes forward as we gaze with interest at the small woman who shuffles forward. Her hair is a short bob of silver threads. Round glasses on her nose and her cheeks as a red as an apple. And even more lipstick on her teeth than on her lips. Her black blazer is only half buttoned, showing off a small hint of ivory and lace. As she carefully takes the steps of the stairs, she clutches a crumbled paper in her hand.

Clearing her throat and adjusting her jacket, even smoothing out her paper with shaky hands, she opens her mouth and speaks. "My father Frank would love to see all these people before him, and I thank you for coming. We, who knew Frank, understood the very few loves in his life. My mother Emily May, poker, and a fine cigar. As few things he loved, there are few things he hated. Peas, telephone solicitors, and of course, our childhood pet, Bailey the dog."

I chance a look at Landon. His lips are in a hard line,

~ ☾ ~

eyes still full of anger. I hope once this is over, he'll
forgive me for springing the funeral on him. I reach out
and place my hand on his knee. He looks down at it
briefly before focusing back on the speaker at the front
of the room as she continues.

"But we aren't here to discuss the obvious; no, we are
here to remember the many other things about my
father. Though his life was full of meaning, his greatest
pleasure was building his store, Hamilton Hardware,
with his two hands, and turning it into a Morningside
landmark. While those long hours running his own
business took a toll on his marriage and his children, we
knew he was doing it all for us.

"I remember always having shoes on my feet and
jackets in the winter, food on our table and money in
our pockets. It was my father's belief that a person
should do everything possible to give their family—their
children— the life you could have only dreamed of
having. And he did that. No matter how hard he worked,
he was home for holidays, school plays and recitals,
sporting events and the like. He made sure that we
always felt his presence when often he wasn't home to
tuck us in and kiss us goodnight. My father did what he
thought to be right, and for that he will always be my
greatest hero."

Frank's daughter stops speaking, then raises her
small hand to her lips. She kisses her palm and blows
the kiss out into the atmosphere. It's like she's hoping
that it will somehow reach her hero.

This hits home for me. Dad did everything he could to
make up for my mom being gone but it was no secret,
his work did hold his attention just a bit more than I
did. But I knew he loved me, even if his long hours got in
the way of father-daughter time. And I'm sure, if I was
into school sports or ballet, he would have never missed
a chance to see me perform. You can tell when the dead

~ ☾ ~

have made an impression on the lives they've touched. The eulogies say it all. Frank Hamilton, a hard working business owner, loved his family and did for them what most only wish they could do. The words spoken were short, sweet, and lacking the fluff most people use to fill in the blanks.

The woman then takes her place back on the pew and another person steps forward and goes to the podium. I'm surprised. The girl now standing at the front of the church, her face mostly veiled by long waves of auburn hair, is most certainly close to my age. Her hands fidget as she unfolds a small square of pink paper. Her lips press tightly together as she closes her eyes and takes a deep breath. Her lungs expand with air, the fabric of her dress stretching taut over hourglass curves. Her perfect figure, satin hair, and sun-kissed glow makes me shift uncomfortably in my chair. She's almost my opposite.

Chancing a look at Landon, I see his eyes are trained on the girl at the front, almost appraising her with his glossy blue irises. Would he prefer a girl like that over me?

Just as her beauty has the whole room mesmerized, the words that flow from her delicate lips are equally beautiful. "Do not stand at my grave and weep—I am not there, I do not sleep," she breathes. Continuing the poem in soft breaths of a small voice, she adds, "I am a thousand winds that blow..."

Though a common bereavement poem, one I've heard many times before, it has much more meaning somehow. Her gentle tone, her voice only slightly magnified by the microphone, holds a huge amount of sincerity. She must have scoured the internet for the perfect set of words, the ultimate way of saying that though we are gone, we are never forgotten and can be remembered every day.

As the poem comes to a close, teary-eyed she finishes.

~ ☾ ~

"Do not stand at my grave and cry, I am not there, I did not die." Then she holds her head up high and looks to the ceiling. As if she is feeling the wind blow on her skin, the gentle autumn rain, seeing the birds in circled flight and the soft stars that shine at night, she says, "For you, Grandpa."

But I don't agree. Mary Frye's words are powerful, eloquent, but they speak a truth I cannot begin to believe, nor do I understand. No matter how many times I say it is so, my mother is no longer here. She is dead. I never feel that she is still with me, watching me; instead, there is an empty whole in my heart where she used to belong. I don't notice the tear that trails down my cheek until Landon swipes it away with a finger.

I guess that's why I'm here, to feel what the girl at the podium feels. To feel that my mother, though gone from this life, is still with me, somehow, every day. If these mourners can find solace in that fact, shouldn't I be able to?

~ ☾ ~

Chapter Twenty-nine

Landon

I had never believed words could touch someone so deeply. I don't even know these people or who Frank Hamilton was, and yet the words that girl spoke sent chills up and down my spine. Even now as I watch the girl take her seat, her words still resonate in my mind.

Xylia maybe doesn't even know she's crying, but the dampness on my finger tells me how deeply she's been affected.

As crazy as it is to even understand, I think I get it. I think finally I understand just that little bit more about Xylia. She's lost someone. The fact rings true in my mind. The pieces of her puzzle are slowly falling into place.

It would seem no one wants to take on the amazing words Frank's granddaughter just spoke. I guess feeling that nothing could top such a moving piece of prose, the pastor ends the ceremony with one last prayer.

Church is awkward. I don't know the words, I don't even understand them, but I bow my head just the same, paying my respects to the family of mourners. When the congregation raises their heads with an "Amen," this time I whisper it through a partly closed mouth.

"Are we going to the brunch thing?" I ask Xylia quietly as others start to shuffle away. My stomach gurgles loud within my ears.

~ ☾ ~

"No, we're funeral crashers, but we aren't going to crash their intimate luncheon," she says, surprising me with a sarcastic tone. I'm starting to think Xylia has a split personality thing going on.

One by one, the guests file out into the lobby of the church. With Xylia's hand clutched tightly in mine, we make a beeline for the door.

Fresh air hits me like a cold slap in the face. The wind has picked up and is forcing the fabric of my pants to whip and lash at my legs. Xylia holds her black skirt tight to her thighs, probably hoping to ward off a Marilyn Monroe moment.

Instead of taking us back to the car where I had expected to go, Xylia leads me around the corner of the church. Another cemetery comes into view. Holding my reservations inside, I follow her through a rickety cast-iron gate.

"I want closure," she says as we come up to a red shale pathway.

"What?" The wind that now seems to be howling in my ears makes it hard to hear.

"Closure. I said it wasn't an option for me, but that's what I want."

I ask the obvious. "Closure from what?" Though from my earlier instincts, I figure she wants closure because someone she loved had been taken away from her.

A few paces down the path a great big marble mausoleum stands tall, with great pillars of stone reaching toward the clouds overhead. Tiny holes filled with stained glass shapes encased in the marble are the only hint of color against the ivory.

She walks toward it. "Here, let's get out of the wind," she says, tugging on the huge gate that stands at the head of the structure, almost out of place.

"Shouldn't it be locked?" I ask curiously as the metal scratches on its hinges.

~ ☾ ~

"Nah...I think they only do that at night to keep the bums out. Bums would kill for a place like this to sleep."

I shrug.

Inside, tiny gold plaques line the walls. In the middle, one long tomb sits center. Roman numerals etched into the stone match that of the rest of the space, inside and out. Xylia strides over, then plops herself onto the casket, using it as a bench.

I take in the space, imagining the people trapped tight inside the walls, hugging their most prized possessions, keeping them for themselves because I imagine that's what selfish rich people do. Take their diamonds and rubies, gold bricks, and secret treasure maps to the grave.

"I want one of these," I say.

"Huh?"

"A crypt. I think it would be totally awesome to have a family crypt, where all the Phoenix's could rest in peace for the rest of time in Silversprings." It would be cool, and if we can't be rich in life, why not give the impression we were from beyond the grave?

"But don't you want to get out?" she asks, then when she notices my confused expression she adds, "of Silversprings, I mean,"

We're changing the subject. The train's derailed, but somehow it doesn't bother me. It's not all about her anymore, I finally realize. She wants to get to know my secrets just as much as I do hers.

"Well, yeah, I do, but that might not be possible. It's hard to get out of small towns."

"But you're All Star. You must have colleges lined up ready to take you," she says, then pauses. "Don't you?" she adds when I shake my head.

Xylia scoots over, tapping the thick marble next to her. I take the space in two short strides, and with a heavy thud, sit down beside her.

~ ☾ ~

"I thought I would," I say. "Or more like, hoped. I needed a scholarship. I was banking the rest of my future on a full ride, one that apparently I'm not worthy to receive."

"I don't understand."

"A brush with death doesn't exactly scream healthy young athlete. I think it scared them off. And my grades, well, they aren't bad since I study just as much as I practice, but they aren't perfect."

"But my father gave you a clean bill of health. He told me you're in great shape, that there is no reason to worry about a repeat episode," she says encouragingly.

"I guess it doesn't matter."

"So you'll just get those student loan things. They give money out all the time. Sure, you'll be paying it off the rest of your life, but you can still go to college."

Her approach is sweet, but it's not just the money that's the problem. "I've kind of realized that without soccer or sports, I don't know who I am. It's always been the thing that's defined me. I was just hoping a scholarship would pave the way for college, that I'd still have sports, and that I didn't have to decide what I wanted to be when I grew up right away."

Her face falls a little as she says in a soft tone, "Oh."

"I suppose you have your whole future planned out?"

"Actually, more like chosen for me. My dad wants me to be a doctor. He's always told me that's what he expects, that I'd become a doctor and save lives side by side with him."

"And you don't want to be a doctor? I think that would be amazing."

"Problem is, I seem better at being on the side that ends lives rather than saves them," she says, twirling a strand of hair around her finger.

"You can't let an experience like mine take that dream away from you. I mean, not if that's what you want."

~ ☾ ~

"It's not just about you. Sure I couldn't save you, but...I couldn't save her either."

I gently squeeze her knee and whisper, "Who couldn't you save Xylia? Who did you lose?"

She looks away, almost ashamed. "My—my mother."

And I'm totally surprised, slapped in the face, because it's not the answer I was expecting. I'd thought a sister, a childhood friend, an aunt or uncle, but not a mother. Most definitely not a mother.

How does one bounce back from that sort of loss? I couldn't imagine life without my mother—she's my rock. She coddles me until I'm blue in the face, but she's there when I need her.

"I'm so, so sorry." I say, knowing it will never be enough. "I don't know why I never knew. I should have known. I'm sorry for that, too." The tears that fill her eyes break my heart but have me relieved. She's just told me something huge, monumental even. She's opening up to me. And maybe even opening up to herself.

~ ☾ ~

Chapter Thirty

Xylia

Tears sting my eyes with salt. I brush the wetness away, concentrating on the tiny gold plaques that line the walls of the mausoleum. Saying everything out loud is one thing, but putting into words the actual explanation for my feelings is one hundred percent a different matter.

I pull my legs tight to my chest, then adjust the fabric of my skirt to cover the bare skin. Resting my chin on my knees, I wait for Landon to say something else. Even hope he changes the subject. But I know deep down he won't. This is why we are here. This is what the whole trip has been about, this moment. At least, for Landon anyway.

"What happened to her?"

I take a deep breath, mentally preparing the answer for the onslaught of questions that I'm sure will follow. "She hung herself. It was Christmas Day."

Landon's sudden intake of air echoes against the stone of the room. His eyes, already stretched as wide as I thought they could get, open even further. "Xylia, I had no idea. I'm sorry."

"Quit saying you're sorry. I know you are, I know everyone is. I don't need your pity."

"I know you don't," he says quickly, then adds "It's not your fault, you know—"

~ ☾ ~

"Of course it is. How could it not be? She didn't want me, so she left."

He's stomping on skeletons and I think he knows it, because his usually gruff, loud voice is full of reluctance. "But how could you have known? How could you have stopped it? Xylia, I don't think it was because she didn't want you." He lifts his hand up to my cheek, then traces the line from my ear to the tip of my jaw. His blue eyes glisten, making them shiny, and a few stray strands of sandy hair fall into his eyes. "Who wouldn't want you? You're...you're amazing," he whispers. His hand is warm against my cheek and smells of faintly of cinnamon gum.

"But she didn't. If I made her happy, why did she leave?" Now I'm having a hard time keeping my feelings in check. It seems the words that have been trapped, closed off deep inside my head, my heart, are pouring out. I know it might not seem like much, but this, the words, admitting that maybe she had never wanted me, is heart wrenching. It tugs and pulls at everything that keeps me sane. But I try and push some of it down, stuff the feelings away, or else I might explode. I try and compose myself, just a little more as I say, "I didn't even get to say goodbye. I didn't go to her funeral."

"Why not?" he asks.

"I wasn't allowed. My father thought it was no place for a child. That I had already been through enough, that hearing about her life and saying goodbye would be too much. But he never asked me, he never let me make that decision for myself. I wanted to say goodbye, I needed to."

Landon murmurs, "The funerals—"

I speak up quickly, forcing the words out, but not the full brunt of emotion that's quickly building, trapped like a dam ready to burst. "They're addicting. At first, I wanted to see if I could say goodbye at someone else's

~ ☾ ~

funeral, pretend like they were talking about my mother. Imagine what they would say about her, picture her casket, what outfit they would put her in, how they would choose to style her hair. But it didn't work. No matter how hard I tried, it wasn't the same. Then the funerals just became an escape. I found it intriguing being able to listen to what others had to say. Even like a reminder of what I'd missed out on."

"Why didn't you just ask your father? I'm sure he would have answered those questions for you. I mean, I think it's the least you deserved."

My father that day, those following days, weeks, even years later...I couldn't ask him. He'd been shattered by what he'd seen that morning. But then again, so had I.

I clear my throat and press on. Landon has to know everything. "I found her that morning, swinging from my favorite tree, her skin cold as ice. I didn't understand it then, hell I still don't understand it. I think now everything has spiralled out of control, sucked me into a black hole and I can't crawl my way out."

"So everything—the funerals, the cemeteries—it's all because you want to understand?"

"I thought it would make me feel closer to her. People said that my mother would live on inside me, that she's not really gone. But I can't feel her, Landon." My voice grows shaky as I try and let everything out. "And I'm angry. I'm so angry that it hurts every day. What was so terrible in her life that she couldn't live anymore? She never said anything, but now...looking back, I think I knew she wasn't happy."

Landon squeezes my leg again and it aches. "It's still not your fault."

I want so bad for him to pull me into his arms, tell me everything is going to be okay. "Maybe, maybe not. But if I'd spoken up, told my dad how bad things were getting, how often she seemed so sad, maybe he would

~ ☾ ~

have done something. He's a doctor, for Christ's sake! It's his job to save people. Even if I couldn't have saved her, he should have been able to."

"After all these years, Xylia, you're still beating yourself up over something that was out of your control? No wonder you are the way you are. You have to let it go."

"Let it go? Let it go?" A tightness in my chest grabs hold of my emotions, and ache in my heart pushes it to sink lower and lower into a pit of sadness and self pity. "I'm so lost. It's dark every day. Even when the sun shines bright in the sky, all I see is blackness."

Then, finally, he wraps an arm around me. "It doesn't have to be that way anymore. You're strong, Xylia. I think you need to just forget about her and move on. You're wasting your life being hurt and angry at someone who isn't around. You can't change the past. You just need to concentrate on the future."

I wipe at my eyes. "It's not that easy." If I let go of her, then what will become of me? I've defined myself by the hurt my mother leaving me has caused. Molded myself into something even I can't understand. Something I don't know how to change.

"Of course it is. Don't worry about the people that aren't around anymore, worry about the ones right in front of you. Like me."

"But you'll leave, too. It's inevitable. When this trip is over, you're going to go back to being the person you were before all this."

Using his other hand, Landon cups my chin and looks me straight in the eyes. "I can't go back to who I was. Because of you, that person doesn't exist anymore."

My eyebrows rise. I don't understand. How could that be a good thing?

He keeps talking. "You've shown me so much, Xylia, in such a short time. The feelings that are growing inside

~ ☾ ~

my heart, they're for you. And I wouldn't let go of that for the world. Nothing is going to take me away from you."

It's sweet, it's so sweet the way he talks, the way his words whisper on my face, but people always leave, don't they?

"I think my therapist would think this is a revelation, talking about my feelings." I let out a small laugh.

"You have a therapist?"

And I praise him because as wacko as having a therapist sounds, he says it with not a hint of judgment. There is no mockery in his tone, no terror in his eyes, just a lopsided grin.

"Well I *had* one. Turns out she thinks I'm unfixable, that I have too much crazy inside my head, that she didn't want to stick around. And I didn't want her to, either."

"Huh. But you know, talking about it might help."

"Oh, no, not you too. I swear, I think all my secrets are out, really..." I say, but they aren't. I still have a few stiffs hidden in my closet.

~ ☾ ~

Chapter Thirty-one

Landon

Xylia never ceases to amaze me. I'm not sure I could hold on to that burden, that feeling that it's your fault, for all these years the way she has. A person is bound to end up a little off. But I get the feeling that there's even more lurking beneath the surface. I'm not sure what it is, but I feel like I'm missing some important information.

"You know, that still doesn't explain everything," I say to her.

"Oh, really? Wh—what's left?"

"You made me sleep in an open grave," I say.

She giggles. "Well, now that was just some good ol' fashion fun."

"Right. Fun," I say, then shake my head. "No, no I don't really see how that was fun. I still think there are bugs crawling around inside my head. Might even get nightmares from it."

"Oh, come on! It wasn't that bad, was it?" She nudges me.

"It was—" I try to file through my brain to grasp the right word. "Kind of—" But there really are no decent words for what I am thinking. So I just say it, no matter the outcome. "Crazy. Okay, it was a little crazy and creepy. Definitely creepy." Then I quickly add, "But I'm not saying you are crazy. I just mean that *that* was crazy.

~ ☾ ~

Not you. Not you at all." And now I want to slap my own face because I'm stammering, fumbling on my own words.

And she knows it because her defensive remark is filled with hostility. "Well, no one made you do it." Her eyes squint, no, *glare* at me as she shrugs my arm away and folds her arms across her chest.

"Oh, don't be like that. Sleeping in an open grave is just not something I'm used to, is all."

"Like I said, no one made you do it," she repeats, then flicks her head to the side. Waves of hair brush the side of my cheek.

I blow out a breath. "Seriously, you're not crazy. I mean it, really. Just look at me, please. I'm sorry, I shouldn't have said that."

Slowly she turns her head to me. A small pout plays on her lips. "I'm not crazy."

"No babe, you're not crazy. You've got some spunk and you're special. You have no idea how special you are," I say honestly.

Her eyes light up a bit. "Spunk? That's the best you could come up with?"

"It was either that or I say you're 'different.' Spunk had a better ring to it." I shrink a little, waiting for a slap in the arm, or worse, the face.

She nods. "Spunk I can handle, spunk is okay," she says and laughs when I straighten up, arch my back and stick out my chest. She adds, "Did you think I was going to like, hit you or something?"

Awkwardly I say, "No, of course not. That's silly." Then, when she tilts her eyebrows, I add, "Maybe..." Her features soften, and she sits up a little straighter too, an air of confidence replacing the sadness from a few minutes ago. It brings a smile to my face.

"You're ridiculous, you know that? Would ya just kiss me already?"

~ ☾ ~

I'm taken back by her forwardness; but her eyes are smiling just as brightly as her lips, which are open and show off a mouth full of teeth. I rest my hand under her chin, then lift it up ever so slightly. Inching closer, I wet my lips, getting them ready.

Xylia's eyes flutter closed. Her breath slows when I wrap my other hand around the small of her back. Her body relaxes against my touch. And when our lips finally meet, there are sparks of sweet tasting magic with an icy cold afterthought.

* * * *

We emerge from the marble crypt. While inside, time felt as though it had stopped; however, signs of its passing show on the outside. The wind has died down to a gentle breeze. The sky is lit up with streaks of pink and gold as the sun dips low, almost disappearing at the horizon.

I look to Xylia. Her lips are dry yet plump from our activities. Her raven black and formerly silky hair is tangled and swept clumsily to the side. And I smile, even hold in a chuckle when I see tiny red splotches on her neck. Little love bites that stick out like a perfectly ripe strawberries against her alabaster skin.

"What? What are you looking at?" she asks. When my eyes zone in on the tiny scarlet blotches, her hand flies to her neck and she whines, "Oh man, you didn't leave stupid, disgusting hickeys on my neck did you? Great. Now people will think I was attacked by a vampire."

I fake gasp. "Or worse," I say, raising my hand to my chest for emphasis, "making out with your boyfriend, cause that would be sooo uncool."

As the final echo of my words find their way to her ears she pauses, drops the hickey shield to rest at her side, and looks at me. Her head tilts to the right just a

~ ☾ ~

hair. "What did you just say?"

"Nothing gets past you, does it?"

"I guess not, because I swear you just called yourself my boyfriend."

Shrugging, I say, "So what if I did?"

"Don't you think that's a little presumptuous? I mean, we've known each other for like, five seconds. Besides, I'm not sure I want you as my boyfriend."

"Really, you don't?" I smirk.

"Oh, just shut up."

I laugh. "Fine. But there's no way I believe you. Not the way you kissed me back." And when she blushes, I know I'm right.

~ ☾ ~

Chapter Thirty-two

Xylia

As we begin to wind our way through the tombstones and back to the church, I reach for Landon's hand, taking it in mine. "Can we watch the sunset?" I ask as I stare off at the pink streaked sky. The sun dips further and further toward the horizon.

As I keep walking, Landon stops, I look back at him and at our clasped hands. He gives me a tug, pulling me into his arms. His hand brushes my cheek and slips a few wayward strands of hair behind my ear. "Only if we can find a better place. I'm sorry to say but a cemetery just isn't that romantic."

I nod, taking in a deep breath. I've always wanted this, from the first day I met Landon, and now he's inches away from me, holding me in his arms. I'm falling, fast and hard, for the one person I never thought could be in my reach.

He leans forward, dipping his head down, wetting his lips, but as my eyes flutter closed in anticipation of his touch, he kisses my cheek instead. My eyes shoot open just as Landon pulls away from me. "I'll race you." He grins and dashes toward the parking lot.

I can't help but stand in place, stunned, as my heart races, trying to keep up with the feelings inside me. But I shake off the feeling just as quickly as I too bolt toward the car, and Landon. Of course he reaches it first. "You

~ ☾ ~

cheated," I say between breaths.

"I did not," he says with that charming lopsided grin of his plastered on his face.

I reach for the door of the car. "You did too." He seems to ignore my response, instead slipping into the passenger seat, still smiling brightly, as though instead of winning a race, he'd won a million bucks.

Instead of driving to the inn, I let Landon navigate us to a spot that would make watching the suns final decent, as he put it, "more romantic," which really is a small hill in a school playground.

Landon sits down and motions for me to follow. "This is much better," he says, wrapping his arm around my waist and pulling me closer to him.

The heat that radiates off his skin warms me to the core, blanketing me from the crisp December air. I rest my head on his chest and focus on the sinking sun. The clouds look as though they are painted with pure gold, as splashes of pink and purple streak with the pale blue of the sky. One by one, the stars pop out, becoming brighter, polka-dotting the sky with shiny diamonds. It's breathtaking. And sharing it with Landon is unbelievable.

The silence that's fallen over us is comforting. There is no need for words as we both stare at the sunset. But my body stiffens when a cold breath of air tickles my skin. I shiver, goose-bumps rising over my flesh.

"Are you cold?" Landon pulls away from me slightly. He unbuttons his shirt and shrugs it off. "Here, take this." He extends his shirt toward me.

I shake my head. "You'll freeze," I say. But he doesn't look bothered by the sudden onslaught of cool air. Instead he looks comfortable in his white T-shirt.

"Just take it, please. I'm fine." He thrusts the shirt to me again.

This time I take it, slipping into the long-sleeved

~ ☾ ~

fabric, letting the residual warmth soak in. But it's not enough. I'm still chilled to the bone.

I hear something. Like a whisper.

Then, "Now can we take him?"

But it doesn't sound like Landon's voice.

I take my eyes off the sky and look at Landon. "Did you say something?"

He turns his head to me. "No," he says, but leans in and gives me a quick kiss on the lips. When he pulls back he looks me up and down. "But I'm thinking you sure do look good in my shirt."

I can't help but smile and look down at myself, seeing my body swim in his button down shirt. I pull it tighter against my skin.

"He's right here. We have to restore the balance. Let's do it now." The whisper again. Low, throaty. Male.

My body stiffens. That definitely didn't come from Landon, who's now back to focusing on the dimming sky, the sun just a tiny sliver on the horizon, twilight fully upon us. I look to my left, then to my right, but don't see anyone.

"I'd rather wait." This voice is different, gruff and distinct. I take a deep breath and look over my shoulder, craning my neck.

Behind us, a few feet down the hill, I make out the shapes of two figures. I let out a gasp and whip my head back around. It's the men in suits. They are here, watching us. Nausea washes over me. They are talking about Landon. They want to take him...somewhere. They said something about balance. What balance? I chance another look over my shoulder, but there's nothing, they're gone.

Suddenly, the nausea in my stomach is chased away with fear. Something isn't right. These men, the voices, the dreams, they are all connected and they all want Landon. I chance a quick peek at him as he sits focused

~ ☾ ~

on the sky, oblivious to everything. But deep down I know something is wrong, and that maybe Landon was never supposed to come back. And maybe he was never meant to be mine, just like my mother wasn't ever meant to love me the way a parent should or else she wouldn't have left either.

My heart drops in my chest, tears sting my eyes because I have no idea how to stop the threat that seems imminent. If I tell people what I believe I know, that someone or something is out to get Landon, I'll just sound crazy. No one will believe me.

Even though my mind is racing a mile a minute, weighing everything that's going on, what might happen, I can't help but feel a small amount of comfort being in Landon's arms. Maybe I'm just not meant to keep him. I know the feelings that I have, so new yet so real, are important. But people always leave one way or another. Whether it's by choice or not, everyone's life has an expiration date. And apparently when Landon came back he brought more with him than just a miracle. He brought back death itself.

And death wants him back.

* * * *

Landon's eyes light up as he drops his body on top of mine. We sink deep into the plush mattress and the squeak made by the bed echoes through our room at the B&B.

"Why don't we just relax. Maybe talk some more," he says. He awkwardly shifts his weight, resting his weight on his knee and holding it off me.

Wrapping my hands in his shirt, tight, I sigh. "Haven't we talked enough? Besides, I'm finding this rather relaxing." I lift my head off the bed and kiss the small curve of his neck. I'm scared. Fear might be

~ ☾ ~

propelling me forward just as much as my need and want to be close to Landon. Since I heard the voices, became convinced that the men in suits have something to do with Landon, and not knowing how to stop them from taking him away, the least I can do is live every moment. It's the only option I have, besides waiting and worrying.

He grunts and pulls back. "You aren't sure you want me to be your boyfriend and yet..." he trails off.

"Does one really need to have their relationship defined in such a way just to have some fun?" I ask, trying to hold my composure.

His mouth twitches to the side. No doubt he's weighing the options in his head. "I don't know. I guess not?"

I grin. "Good." His body relaxes as he lowers his face to mine. Ever since the cemetery I've been thinking about this, have been waiting to feel his lips pressed tightly against mine again.

My experience in this department is lacking. My first kiss was on Landon's dead body. It seems, at least for me, a little out of character, as I thought I *would* be in love and I *would* be in a defined relationship the first time I kissed anyone. Yet, I've also come to terms with the fact that anything could happen. Landon has shown me the whole live-each-day-as–though-it-is-your-last aspect, because anyone could drop dead at any moment. Unlike him, not everyone gets a second chance. And not everyone might get that second chance taken away either.

I realize I might be over thinking things. I close the last inches between us and let my lips touch his. They are soft, supple, and like earlier, very different from the lips I'd felt in the morgue. Those were cold, icy, and dry.

Relaxing my hold on the fabric of his shirt, I sigh, then let my hands slide around to his back and pull him

~ ☾ ~

in even closer. He shifts his weight, pressing against me in a delicious way.

It takes Landon a few seconds to respond to my kiss, but when he does it's with an urgency I didn't anticipate. His tongue parts my lips and explores my mouth. He cups my cheek, his fingers lightly caressing the strands of my hair within his reach. His touch sends shivers down my spine. When his warm hand leaves my cheek to trail down the side of my neck, my breast, my stomach, I gasp and flinch.

His fingers trace the length of my body, caressing my thigh for a moment, before inching toward the hem of my skirt. Goosebumps pebble my skin when his hands slip underneath the fabric. I help myself to his shirt, untucking the material and running my hands up his back, which is warm, smooth. I catch a whiff of my scent that still clings to the fabric from when he'd taken the shirt off his own back and placed it over my shoulders to keep me warm while we watched the sunset. With a deep breath and a whole lot of confidence, I move my hands around his waist until I'm touching his toned stomach.

Pulling slightly back until my head touches the soft quilt beneath me, I gaze into his eyes. They are bright with emotion and teenaged lust. A lopsided grin plays on his lips as I shakily undo the buttons of his shirt. I drag my hands higher, over his shoulders, then push the fabric of his shirt down his arms.

Landon lifts himself off my body and leans back on his heels. He takes his shirt the rest of the way off, then tosses it to the floor. I can't help but to stare.

"Like what you see?" he says, obviously noticing my ogling.

Heat rises up my neck and spreads over my cheeks. "Well...um...yeah," I say, then swallow thickly.

He tilts his head to the side, frowns a little, and says

~ ☽ ~

with concern, "Sorry, babe, I didn't mean to embarrass you."

But I'm not sure what's worse, being embarrassed or having him point it out. I just nod and smile in response. Taking this as a sign to move forward, Landon, still on his knees, tugs up the material of my shirt, pushing it past my navel until my simple white bra is exposed.

I know I'm inexperienced, and should enjoy this. But with my shirt pushed up, a small amount of panic rises in me. I'm the only one who's seen me so exposed, and now to have someone else taking in the peaks and valley of my chest, I feel self-conscious.

Pushing all self doubt out of my head, I ignore my own thoughts of warning, ignore the panic that is clouding my mind and possibly my judgment, because this is what I want, ultimately. But the thoughts keep coming. Am I doing this for the wrong reasons? Is it because I've daydreamed about what it would be like to have Landon kiss me, to gaze at me with those big blue eyes and see me, really see me for who I am? Or is it the worry, the fear that I might lose him, again, that's freaking me out? My head is spinning out of control, my heart pulling me in a million different directions. This is Landon, my crush, the one person I've always thought I could never have. I want this, don't I? I think. I'm pretty sure. Almost positive.

My eyes flutter closed. I wait for his lips to find mine again. Until then I name every cemetery I can think of within a fifty mile radius of my house in an effort to let my worry fade away.

Once he's kissed my torso, collarbones, the hollow of my throat, his lips find mine. My hands wrap around his neck, fingers lacing into his hair as I caress the soft waves at the nape of his neck. How could this possibly be real? I want to pinch myself just to make sure I really am awake. If I'd been asked two weeks ago if I saw

~ ☾ ~

myself here, making out with Landon Phoenix, I would have laughed. But here we are. Landon's alive, and he's kissing me like there's no tomorrow.

* * * *

As I lay in the crook of Landon's arm, my hand across his chest, I realize I've never felt happier. His warm body is slightly damp with beads of sweat that are wiped away as my fingertips gently swirl and caress every inch of skin they can reach. The soft sheet of our bed hangs loose around our entwined bodies. Landon's breath comes fast and shallow, as though he's just ran a marathon. His heart beats loudly in my ear, even thumps against my cheek. I lift my head up slightly, looking at the thick draperies that hang alongside the only window in the room. The moon, big and round, shines light that streams across the hardwood floor.

But though some clothes had been removed, a few boundaries even pushed, my virginity is still intact. I thought I was ready. In the end, however, I just couldn't go through with it. Landon was ever the gentlemen and settled for a hot and heavy make-out session instead.

"Can I ask you something?"

I adjust my head a little more until I can look up at his face, into those blue eyes that are hooded slightly by his lids, which gives his features a more mysterious tone. "Of course."

"Where are we going tomorrow? 'Cause this 'haunted house' isn't very haunted." He smiles.

Hastily I lift my head up, let my eyes grow wide with astonishment, and say with a gasp, "Wait! Did you hear that?"

"Funny. I didn't hear anything. This is so not a real haunted house."

Laying my head back down I reply, "You're right, it

~ ☾ ~

does kind of suck. I was totally expecting creepy sounds, rattling doorknobs and floorboards, even lights flickering on and off." Then I add, "You know, I was thinking I'd let you have a turn at the map, let you give us a destination tomorrow." Worry creeps over me. "That is, if you don't need to go home yet?"

"Really?" he says with surprise, "But I thought this was your trip and that I'm just tagging along."

"You know it *was*, until I realized it was kind of a stupid idea. I mean, who would waste their winter break driving around looking for cemeteries, spooky churches, and lame haunted houses? That kinda sounds like something a crazy person would do and...I'm not crazy." I take a deep breath. "I'm just happy spending time with you."

"Great. Because I'm not sure I could take many more funerals. Or cemeteries, for that matter."

"Tomorrow it's your day. We will go wherever you want."

And like a typical guy, Landon says, "Sweet." But then adds, "Have you talked to your dad at all? I mean, since we left?"

Realization hits that I haven't talked to Dad, returned his texts, or even so much as thought about him since we left. I actually feel kind of guilty. "No, I guess I haven't," I mutter.

"He's probably worried sick, Xylia," Landon says, almost sounding stern. "It's too late to call now, but I think you should at least call him in the morning, let him know you're safe."

I sigh. "Yeah, you're probably right. But you should call your folks too."

"Yup...you're probably right." He sighs too, letting his chest rise and fall dramatically.

Silence fills the air. Maybe we are both thinking about our parents. I know Dad is worried, probably wearing

~ ☾ ~

through the floorboards with his pacing. Tomorrow. I'll call him tomorrow. Right now, I just want to lay next to Landon and pretend this moment will never fade.

We lay in silence for a while, then Landon swallows loudly. I can hear it, feel the motion, then he says, "Can I ask you something else?"

"Sure, unless you are going to ask me if you can drive."

"No, no that's not it. But now that you mention it, can I?"

I swat him in the ribs. "No, you can't."

"Ouch, okay. But seriously…"

"Alright, seriously, you can ask me anything you want."

"If you don't want to be a doctor, then what do you want to be?"

I think about it for a few seconds. "A mortician."

"Get out, seriously?" he asks, flabbergasted.

"No, not seriously, but glad to see you would have been on board if I was," I reply sarcastically.

"Sorry, it's just—"

"If I was a guy and said I wanted to be a mortician, some would think it odd, but most wouldn't even bat an eye at it. Sometimes I hate being a girl. We seem to get judged way more than guys."

"You're right, it isn't fair." He kisses the top of my head. "If that's what you want to do, then I'd be okay with it."

"Not that you'd really have a choice in the matter," I scoff.

"True. So really, though, what do you want to be?"

"It's probably not as bad as a mortician, but not much better," I say. "I think I want to be a Medical Examiner."

"Like on CSI?"

"Yeah, kind of. Though there aren't many big crimes to solve in Silversprings. But I think"—I stall, looking for

~ ☾ ~

the right words—"I think I want to help people. If not by saving the lives of people directly, I can at least give a sense of closure for those left behind."

Landon nods. "I can see how that can help overcome the grief you have, by helping others get closure, even though you still don't quite have yours, yet."

A small smile overcomes the sadness that weighs on my heart. He gets it, at least, a little bit. "I might not always be able to tell the families why, but I can at least tell them how. How their loved one's heart stopped beating, what they were experiencing as they took their last breath. But mostly, at least some questions will be answered."

Landon pulls me in tighter, comforting me. Maybe he senses that what's going to come next will be hard for me to say.

I swallow and take a deep breath of air and exhale it, readying myself. "I wish every day I knew why Mom took her own life, why the night before she had been so determined to find that length of rope—for a project, she had said—but especially why she just couldn't bear to live another day."

I have to take another deep breath. Water wells in my eyes, and I reach up, swiping away the wetness.

"You don't have to continue," Landon says.

"No," I strangle out. "I want to. At least I know how she died. I know that it was instantaneous. That her neck snapped like a dry twig. That her body froze from the near frigid temperature. And I know that she was clear headed. She knew what she was doing." Which makes her death all the more painful. Had she been drinking, or on drugs, if her mind was confused, it wouldn't hurt so bad. She killed herself, and did it on purpose. And I'll never know why.

"It's still not your fault," Landon says, then lets silence fill the air, waiting for me to push forward.

~ ☾ ~

"It's taken me so long, but I think now I can finally forgive her. For so many years I was hurt and angry, cast aside as if I meant nothing. But I think I just needed something, something to keep myself going, to make a small amount of sense in my life."

Landon's eyebrows quirk in question but he doesn't speak. He just waits with those adoring eyes for me to continue.

"However morbid, I think everything death made me feel closer to her, because I didn't believe she was still with me. But her life was important—her greatest gift to the world was me. Even though she failed to see that, in a way I believe everyone deserves some amount of closure, and that's the least I can do for others. And now you've shown me that there are other things to worry about and care for in life." The tears that have pooled in my eyes break free and begin to stream down my cheeks. A simple explanation turned into even more than I was expecting. It's funny how some things happen without much thought, or control. I've just managed to say some of the words that have been caught in my throat since Mom left.

Landon's hand finds my cheek, and with a gentle touch he wipes away the tears.

I sniffle, compose myself again, and say, "I read in a book once a quote that only now makes sense. It's stuck with me, waiting for the moment when I would finally understand." I take a deep breath, then I recite the powerful words, *"Just because you're giving up doesn't mean you're weak, it means you're strong enough to walk away.-Anonymous."*

"Xylia, beneath the spunk, the black clothes, and the tough exterior, there's this person I'm thankful to have gotten to know. Because even though you have had some unbearable pain in your life, you still manage to see the light and want to help others see it, too."

~ ☾ ~

Landon gently leans over, and kisses me passionately.

Time stops for me again as all of what Landon just said is poured into that kiss. And when he pulls away, I do not whimper. I do not show the sorrow that still lies in my heart for the mother who left me behind, but rejoice in the fact that I have finally found someone who understand me for who I am.

Landon then takes me in his arms, squeezing just the right amount, and his comforting touch lifts a weight off my shoulders. He releases one arm and pulls the covers up. The soft cotton surrounds me but it's his warmth and compassion that lets me settle in for the night.

I wait until Landon's breaths become slow, shallow, before I chance movement. I raise my hand up, in front of his face, and wave it frantically. He lays still, his eyes don't shutter, his rhythmic breaths don't waiver. He's fast asleep. Nuzzling closer, my head still resting on his arm, I whisper, soft and sweet, into his ear, "I love you." I know he can't really hear, that he probably won't have any recollection of my words, but somehow I think he senses it because as I look at his face, a hint of a smile creeps up his cheek.

Then I shed all the tears I was stubbornly holding in, because that's what closure does. It lifts the skeletons that have been weighing you down off your shoulders, pushes them out of the closet and back into the ground where they belong, but not because those skeletons need to be buried deep and forgotten. They need to allow you to move on. And I see that now. These tears are both because I am happy and I'm relieved.

I forgive her.

And I forgive myself for believing her suicide was my fault and that I could have done something when I couldn't. Not really. Landon has shown me that. It's because of him that the world makes a fragment of sense than it had before.

~ ☾ ~

Chapter Thirty-three

Landon

Light trickles in through the window, creating shadows that dance around the room of the B&B. I smile when I see Xylia, still fast asleep while nestled against my chest, enveloped in blankets. The thick papered walls glow even brighter with the sun's light, while several wall sconces still glow warm.

The small clock on the nightstand reads early, too early to be awake after such a great night. It always works that way. I find that when I want nothing more than to sleep in, that's when I awake at the crack of dawn. But then an idea pops in my head.

Stealthily, I rise from the bed, hop silently when my feet touch the cold hardwood floor, then slip into my clothes.

When I reach the door, I turn back. Xylia's raven silk is splayed across the pillow. A small amount of supple skin peeks out from the covers to stare at me, and I worry what she'll think if she wakes up and I'm gone. I would if I were her. Tiptoeing back to the antique nightstand beside the bed, I pray there is a pen and paper so I can scrawl a note.

The drawer creaks, whines with protest as I slide it out, but I'm relieved when I see the inn's stationary lying inside. I take a crisp sheet of paper and write a brief message, but I hope Xylia stays sleeping and

~ ☾ ~

doesn't see my note. My surprise would be much better if I'm back before she wakes.

Outside, the crisp morning air fills my lungs, birds chirp with enthusiasm, and off in the distance, sounds of other early risers can be heard.

The inn is set against trees, shrubs, and flowers, and is just off Valley View's main street. I think I remember a bakery a street over and a few blocks down.

The walk is peaceful, slow. That's something else I can thank Xylia for, patience. With no real schedule in place, the whole world has slowed down for me. It's crazy how my life has changed in such a short time. Normally, I'd have an intense schedule to follow—taking early runs down Silversprings winding walking paths, spending hours of gym time to stay in shape and bulk up, or studying like mad. Now I can take time to feel the gravel beneath my feet and the sun warming my face as I cut through a short alleyway.

My chest tightens, though, as my mind swims with the loss of soccer. I don't know what to do. I don't know who to become now that I've lost my chance with soccer. This is nice, taking the walk in slow strides, but part of me is pulling me forward, wishing to speed up and burn off energy, because that's what I'm used to. I suppose on the bright side, I can be anything I want. I can start over, and I can always try for late admission, hope my grades are enough to get me into another school. I've always liked computers, maybe that's an option. Though I'm not sure I can picture myself stuck in a stuffy cubicle all day. I need to come up with something, because Silversprings is too small, suffocating. I don't want to be a lifer, I want to get out and see the world. And if not with soccer, then with some other career.

I know when I'm close to the bakery because the air is full of the warm, tangy and sweet scent of yeast and sugar. But I don't walk straight there.

~ ☾ ~

It's because I'm walking slow and checking everything out that I notice a small gift shop on the other side of the street. The shopkeeper, a plump lady, is out on the sidewalk, placing a sandwich-board sign out that says "Sale" in big letters. Then she flips the Closed sign to read Open. Maybe a gift for Xylia is just the special touch my breakfast in bed plan needs.

Crossing the street, I wave to a small red VW Bug that stops and waits. The driver politely raises his hand back. Once on the other side of the street, I head straight for the small shop. The door opens with a jingle, then strong perfumes and incense overwhelm my senses.

The store is cluttered with gifts. No real aisles separate the space, just shelves and racks, swirly stands, and things hanging overhead or piled on the floor. How would I ever find something for Xylia in this mess?

As the morning sun rises in the sky and slides through the window, dust particles swirl in the air, landing on various kinds of smelly candles, stuffed bears, homemade preserves, and greeting cards. I need to hurry up and get back to Xylia before she wakes, the rising sun is my only measure of time since I have no phone or watch.

Slowly, I sidestep through the store until something catches my eye. Hanging on a small stand that has curly wires like branches of a tree are necklaces. Each one different, hand crafted and unique. Exactly what I want. I pick one up. I hold it in the palm of my hand, looking it over.

A thin black cord holds a small smooth flat rock, pierced with a hole that lets the cord through. Etched on the surface in elegant black script is the word *Dream*.

Perfect. It's sentimental, yet simple enough for our still undefined relationship. I can't wait to give it to Xylia.

"Did you find what you were looking for?" the

~ ☾ ~

shopkeeper asks as I approach the counter.

"Just the thing." I lay the necklace onto the counter. A few presses of the register and she says, "That'll be nine fifty-seven."

I nod, reach for my wallet, only it's not there. Panic makes my eyes grow wide as I shove my hands into all the pockets. My cheeks heat up with embarrassment. "I-I seem to have left my wallet behind." I curse in my head a dozen times. "I'm staying over at the inn and snuck out in a hurry to get breakfast. I wanted to surprise my girlfriend. Would you mind holding this for me until I can come back and buy it?"

She rubs her chin, then smiles and says, "I trust you'll come back. If this is meant to be a surprise, I think you should take it now."

The heat quickly leaves my face, though I'm not sure she's serious. "Are you sure?"

"I'm sure. I know an honest face when I see one, and you, young man, have a *very* honest face." She hands me the necklace, adding, "I hope she likes it."

Then with a quick afterthought I say, "Do you happen to have a permanent marker around?"

"Yes..." she says, a quizzical expression on her face. She reaches into a drawer and produces a Sharpie. I take it from her and with the steadiest hand I can, manage to write on the back of the stone.

Sliding the marker across the counter I say, "Thank you. I know she'll love it. I'll be back soon to pay you."

"You have a good morning, ya hear."

As I walk through the door, I carefully place the necklace in my pocket. With an extra hop in my step, I head toward the bakery.

"Landon? Landon is that you?" I hear a voice from down the street calling my name. Strange. I swear I recognize the voice, but that's impossible. She can't be here. Slowly, I turn around, and when my eyes confirm

~ ☾ ~

what my ears heard, I feel the blood sink to my feet.

"Oh, Landon, we've been worried sick about you," Charity calls out as she gallops toward me. I moan inwardly and roll my eyes. When she gets close I expect her to stop, only she doesn't. She runs right into me, throwing her arms around my neck.

"What are you doing here?" I ask through gritted teeth.

Still holding me in a bear hug, Charity giggles. "Silly, don't you remember? My grandmother lives here. I'm just up visiting."

I want to think it odd, but I do remember her grandmother lives in Morningside. What are the chances? Something seems off, though. And all I want is to get back to Xylia.

"Right, well, I'd better be going," I say, attempting to pry Charity's arms from around my neck.

"Oh, I just knew you'd come back to me," she says. "When your mother called and said you were missing, I just knew you were on your way here. I felt it in my heart."

What the hell is she talking about? Why would she ever think I'd come to Morningside? I've never even met her grandmother. I've never even been to this town before. No way would Charity have ever thought I'd come here. No way would she come track me down.

"I-I'm not here for you," I say. But when I manage to get her arms free from my body, she comes at me, this time with her lips.

I stagger back a step as she grabs my face in both her hands and plants the biggest, sloppiest kiss ever on me. I attempt to push her away but she holds on tight, moving her mouth against mine, even making dramatic kissy noises.

I want to gag, throw up everything that is in my stomach, because I swear it is just begging to come out.

~ ☾ ~

My head bellows, loud with frustration, then I feel an unusual sensation. It starts at my feet and swiftly reaches the top of my head. I think I close my eyes and that's the blackness that I see, but I'm lightheaded and everything, including me, is spinning uncontrollably. What's even worse than a spinning world? That rush you get when you are falling, *fast*. And I'm falling.

My body lands against something with a bone-crushing thud. The wind is knocked from my lungs and I struggle to gasp for air. The ache in my head, that pounding pressure, is almost unbearable, like I fell from the sky and landed on the pavement only to have a semi-truck run me over a few times.

My eyelids quiver as I force them to slowly open. The throb in my head is intensified with blinding light that surrounds me. I pinch my eyes shut again, shielding from the brightness.

"They're always tempted by the pretty girl in a red dress," I hear a man say.

Trying to focus my eyes, to adjust to the light, I hear someone else's muffled tone. "Were you even watching? She wasn't in a red dress, you idiot. I don't even think she was in a dress at all."

"Don't call me an idiot," the first voice, boyish sounding, replies with attitude.

The second voice tosses back quickly, "Then don't make idiot comments."

"Quit it! Hey, I think he's waking up."

Voice number two says, "It's about freaking time."

"Can't you say anything nice? Ever?"

I'm confused. The banter between the two voices seems out of place, or maybe I'm the one that's out of place. There should be sirens sounding, frantic voices, something, anything that suggests I've been in a terrible accident.

"Hey there, sunshine, you might want to tune in," the

~ ☾ ~

second voice says. I feel my leg being nudged.

I blink my eyes rapidly and a face, inches away from mine, comes into view. This man has piercing blue eyes, pale skin, and hair just as black as Xylia's, tied back into a ponytail. A toothpick dangles from his mouth.

"You with us?" he breathes in my face. I nod.

Forcing myself into a sitting potion, I am startled by what I see. The White Room. The same never ending space of pure white that has no beginning and no end, but this time it's muddled with the presence of this guy and the one hovering behind him, who has red hair and is young. Both have matching, unnaturally blue eyes, and both are in suits, charcoal gray. But unlike my last memory of this place, I'm in the same clothes I was in before.

Then I wonder if what I've experienced with Xylia was just a dream. That this whole time I've been here, wandering, searching for something, and only now have found it. My heart clenches with tightness, sinking to the bottom of my stomach. Nausea washes over me as bile rises in my throat. It can't be a dream, Xylia was real, what we shared, had to have been real. I've never felt—she's perfect.

"Is—is this heaven?" I ask, though I know it's not, just like I knew it the last time I was here.

The man with the red hair and the boyish voice laughs, doubling over as he says, "No, kid, this isn't heaven."

"Now"—Toothpick Guy points his slobbered-on toothpick at me—"let's get on with it. We're a little short on time here—"

"Are you guys angels or something?" I say, still not completely sure what is happening.

Toothpick Guy, obviously the leader of the two, throws back his head and laughs. The skin on his neck ripples. He points the toothpick again. "Sure, whatever

~ ☾ ~

you wanna think." Redhead says, "But we're—"

"Shut it." Toothpick Guy pauses awkwardly, fist raised in the air, almost like he wanted to use a name but chose at the last second not to. Instead, he slides the small wooden pick across his lips. Redhead timidly backs away a few steps, even has his hands raised like a white flag, but he's still grinning.

"As I was saying before I was interrupted," Toothpick Guy says to me, refocusing, "you managed to go and cheat death. The *powers* are none too pleased about it."

"Cheated death?" I whisper.

"Yeah, you know, you were dead, and then *BAM*"—he pounds his fist into his other hand—"you're alive."

"So it wasn't a dream?" I ask.

"No, not a dream. Very real, in fact, but it's caused an unsightly rift that needs to be fixed."

My head is spinning like a top. "Uh, fixed how?"

Toothpick Guy takes the wooden spear from his mouth and snaps it in half. "The world needs balance. Without it, things go astray. You were supposed to die, plain and simple. Your time was up. But you managed to"—he gestures with his hands—"come back to life somehow. I had fun watching you for a while, but now it's time to right the balance. I'm going to make you choose."

"Choose?" Redhead says, his brows raised to his hairline. "What are you doing? This isn't the way we're supposed to do things. It was bad enough you wanted to hang out and watch him, but now you want to completely change the rules?"

"I'm in charge. My decision," Toothpick Guy says.

Redhead just shakes his head, that perplexed look still on his face. I focus on Toothpick Guy—after all, he's the one in charge.

"I don't understand," I say. I'm sick inside; my stomach feels as though I am riding the fiercest waves of

~ ☾ ~

the ocean. I was *supposed* to die? "But I didn't do anything. I don't—"

"It doesn't matter if you directly or indirectly did anything to give yourself life again. When you were supposed to die, someone else crossed the boundary between life and death and ended up with your life in their hands. Guess you could blame that person, but it's a moot point. As I said, the world needs balance, so now you have to choose: your life or someone else's."

"Someone else's?"

"Is that your choice?"

Redhead sputters, then says, "Of course that's not his choice! You have no right. Why are you making this personal? This isn't who we are, what we are about. We do our job—we don't play with people. We don't get to decide who lives and who dies."

I say, "No. I don't know. Who—who would die?"

Toothpick Guy's lips take on a grin, one that terrifies me. "How about that little squeeze of yours?"

My chest tightens and my eyes fall shut as anguish fills my core. "Xylia...no," I mumble.

"So what'll it be?" he asks, pulling another toothpick from his inside breast pocket and sliding it between his teeth.

My heart plummets to the ground. Either Xylia dies, or I do. How could someone make a person choose whose life is more important? How can this be the only option? Who's running this show? I don't even know who these guys are, and yet in a place with no walls, no ceilings, and no place to hide, they've managed to back me into a corner. If I was on the street I'd run, hide from them, but in the White Room, nothing can disappear.

There is no easy answer, no easy choice. I'm not ready to die. And yet, how can I make that choice for her, without her knowing? She has just as much of a right to live as I do. She has plans of her own—she wants to help

~ ☾ ~

people, change the world with her kindness.

I've only just found her and now we're being forced apart. I thought this was it—I was so sure I had found someone amazing. Someone who is not only hot, but who understands me. Xylia doesn't care about my soccer star status, and doesn't care that I might never go pro. She wants me for me.

Before I came here, I was so sure she was the one. That we were meant for each other. Soul mates.

Toothpick Guy says, "Time's a ticking."

And just like that, it comes to me. I know what I have to do, because I'm *not* a selfish person. "Can I say goodbye? Please, just give me a few more minutes of time. I didn't say goodbye."

I'm thankful when the Redhead, who has remained silent the past few minutes, speaks up. "What's a few more minutes delay?" he says.

"It's not policy."

"Policy?" Redhead snorts. "We're way beyond policy."

"I need to see her again. Please. Then you can take me," I say to Toothpick Guy.

"So that's it? That's your choice? You will give up your life for hers?"

I swallow and hope to God that this gets me into heaven. If it even exists. I have no clue what this White Room is or who these oddballs are, but somehow I can't see them as part of what I've always believed to be an afterlife. "Yes. You can take my life. *Again*," I say, thinking it seems like the only choice. If I was already supposed to die, why should I take Xylia's life away? And besides, I know she'll do greater things than I could have ever dreamed for myself. I'm just a has-been jock who would be stuck in a dead-end life. Xylia has all the potential.

"There, he chose. Now just for once, have a heart and give the guy what he wants."

~ ☾ ~

Toothpick Guy thinks it over, sliding the toothpick from one side of his lips to the other. And I wait, tearing myself up inside because I had been more worried about a stupid surprise for Xylia than waking her up and saying goodbye.

"Alright," he says, "but first, I want to show you what you probably just prevented."

"Did. *Did* prevent." Redhead squirms.

"Like that movie? The one they play on TV at Christmas?" I ask.

Toothpick Guy nods.

"Uh, okay," I say with hesitation.

With a wave of Toothpick Guy's arm, a screen appears out of thin air. Redhead moves aside and there, taking up a large amount of the expansive space is Xylia, walking down the street. I watch on with confusion as she stops abruptly. Like a movie, the camera pans out over the set. And there, wearing the same clothes as I am now is me...with Charity. From the angle of the camera, we are kissing, but what isn't shown is the struggle, the force I was using to push her away.

The camera goes back to Xylia. Her face is torn up with tears that fall as she watches me kiss another girl. She turns on her heels and runs at top speed without looking, right onto the street. Out of nowhere a truck comes barrelling down the road. And as though I'm there, I hear the tires screech, see the impact that sends Xylia flying. My heart stops, panic spreading over my body. Bile squirms in my stomach working its way up. "That's enough. Stop." My own eyes well with wetness.

But the screen never falters and Xylia is laying on the pavement in the most unnatural position. Blood, gashes, and dirt cake her body. I shut my eyes, horrified.

Then the voice cuts through the silence and says, "I'm sending you back. You say your goodbyes, though, might I suggest not to. It always makes things worse. And after

~ ☾ ~

that, you're mine."

"How long do I have? And then what happens?" I take a deep breath, attempting to hold back the building panic.

"I assume you mean how will you die for the second time?" Toothpick Guy asks. When I nod, he says, "Well, that's simple. When we start the process, we do something sort of like rewinding the reel of a movie. When that happens, you'll no longer have any memory of what had happened after you died the first time. Neither will your girl, nor anyone else. Think of it as a do-over. As for again how much time you get to re-live? That's the funny thing about time...it could be a minute, or five. An hour, or weeks. It's hard to say. That depends on how well genius here can push the stop button." He motions toward Redhead and rolls his eyes almost with disgust.

"Alright, I get it. Just do it." I say and close my eyes, waiting for myself to be dropped back into reality, knowing at any minute I could be taken right back out again.

~ ☾ ~

Chapter Thirty-four

There's a whoosh of air, like someone opening the door to the outside and the wind blowing at you. Opening my eyes, I find myself standing by the door of the hotel room. It's like I never left. Xylia is still curled up in a sea of blankets. I glance at the clock. 8:32 am.

I stand still for a moment. Should I wake her and say goodbye, or just relish these last few moments with her and leave it at that?

Placing my hands in my pockets, I struggle with how best to proceed. Having no idea how long this life of mine will last, is it worth even moving? It's that second I feel something smooth and cold against my hand. Rubbing my thumb over the surface I realize it's the necklace. I'm surprised, then curious to know how the necklace made the trip since technically I haven't even been to the store yet.

That's when I realize I have to wake her. It's my last chance to say goodbye.

Worried that the men from the White Room are watching, I wipe all emotion from my face and stride over to the chair. Xylia's ratty old messenger bag hangs over the back. When I pull the chair out, the legs screech across the floor, but Xylia doesn't wake. Taking a seat, I try as stealthily as I can to slip the necklace in her bag without giving myself away. I'm not really sure if it will

~ ☾ ~

make another trip through time, but I have to try. If I'm going to die, I want her to have this.

Two minutes have passed. Now, with all the nerve I can muster, I reach a shaky hand out and touch Xylia's bare shoulder. Giving her a slight nudge I whisper her name. "Xylia...Xylia. Babe, you have to wake up."

She stirs, her eyelids flutter as she stretches out her body. Letting out a big yawn, she shows me her emerald green eyes and smiles wide. But I can't bring myself to smile back. I know what's coming, and it pains me to have to do this.

"Landon? What's wrong?" she asks, face full of worry. Sitting up, she pulls the blankets tight around her body and asks again, "What's wrong?"

My eyes grow blurry with moisture. "I love you," I say simply. I shake my head and press my palms against my eyes, forcing the water back.

"I—I love you too, but please tell me what's wrong."

She wraps her tiny hands around my wrists and pulls my hands away from my head. Not being able to grasp any better words I say, "I have to go."

"Go? Go where? I-I don't understand."

"I know you don't, but it's the way it has to be." My heart breaks because tears fill her own eyes and roll down her cheeks.

"Please, please just tell me the truth," she says. "If you really love me, you owe me that."

"I was supposed to die, Xylia. I don't know how I came back, but it's not right. It's not how the world's supposed to be."

"No, no. You came back. You were given a second chance."

I reach out and wipe tears off her cheek, tucking hair behind her ear. "It wasn't a second chance I was supposed to have. I've been shown that. Something went wrong, Xylia. I wasn't supposed to come back."

~ ☾ ~

"Don't say that. How can you say that? We're supposed to be together, I know it. We were meant to find each other."

"No, Xylia, my coming back was an accident. Something happened after I died, but it shouldn't have. It isn't supposed to be like this."

"Something happened? What happened?"

"I don't know what it was or how it happened. But someone got into my death space or something when I was dying, I guess. Somehow someone got attached to my life force and brought it back to me."

Xylia gasps, bringing her hand to cover her mouth. "I kissed you," she whispers. Closing her eyes, she shakes her head. "I thought it was a miracle...a sign," she whimpers.

"Kissed me? When?"

"The morgue, you were in the morgue. I was there. I lied before. I'm sorry. I *was* there and I kissed you when you were dead. I'd had a crush on you forever and I hated that you were dead. I just wanted to say goodbye. That's—that's when you came back. Your heart started beating and you gasped for air, then you sat up. Landon, you looked at me. You looked right at me."

I'm astounded; I let my fingers trail across my lips. That feeling, that last feeling I had before I left the White Room. It was of her, kissing me. Those green eyes and black hair—it's always been her.

Suddenly I wish I'd fought harder to save my own life, that I hadn't given in so easily, because Xylia's right. I came back. I came back for her because we're meant for each other. But I can't continue to live. If I do, she'll die. But I'll never tell her.

I shake my head. "It's too late. What's done is done. I have to go back." I wish I didn't. I've found the one person that I was meant to be with and she's going to be taken away from me.

~ ☾ ~

"When? Now?"

Looking at the clock, even though I don't know for sure I say, "Soon."

"It's not enough time. We can fix this. It doesn't have to be this way. I-I brought you back once, maybe I can do it again."

I gather her up in my arms, squeezing. "No, you can't." I let go, then take her head in my hands and kiss her. I pour every emotion into the kiss, maybe hoping she'll remember, that she at least will carry the feeling that someone loved her with all their heart.

Xylia pulls away and throws her arms around my neck. Her eyes are red rimmed, pained, her face blotchy, but she's never looked more beautiful.

"It's not enough time, Landon. I'm not ready to say goodbye."

"I know."

Resting her head on my shoulder, she cries, "I don't want you to go."

"I know, baby." And I hold on tight, just waiting for life as I know it to disappear.

But nothing disappears, and least not now. I pull away from Xylia, take my fingers and wipe them across her cheeks, soaking up the tears. "I'm taking you home," I say simply.

She looks at me. "I don't want to go home. I-I want to stay with you."

"I don't know when it's going to happen, but when I go, I don't want you to be alone. So, please, get dressed, and let's go. I don't want to risk time I don't have."

Xylia stays silent for a minute, and then she nods. She gathers up the sheets from the bed and heads for the bathroom, grabbing her duffle bag as she passes by it.

I can't help glancing at the clock. I wish they had told me when it would happen, how much time I really had. They said I could say goodbye. That they needed to

~ ☾ ~

reverse time to when I died in order for them to take me, again. But I still don't like not knowing. I could leave right now, or five minutes from now, a day, or two. Or more. Maybe I shouldn't have told Xylia. Maybe I should have let them take me then and there.

I begin to collect our belongings, shoving them into bags as I wait for Xylia to come out of the washroom. When she finally emerges, her black hair is pulled up into a messy ponytail. Her eyes are still red rimmed, cheeks blotchy, and it pulls at my heart, seeing how upset I've made her. She's thrown on a pair of black cargo pants and a band T-shirt, clutched to her side is the duffle bag. Quickly, she makes her way to the chair and slings her purse over her shoulder and meets me at the door.

We both stand there for a moment, in silence. I know I'm trying to commit everything to memory. Bracing myself because I know last night was the happiest I'll ever be. Because I know that soon I'll be gone, dead again.

* * * *

I've been driving now for over an hour. I know it might not have been the best idea to take the keys from Xylia when she offered them, but she had so much hope in her eyes, she believes maybe I won't just disappear.

"How's it going to happen? When? How do you know for sure?" she asks. I hold her hand tightly in my lap.

I shake my head. "I don't know."

"But you know something, you must. I don't understand."

Neither do I. And she's right. I do know, but when I try to speak my mouth begins to taste like ash. The words bubble at the surface but are unable to be spoken. Apparently I'm not allowed to share my secrets. I try

~ ☾ ~

again, however, opening my mouth to say the words that are so clearly in my head. Explain to Xylia about the men, the balance, that time will be reversed. But I still can't speak the words that remain trapped by something is forcing them back down my throat. I'm pretty sure if I tried to write out what had happened, no words would form either. I can't tell Xylia anything, so instead all I can do is say, "I don't know. I'm sorry."

There is so much that I want to say to her, there's so much that I still want to do. I don't want my life to end just as much as she doesn't want it to fade away. But, it's clear as tears silently fall down her cheek, as she presses her head against the window, that she's not able to bear looking at what she's going to lose, so I say nothing. I drive the rest of the way in silence, hoping that time doesn't suddenly stop as I drive. If I'm going to go down, no way do I want to take Xylia with me.

When I pull up outside my house, I put the car into park but leave the engine running. I open the driver's door, pull my things out of the trunk, and walk around to Xylia's side.

She opens the door, stiffly crawls out of her seat and stand in front of me. "We're going to figure this out, okay?"

I nod, dropping my bags, and then I circle my arms around Xylia's waist and pull her to me, crushing her against my chest. I stroke my hand down her cheek and kiss the top of her head. "I know we will, I'm sure of it," I say. But I know it's not possible. The deal's already been made. I'm giving up my life so she can live.

"Meet me at the soccer field tonight," she says. "After your parents go to bed."

I nod, agreeing to sneak out to meet her. If the soccer field was where my life with Xylia started, then I hope at least that's where it will end.

~ ☾ ~

Chapter Thirty-five

Xylia

As I pull away from the curb and look in the rear-view mirror through tear streaked eyes, I see Landon, looking sullen. He lifts up a hand, giving it the tiniest shake. I watch him probably more than I watch the road until his form disappears completely from my sight.

I know I should go straight home, or at the very least, call Dad and tell him I'm back in town, but getting yelled at isn't what I need right now. So instead I maneuver the car through the streets of Silversprings until I find myself at the hospital. If Mom was around, I'd probably go to her for help, but since she's not, I've got the next best thing. Evelyn. And the truth is, I just can't bear to be alone right now. I know I will see Landon again, shortly, but it's not enough. Seeing the hurt in his eyes, hugging him goodbye at his house, just about tore my heart out. It took all the strength I had to get into the car and drive away.

I know so little about what's going to happen to Landon that I hope Evelyn can help. Since she was the one that believed Landon and I were meant for each other, then maybe she has some insight as to why he's being taken away from me.

I waste no time making me way up to the geriatric ward. I find her sitting in her pink bathrobe, sipping a cup of tea, the TV blaring in the background.

~ ☾ ~

"Evelyn?" I say.

Her head turns toward the door, and at first her face beams with happiness at the sight of me, then suddenly her face falls flat. "Xylia? What is it, dear?"

I race to her side and throw myself at her. I fling my arms around her neck. Within seconds, the tears that I'd been trying to force back break free from the dam and pour out. "I'm so scared I'm going to lose him," I sob.

Evelyn pulls me to her, pressing her cheek against my head. Her hand rubs circles on my back. "Shh, dear," she coos.

I fight to regain control. The comfort that Evelyn brings is immeasurable. The scent of her wafts around me like a blanket, roses and vanilla. With another breath of air, I smell the tangy mint of her face cream, the sour-strong smell of nail polish remover, and tea. Her warm hand wipes tears from my face, and finally, after a few more heaves, I'm able to pull back.

"Everything is out of balance," I say, my eyes tear-streaked.

"What's out of balance? What's got you so upset?" Evelyn continues to rub circles, but every once in awhile a long pointy pink nail catches the fabric of my skin, ruining the rhythm.

I curl as much of my body onto her bed as possible. She moves over, giving me room, tucking my head under her chin.

"Something terrible is going to happen Evelyn. And—and I can't stop it."

"I don't understand."

"I-I ran away from home. Well, I didn't run away, I was planning on coming back, but then I brought Landon with me—"

"Landon?" Her voice perks up.

"You were right—we're meant for each other. I know it, but then he said he had to leave. That he wasn't

~ ☾ ~

meant to come back, and the world is off balance."

"Off balance? Whatever do you mean?"

I explain to her as much as I know. How Landon was never suppose to come back. How when he died, I must have interfered with the balance. How me bringing him back changed the course of the world. I told her about our trip, how together we both found things that we had been looking for. How he wanted to know what I had to do with his death and his awakening and how he'd found the answer.

"But I realized something, too. Landon made me understand so much about myself, things that I didn't even know. I always thought I needed to know what happened to my mother, why she left. I understand now that I'm not supposed to know. She chose to leave, and I owe it to her not to question it. I no longer need to know what happens when someone dies. I just need to know that life is worth living."

"Of course it is, dear. Life is always worth living. If we were meant to know what was in store for us once we've passed on, then it wouldn't need to be a secret. There are bigger things out there than any of us could imagine. We'll only understand it when it is our time."

I nod, knowing she's right, that this journey with Landon as shown at least a little of that. However, the knowledge doesn't ease the pain that still stabs at my heart.

"Then why does Landon have to leave again?"

She shakes her head.

I'd believed she'd have all the answers. I'd counted on her to share her own deepest thoughts, because if anyone has a connection with the world beyond it has to be her. She seems to know even more than she ever lets on.

But instead, she says, "That is one answer I don't have."

~ ☾ ~

"But you said we were soul mates. That my bringing him back meant something. That God—" I cringe at the word God. I always have because I've never been given the reason to believe there is in fact an almighty. "That God didn't let people come back for no reason."

"I did. But Xylia, I can only say for sure what *I* believe. And if you are only meant to have a short time with Landon, then it's because that's what's meant to be. You said life is worth living, than you need to live it with him as long as you can."

I'm quiet for a moment, taking in her words. She's right. "I get it. I owe it to him—to us—to appreciate each second."

The smile that plays on Evelyn's lips is big. "See, it must be true love. I know it is. And it will all work out. I know it will."

I pull Evelyn into another hug. It pains me just a little, because I don't see how things can work out, but if a few more days, weeks, or even months with Landon is all I have left, than I will take it. The way his eyes light up when I'm near, the smile that covers his face, the one that's crooked and dimpled, is worth it. He's worth it.

"I better get going. I've got some damage control to do with my dad, and I'm meeting Landon at the soccer field tonight."

Evelyn pats my head, kisses my forehead, then releases me. She's still beaming. "Go. Go make the most of it."

"I will," I say. I slip off her bed and head to the door. I stop just shy of the threshold and look back to Evelyn. She lifts a hand off the bed and motions it in a way that tells me to just go, to stop wasting time. I give her a small wave and walk through the door and down the hall.

I take the long way home. I know the talk I had with Evelyn lifted a huge weight off my shoulders, and the

~ ☾ ~

anticipation of seeing Landon again is the only reason why I know I have to face Dad. It's not going to be easy. But it has to be done. If I'm ever going to get better, if I've learned nothing besides accepting that which I have no power over, then I have to accept that Dad is going to be furious. But in time, he will forgive me.

I pull my car into the driveway next to Dad's Smart Car. I turn off the engine and take a deep breath, thinking, this is it. If I can just get through this last hurdle, I can be with Landon again. Taking the stairs two at a time, I hesitate for one second at the door before I place my hand on the handle and push it open.

"Daddy?" I call out. My voice echoes off the marble of the foyer. I hear his loud steps before I see him or hear his voice.

"Xylia?" He emerges from the kitchen. My heart lurches. It looks as though he's aged ten years since I last saw him. His clothes are wrinkled. His hair, normally combed, is dishevelled. Dark circles rim his eyes.

"I'm—I'm sorry." I say. Dad closes the distance between us, taking long strides. He pulls me into him, crushing me against his chest. He hugs me tight, but just when I think I'm going to get off easy he pulls back, holding me at arm's length.

His tone is a little tortured. He lets out an exasperated sigh. "Xylia."

"Daddy...I'm sorry. I'm so sorry."

"You scared me. Don't you ever scare me like that again. I thought I'd lost you."

"I know." The look on his face is something I've never seen before. It's so pained, as though he can't even bear to be mad. I've done to him something terrible. He really did think he'd lost me, just like he'd lost my mom. I can see just how badly I've hurt him, the stress that I've put him through the last couple of days.

~ ☾ ~

"I want you to go to your room and stay there. We'll talk later. But—"

"I have plans. I need to meet someone." I say.

"Not tonight, you don't. Xylia, honey, you're grounded."

A rock plummets to the bottom of my stomach. I never thought he'd ground me, not really. "But Daddy…

He pulls a shaky hand through his already tousled hair. "Xylia, please. Just go. I can't deal with you right now."

His voice isn't stern, it's not raised, but seeing that look in his eyes, I know I can't talk my way out of this one. He's so mad, so upset that he can't even yell at me. I feel terrible. I turn from him, hanging my head, and begin to ascend the stairs.

I'm almost at the top when I turn around. Dad is still standing there. Our eyes meet. I open my mouth, and he shakes his head. He doesn't want to hear what I have to say, but I don't care. I say it anyways.

"I've let her go, Dad. I understand if you can't, if you're not ready…but I can't let what she did bother me anymore. I know it's not worth it. And I'm sorry I hurt you, but this was something that I had to do. I needed to understand, and I think…I think I finally do. It's okay, Daddy. I forgive her."

He nods, his eyes glistening with wetness, then turns away from me and walks back to the kitchen.

I stomp up the last few stairs and head to my room. Inside, I plop down on my bed. I feel so relieved, saying that out loud. Telling Dad that I forgave Mom. I could see my words had touched his heart. I'd done the right thing, but I can't help but feel a bit angry too. I'm grounded.

I pull out my phone and call Landon. There's no answer. He's probably in trouble, too. We're supposed to meet in a few hours. I have no idea how I'm going to get

~ ☾ ~

to him. I untie my boots and kick them off. Grabbing a pillow, I curl up under my duvet, my phone still clutched in my hand.

Sleep begs to consume me, but I try to force it away. I just need to bide my time. Wait for Landon's call, and everything will be fine. Together, we can figure out how to stop him from leaving. I know we can. He just has to hold on just a little bit longer.

The shrill ring of my phone pulls me back to the present. I flip it open and answer.

"Xylia? I'm sorry. I got into a little more trouble than I thought I would. I'm grounded."

"Me, too," I sigh into the phone.

"We're going to have to meet tomorrow morning, at the soccer field. I don't think I can get away until then."

My heart begins to speed up. "But—but we don't know how much time you have!"

"I know. I'm sorry. But my mom thinks I've lost my mind. She's not going to let me out of her sight. I won't even be able to sneak out. Meeting in the morning is the only option I've got right now."

Tears sting my eyes. "But..." I want to fight against our parents, but I know right now that's another problem we don't need. If I snuck out tonight, I'm sure to find bars on my window, my door will lock from the outside, and Dad will never let me out of his sight either if I sneak off again without him knowing. If Landon and I are meant to be, then we have to fight together whatever comes our way, even if that is being grounded. It's not ideal, but I have to have faith. "Okay, tomorrow morning." I say.

We talk for hours, learning everything there is to know about each other. He tells me how his mom was hysterical that he'd run away, and that if it was humane enough to put tracking collars on humans, no doubt his mother would put one on him. I laugh, thinking my dad

~ ☾ ~

would do the same thing to me. I tell Landon how I'd told my dad that I'd forgiven my mom and how good it felt to get it off my shoulders. I also tell Landon that Evelyn still thinks we are soul mates. I'm still not sure I believe one hundred percent in the term, but I know Landon and I are meant to be together. That my kissing him was the best thing that I ever could have done, even if it does mean I'd kissed a corpse.

Eventually, our conversation becomes less enthusiastic, and through the phone I can hear his levelled breathing, then his yawns, and even though I'm not ready, I whisper, "Good night. I love you."

"I love you too, Xylia Morana," Landon whispers back.

I pull the phone from my ear and close it. Tomorrow morning I'll wake and everything will be better. I can feel it.

~ ☾ ~

Chapter Thirty-six

Xylia

The championship game is at halftime, and when the team runs off the field, I'm ready to dig my nose into my book. Dad's finally forgotten that he was mad at me earlier in the day for skipping school. With winter break coming up in a week, I'm glad Dad's no longer mad, because now I'm pretty sure he will let me go on the trip I have planned over break. The trip I'd finally convinced him to let me take alone—the one where I tour cemeteries and haunted houses. Weird, but so very me.

The team's ahead, and the crowd's insanely happy. Nothing like a championship game to get our small town hyped. I'm even excited, but mostly because I've been able to check out number 17. I may hate watching a bunch of guys kick a ball around, but I love checking out Landon Phoenix. He's beyond gorgeous. Amazing, really. Even though he has no idea I exist. My fault, totally.

Soccer isn't really my thing, but the games are the one time I feel I can bond with my dad. And as a bonus, I get to check out Landon without getting caught. At school I keep to myself and only sneak peeks when he walks by. But at the games, I practically drool when he runs down the field, his shirt clinging to his sweaty body, his winning grin flashing at the screaming fans. Nobody knows that I gawk at him. That I wish he were mine.

~ ☾ ~

That I hope one day he'll look at me as intently as he looks at the soccer ball.

Hey, a girl can dream.

I scan the crowd for Dad. He's juggling food that will probably have me break out in zits, add ten pounds, and keep me up all night with indigestion. A traditional soccer game meal.

I should have gone with Dad to help carry all the junk, given the trail of popcorn, French fries, and nachos he's leaving behind. He sits next to me and I offload the food, setting it on the small space between us. "Think you got enough?" I ask.

"I figured if this was our last game, we should go out in style, so I bought most everything they were selling." Dad raises his eyebrows, gives me a shrug and adds, "Too much?"

I let out a belly laugh. "Yeah, Dad, you went a little overboard."

"Huh...and here I was prepared to make a second trip."

"I think you got it covered," I say, munching down on a chilli-covered fry. Now my fingers are covered with sauce. I ask, "Did you grab any napkins?"

"Damn. I knew I forgot something," he says.

I lick my fingers, then reply, "I could go get some."

"You sit and eat. Read your book." He gets up and starts making his way past the wall of knees in front of him.

"Daddy?" I ask.

"Yeah, honey?"

"Could you bring back some cotton candy?" I finish off a fry and lick my fingers.

"Of course. Is that all?"

"Yeah, that's all. Thanks, Dad." I settle in to wait for my treats: cotton candy and Landon Phoenix.

When the blue and yellow pants disappear into the

~ ☾ ~

crowd, I reach for my bag to pull out my book. The bag was my mother's: it's army green, tattered and torn, with safety pins and patches stitched onto the fabric. Ugly, but I can't let it go. I figure I got at least two chapters worth of time before the second half starts.

Digging in deep, I grab my book. It's a hardcover murder mystery, heavy on the murder and mayhem. I pull it out, then sigh deeply when I notice my bookmark, the all-important place holder, is missing. It was a gift from Dad, a thin-as-paper metal bookmark he picked up from the airport gift shop when he went out of town for a conference. A peace offering when I threw a fit because I couldn't go with him. It was the first time I was old enough to be left on my own. Guess I'd hated him for leaving me alone. Hated my mom, too, for the same reason.

Worried that the bookmark has been lost forever, I grab my bag and plunge my hands into it. I pull out some crumpled paper that I toss to the ground. Pens follow, even a few empty packs of gum. I bring the bag closer to my face and rummage through more garbage and even a little make-up. At the bottom of the bag I see silver and...something else. Something unfamiliar.

Setting aside the bookmark, I reach back in, grab the mystery object, and yank it out. It's attached to some sort of string or cord that's tangled in a few paperclips. I disentangle the cord and hold what looks to be a stone on a string in my hand.

The rock with the black cord running through a hole is meant to be a necklace. On the surface, etched in elegant black script, is the word *Dream*. Butterflies tickle my belly as an intense warmth swells over my body. It's odd. I've never seen this item in my life, yet somehow I know it's mine.

The rock is smooth, heavy. I bounce it in my hand, trying to remember where it might have come from. I

~ ☾ ~

see more writing as the rock lies sideways in my palm. Turning it over completely, I read the inscription.

Love Always, Landon

I stare, because I can't believe what I'm reading. I repeat the words in my head again and again. The more I repeat the words, the more a warm feeling spreads over my body. I've always had a crush on Landon Phoenix, and must have wondered a million times what it would be like to get something like this from him. A small amount of worry fills my head at the thought that this might not be meant for me. As far as I know, Landon is taken. Charity makes that perfectly clear every single day. This necklace must belong to Charity and ended up in my bag by mistake somehow.

Bringing the rock closer, I want to touch it against my cheek, because this might be as close to him as I ever get.

I'm startled when the rock touches my skin. In my hand the rock feels smooth and warm, but against my face it's cold—so cold it almost stings. Quickly, I pull it away and say "ouch." But the coolness doesn't go. I bring my fingers to my face and rub my skin, but cold travels from my cheek to my lips, making them frigid and dry, cracked.

That's when it hits me.

My eyes slam shut as I'm pounded with emotions I've never experienced, yet emotions that feel so real. Then comes images: they fill my head, thousands at a time, like drops of rain in a storm. I gasp with a jolt of disbelief because as quickly as the pictures appeared, they are plucked from my mind just as quick. And then I'm left feeling empty.

I swear my heart shatters into a million pieces, the sharp edges stabbing me with sorrow and pain. Tears fall from my eyes with the feeling of the greatest loss. As though my other half, a piece of me, has been torn away,

~ ☾ ~

leaving me alone and heartbroken.

But what's even more incredible, mind blowing even, is that I remember.

Through the sadness, the pain, and the tears, my heart leaps with joy. And fear. I remember everything. Landon, playing the game of his life. Landon, collapsing on the field. Landon, his life slipping between my fingers.

But that's not all.

I remember desperately wanting to say goodbye to Landon. Sneaking into the morgue. Kissing him alive.

But I also remember the men, the two of them. The ones who'd threatened to take him back.

I swipe away the tears, letting all the memories fall back into place. There's so much to take in—the kiss, the trip, and Landon saying goodbye, saying he had to leave. When I kissed him, I must have interfered with his death. He wasn't suppose to come back, but the kiss must have pulled Landon back from crossing over.

Then just as I become grounded and realize the truth, that Landon maybe wasn't supposed to come back, I'm not sure what to do. I could sit here and do nothing, letting the past—letting what might have been—float by. At least I'll always have these memories. But I can't ignore the feeling that's deep inside my heart. Something inside me changed on that trip, and Landon helped me understand things.

I'd been able to move on, to forgive my mother for abandoning me. But I'd also fallen in love. It was quick, almost unbelievable, but Landon had become more than just a crush. We'd shared something special, and I know he'd felt it too. I swear it.

A small twang of fear tugs at my heart and my conscience. If I interfere again, will something bad happen to me?

I shake my head, clench my hand tighter around the

~ ☾ ~

smooth rock necklace and feel how its warmth replaces all sense of reason. I don't care. I love Landon. I want him to live.

I grab my bag then race down the stairs. The metal bleachers shake with the hard falls of my feet. I push through the crowds of people milling about, waiting for the second half to start, then head to the concession stand.

"Dad! Daddy!" I shout. Heads and bodies turn, but I'm still too far away. I push my legs to move faster as I sprint. I collide with a Rams fan and fall hard on my knees. My heart aches and my lungs burn as I gulp in air. The fan extends his hand to help me, but I push it away, standing on my own. I focus back on Dad and start running again, pushing myself faster and faster. Tears sting my eyes, blurring my vision, as my heart pounds loud in my ears. I take a deep breath of air and scream, "Daddy!"

Dad turns, startled, a bag of cotton candy in his hands. When I reach him I have to bend over, place my hands on my knees, and try to catch my breath.

"What? What is it honey?"

"I—I need your help," I gasp out. Standing straight, I grab his arm, then drag him toward the gym.

"Help? Why, what's wrong?"

He's resisting my pull, so I say, "Please, Dad. Please just trust me." And I know he will. He may not understand, may question my plea, but no matter how much I've done in the past, no matter how much trouble I've gotten into, he's always trusted me when I needed it most.

"Okay, I trust you, but you have to tell me where we're going."

Letting go of his arm, I frantically say, "We have to stop number seventeen from playing." Looking back, I see Dad's mouth is in a frown. "Are you listening? He

~ ☾ ~

can't play, Dad. Number seventeen, Landon Phoenix, *can't* play."

"I don't understand. Why is it so important that he doesn't play?"

"I can't explain it right now, but please, you have to pull some sort of doctor card and force him out of the game."

"Honey, he's not my patient. I have no clue what I could say."

I'm panicking. "Then just get me into the locker room and I'll do the rest."

I push hard against the door to the gym. It swings open loudly. "Hurry, Dad!" I call out as I run down the long stretch of hallway. I hear him pant—he's on my heels.

We reach the coaching offices first. They stand between me and the locker room, and there are three coaches milling about.

"Just distract them or something," I whisper as we slow to a walk.

Dad falls into step at my side. "Distract them how?"

"I don't know, I just need to get in there."

Dad takes a big breath of air then says hesitantly, "Okay, I'll do my best."

He walks straight toward the coaches. I crouch behind a drinking fountain and wait. Dad's always been a talker when it comes to sports. Put him in a room full of other avid fans and he can keep them chatting all night about scores, play strategies, even mascots and team colors. So I'm relieved when he manages to corral the coaches into an office.

Taking my cue, I rush past the doorway, hoping Dad keeps them engaged so they won't notice me. I pass by a few more offices until I see the door to the boy's locker room.

This is sort of where my plan ends. I haven't had

~ ☾ ~

enough time to think about the second part of the plan. I have to somehow get Landon's attention and force him to sit the game out. It's a weak idea, but I hope it works. There are only so many reasons why someone, even Landon, would drop dead during a soccer game. I'm putting all my hopes and dreams into my *casket* and praying the reason Landon had collapsed and died the time before had something to do with physical exertion. Maybe if I can stop him from playing this game, I can stop him from dying.

The door to the locker room opens up to a crowd of laughter, stinky socks, and sweat. The team is all suited up in shorts and jerseys, cleats and shin guards.

I see the back of Landon, the 17 stitched in blue against his yellow jersey. Taking a deep breath I call out, "Landon!"

The room grows silent as an entire team of heads turn to me. Mouths drop open, a few pairs of eyes go wide. Landon steps forward awkwardly, confusion on his face.

"Can I talk to you for second?" I reach out my hand, but when Landon's face turns from confusion to disgust, I pull it back quickly.

"Uh, no," he says, looking over his shoulder. Numerous guys have their eyebrows furrowed, and a couple whisper to Landon. He shrugs, then turns back to me. "I don't even know you."

My heart lurches. Of course he doesn't. He doesn't remember. "Please. It'll just take a second. Just come with me." I ignore his glaring eyes and take a step forward, reaching out my hand again.

Only Landon steps back, bumping into one of his teammates. He reaches up and grabs the back of his neck. Another one of his teammates, Daniel, the goalie, says in a mocking girly tone, "But it'll only take a second," and wags his eyebrows up and down.

Red flushes on Landon's cheeks. "Look, I can't. I've

~ ☾ ~

got a game to play," he says and turns to leave.

"Please, it's important, I swear. Just—just talk to me."

Landon begins pushing through the crowd, but the guys aren't letting him leave. Daniel pushes him back, saying, "Maybe she wants to do more than talk, if you know what I mean."

Landon looks over his shoulder and at me. "Let me through. I don't even know who this chick is."

I begin to lose hope. I don't know what I was thinking. Why would I have thought he'd just come with me, no questions asked? I can't help looking down at myself, seeing what they must see. That I'm a freak. Ripped yellow fishnet stockings, blue tutu. Black Doc Martens. Someone not to believe. But this is important. Landon will die if I don't stop him.

What do I have to lose? Quickly, I spit out, "If you play in the second half, you'll die!"

Landon stops trying to push through the crowd of players and stops. His fingers scrape through his hair. But he doesn't turn around. Instead, he stands silent while the rest of the team doubles over, howling with laughter.

"Do you hear this chick? She's seriously wacked!" Daniel says.

"I'm serious, Landon. Please, you can't play. If you do, I swear, you'll die."

Slowly, Landon begins to turn around. This time, instead of disgust plastered on his face, it's covered with red and his eyes are filled with rage. "Listen, I don't know you, and this is the most important game of my life, so of course I'm going to play. Please, do me a favour before you make an even bigger of a fool of yourself. Just get out of here."

My lip quivers. "But—"

Landon's voice booms with anger. "Out."

His voice carries so much finality it hurts. Tears well

~ ☽ ~

in my eyes. It's hopeless. It was stupid of me to come here and try to stop him, even stupider to tell him he's going to die. That just makes me look like even more of a freak. My own cheeks flush, my head fills with pain and sadness. Landon's going to die, and there's nothing I can do. If I can't get him to listen to me, to talk to me, I can't prevent his death.

Heaviness weighs down my shoulders as I stand in awkward silence. Obviously, the love I have for Landon isn't enough to fix this mess.

A look of pity crosses Landon's face. Had I blinked, I might have missed it, but then he says over his shoulder, "Come on guys. It's game time."

"Yeah, let's get out of here before that freak points the death finger at one of us too."

Maybe I'd been wrong about Landon the whole time. I thought he was different, but seeing him now, with his friends, he's just like every other jock. He's no different.

But he is. He *is* different.

And I know him. I know the true Landon Phoenix.

When I reach him, he's beyond startled. Almost pissed. But I grab his shoulder, pulling him around with all my strength. Then when he's fully facing me, I reach for one of his hands and place the rock in it. The same rock I'd been gripping the whole time, hoping it would give me the strength I needed. The one he had to have put in my bag back when we were together. He holds onto the rock and I'm thankful when he doesn't throw it to the ground. I then take his face into my hands.

If a kiss brought him back to life, a kiss can make him remember.

I lean in swiftly to his face, not giving him a chance to flinch out of my grasp, and lay my lips on his.

There's a lot of commotion, hoots and hollers, even some derogatory comments from the team, but I don't let it mess with my focus. I think of every single feeling,

~ ☾ ~

every single picture I saw on the bleachers, and pour it into the kiss. Landon's lips feel hard and cold, chapped. His body is stiff against mine—bone straight as I press myself against him, deepening the kiss. Landon's smell envelopes me, assaulting my senses with a mix of sweat and cologne, sweet like cinnamon with a tang of something else. So familiar. The aroma sends a flood of images of him and I together to flash in my mind.

Then the tension eases from his body, and slowly I feel him sway toward me. I repeat over and over in my head, *remember, just remember*, until I feel I've done all I can.

Stopping the kiss and pulling away from him, I gaze into his eyes.

Landon pushes me away, his face contorted and full of confusion. My body starts to shake, because it wasn't enough. What I remember, what I feel, isn't enough to pull the shroud that has covered up Landon's memories. It's over.

I've failed.

~ ☽ ~

Chapter Thirty-seven

Xylia

Still holding me at arm's length, Landon's eyes close and he shakes his head, his mouth opening and closing. My knees feel like they're ready to dump me on the ground. Landon's teammates are still laughing, but I'm too heartbroken to be ashamed. I back off and turn to leave. There's nothing more to do.

"Wait," Landon says.

I stop.

He comes up to me from behind, then tugs at my shoulder until I'm turned around and facing him.

"Do that again," he says.

"Do what?" I ask.

"Kiss me."

He doesn't have to ask twice. I grab him and kiss him the way he kissed me the first time, that morning in the inn, when it was just the two of us alone. I wrap my hands around his neck and suddenly there isn't a room full of sweaty guys laughing—there's just me and Landon. Just us.

When the kiss is over, Landon pulls back. His eyes open and there's something—a shimmer, a brighter blue perhaps—*something* in his eyes that sends relief over my body, warming it.

He stares at me for what feels like forever. His teammates have all shut up and are silent—so silent I

~ ☾ ~

can hear Landon breathe. Suddenly he sucks in air, then steps closer. He pulls me to him and whispers, "Xylia?"

I throw my arms around his shoulders. "You remember?" I ask, nuzzling his neck in pure happiness.

He wraps his arms around my back and lifts me up. "I remember everything, but—"

"Shh," I say. I don't want to ruin this moment, this second, because it feels like my heart, my body, is melding back together with his. That I've finally found my other half, my soul mate, and I can't bear to think about losing him just yet.

"Hey, Landon, we got a game to play," Daniel says, stepping through the crowd.

Setting me down, Landon closes the distance between them. He looks back at me, smiles, then turns to Daniel and says, "I'm going to sit this one out."

Daniel's eyebrows raise. "You're kidding, right? The championship game, and you're going to just *sit this one out*? What about the scouts? Your soccer scholarships? Your frigging *future*?"

Landon raises an arm and pats Daniel on the shoulder. "Yup. Suddenly I'm not feeling too great." He nods with finality, then adds, "I've realized there are things more important than soccer."

Watching them, there's some sort of exchange, one that's not shown on the outside but rather the inside, because Daniel looks over at me and smiles, even giving me a wave as he says to Landon, "Alright then."

There's some definite anti Xylia and Landon people, because I hear someone say, "I wouldn't feel too good either if I'd just been kissed by that hag." But I ignore the comments tossed out; they don't bother me.

As the team files through the door leading to the field, Landon yells out, "You guys are going to win!" Minus their star player, of course, and who knows if they will pull off a win without him. But I don't care. I have

~ ☾ ~

everything I could ever need. I will know now, for the rest of my life, that no matter what the world has in store for me or Landon, at least we found each other, again. We share the greatest gift of all. Love.

* * * *

Sitting on the bleachers, Landon holds my hand in his. To his left, his parents sit, still in shock over their son throwing away his future by sitting out the game. I was worried for a second that Landon would give in to his father's pleas and play. But when he threw his arms around me and stood his ground, I'd never been prouder. Sure, his dad yelled, threatening to ground Landon, but at least Landon's alive. Dad sits on my right, biting his nails as the second half starts up. He's still confused why the star player had to drop out of the game at the last second. I suppose one day I'll have to tell him. It might just make me sound a little crazy.

A familiar face makes its way toward us. Dad stops biting his nails. His face turns a slight shade of red and he stands, extending his hand.

"Dr. Evans. I didn't know you liked soccer."

Doc Stephanie smiles warmly at him, and instead of taking his hand, she touches his arm and giggles. "You always said I needed to support our players."

There's a moment of silence between the two of them, and although I'm laughing inside, knowing what could have happened between me and Dr. Stephanie Evans, I realize this might just be what my dad needs. I nudge him with my elbow, pulling him out of his awkward stupor. He looks back at me and I smile encouragingly. If I can move on, if I can understand that I don't need death to give me the emotion I need to push forward, then maybe Dad can, too. He might even realize that an occasional date could help.

~ ☾ ~

Dad turns back to Doc Stephanie and says, "Would you, uh, like to join us?"

She grins, and I know she'd had this planned. No fool, that Doc Stephanie. When her rear is firmly planted on the bleacher, Dad offers up his popcorn and cotton candy and wastes no time explaining the rules of the game. I hope she knows what she's in for. Dad is relentless when it comes to sports. But I'm happy. This is his chance to move on, accept what happened and what we can't change. The two of us need to forgive my mother for leaving and understand that her decision hadn't been about hurting us. Even though she took her own life, it was her decision. If Landon can help me to see that, I'm sure my Dad can figure it out, too.

We settle in to watch the game, Landon and I both worried and tense. As the moment where Landon collapsed the last time this game played approaches, he squeezes my hand. We're both worried he could still die.

A ferocious wind picks up, coming from nowhere and yet everywhere. It raises my pigtails and whips them across my face, stinging me. I look to the field and the blood that runs warm in my veins turns cold. The hairs on my arms stand up. I'm frozen to the core, from skin to marrow.

Centerfield, standing pin straight, arms folded across his chest, is the guy in the gray suit. His eyes are penetrating, his expression smug, and a toothpick dangles from his lips. This time there is no question—he sees me. However, I wonder, is he here for me or Landon? But when the clock keeps ticking down to the end of the game, Landon's heart still beats.

The team takes the championship without Landon's excellent soccer skills helping them out. Apparently, that was meant to be either way. But I don't know what seeing the man with the toothpick means.

Dad's pocket begins to chime. It's hard to hear over

~ ☾ ~

the excitement of the fans. I nudge him with my elbow. "Dad, I think your pocket is singing."

He raises his eyebrows. "What?" Then it dawns on him and he reaches into his pocket and pulls out his cell phone. He flips it open, but just as quickly, he shuts it and slips it back into his pocket. I can see the dramatic change in his facial expression as his body grows rigid.

"What was that?"

He shakes his head. "Nothing."

"Dad? What's wrong?" I say, my stomach tightens with worry.

"We'll talk later." He begins to stand, but I reach out and grab his arm.

"Please, just tell me."

Dad heaves a sigh and sits back down. He puts a hand on my knee and gives it a squeeze. I look over at Landon. He's just as concerned as I am.

"It's Evelyn. She's passed away. I'm so sorry, honey."

I close my eyes as sadness washes over me. Evelyn was old, it was going to happen, but it still pulls at the strings of my heart. I take a deep breath, then look up, opening my eyes.

The man with the toothpick is back, but this time, instead of glaring at me, he smiles and winks. I blink my eyes, and when I refocus on the field, he's gone.

"Evelyn," I breath. Was this the balance the world needed?

"Are you going to be okay?" Dad asks.

"Yeah. I'm okay." I say.

Dad squeezes my leg once more, giving it a few pats, then says, "I'm going to walk Dr. Evans to her car."

"Okay. I'll meet you out there."

After my dad and Doc Stephanie walk off, Landon sighs, putting my happiness on hold.

"You know this might not mean this is over, right?" he says. "I might not be free and clear?"

~ ☾ ~

"Maybe the world found its balance another way," I say.

"You know what? I don't care." Landon smiles and pulls me to him. "I have the most important thing right here in my arms. If I'm going to die, I at least can remember I loved you."

It's true. The first time Landon died we weren't together. Heck, he probably didn't know I even existed. The second time around, Landon would have died without the memory of ever having loved me. At least this way, even if God or the great balancer or whatever it is that makes these decisions commands he dies tomorrow, we will both know that we loved each other with all our hearts.

But I'm thinking about what Evelyn said. How I am Landon's knightess in shining armour.

The wind goes away and the night air turns balmy. Landon tips my chin up and wraps me in a deep kiss that swirls stardust around me. And Evelyn's final words drift over my memory like the warm breeze that drifts over my skin. "*Believe, Xylia. This is meant to be.*" And I think to myself, maybe she was right all along.

The End

~ ☾ ~

Acknowledgements

I admit there was a time when I never thought I'd be in the position to write a novel, let alone the acknowledgments section for one that I had written and for one that was going to be published.

So, I wish to thank my family, my friends, and my husband for giving me everything I needed to make this dream of mine a reality and for standing beside me every step of the way.

There is a lot that goes into a novel besides the work I put into it. I need to thank all the great Critique Partners and Beta's that have helped me along the way and did their best to make this novel what it is. Thank you, Jean H, Becky W, Brandy B and Dana-Lynn. I do wish to single out one person in particular, Steven W: you mean the world to me, and I wouldn't have gotten here without your friendship and guidance. Stop shaking your head, because it's true!

I also have to thank my editor Rochelle F. You were amazing to work with, you listened, you taught me, and you truly went above and beyond. I will always be beyond grateful!

Since a cover is one of the most important aspects of a book, and my cover ROCKS! I need to thank Taria Reed.

A huge thank you goes out also to Bryant H. McGill for allowing me to use his quote at the front of the novel, as well as William Blake for his poem "The Poison Tree," and to Mary Frye for her poem "Do No Stand at My Grave and Weep," These powerful words really helped A Stiff Kiss become what it is, even if I had to borrow them!

My publisher, Crescent Moon Press needs a huge shout out as well. They've truly made me feel at home and have done great things for me and my novel.

And of course, I need to thank the readers, from near and far.

Avery Olive

Avery Olive is Canadian. She is married, and when she's not helping raise her very energetic and inquisitive son, she can be found working on her latest novel—where she devilishly adds U's into every word she can.

When she is looking for a break, Avery enjoys cake decorating, losing herself in a good book, or heading out to the lake to go camping. She can be found at http://averyolive.blogspot.com/, on Facebook, or you can follow @AveryOlive on Twitter.

CPSIA information can be obtained at www.ICGtesting.com
Printed in the USA
LVOW062120290212

271036LV00001B/11/P